I0760775

DISCOVERING ME

book 2

dating WASHINGTON

ANN MAREE CRAVEN

MICHELLE MACQUEEN

This is a work of fiction. Names, characters, places, and events are used fictitiously and any resemblance to actual events, locales, or persons is entirely coincidental.

 Printed in the United States of America

Cover by Daqri Bernardo at Covers by Combs.
Editing by Kelly Hartigan at Xterraweb

For the ones who struggle with the shades of gray.

Chapter 1

Kenny

"Life sucks and then you die."

Wasn't that what people said? Boohoo, right? Kenneth James Montgomery didn't get to mope. He didn't get to wallow or claim no one understood him. Who cared about the problems of a spoiled rich kid at a fancy boarding school, right?

Kenny lifted his eyes to the seats surrounding the ice surface of the Defiance Academy arena. Their hockey team, the Knights, had every advantage. Top facilities. Knowledgeable trainers. Actual fans.

Not to mention the constant train of National Hockey League scouts looking for their next draft star.

Was that Kenny? It could have been…if a single picture hadn't ruined his chances.

Kenny was bisexual. Only two short months ago he'd been caught on camera kissing Nicky St. Germaine beside the pool in his backyard. It should have been a private moment. A private moment with the boyfriend of Beckett Anderson, country music golden boy—not to mention, the son of an NFL legend, too. At least no one in the media learned the entire truth. For two years,

Kenny dated Nicky without anyone knowing, terrified that the people in his life might learn his secret.

The son of Ohio's conservative, anti-gay, full-on hateful senator liked boys every bit as much as he liked girls. He kissed them and fantasized about them, and he wasn't going to apologize for it.

At least, he didn't want to. Maybe one day, he'd grow the courage to tell his parents to take their asshole ideas and shove them where it hurt.

Today was not that day. No, today was the first game of Defiance Academy's hockey season, Kenny's last season before leaving for college. He already had his scholarship to play for Boston College—if he didn't screw it up. His "family advisor," Kyle, told him he had a shot of going in the late first round of the draft. Really, Kyle was his agent, but amateur players weren't legally allowed to have agents, so they called them "family advisors" instead. He trusted Kyle as much as he trusted anyone—only slightly.

Kenny pumped his legs, trailing the St. Mary's winger after getting caught behind the play. He could have cursed himself but knew Kyle would do it enough for the both of them. *You get too much in your head,* he'd say. He wouldn't be wrong.

Scanning the jersey number up ahead, he skated faster. There was no way he'd let Eric "douchebag" Morrison put their team up one to nothing.

Killian "Killer" James, the Defiance goalie, squared himself to Morrison, waiting for the shot. It didn't come. Morrison skated behind the net, anticipating his centerman streaking down the center of the ice right through two Defiance defenders. The puck slid toward the center, but he couldn't stop his momentum and slammed into Killian, pummeling him into the ice.

Kenny reached the collision first, pulling the center up and shoving him into the goal post. Morrison, taking issue with that, swung at Kenny, but with Kenny's height, he barely stood a chance.

Kenny deflected the blow off his shoulder before driving his fist into the side of Morrison's helmet. Both skaters yanked their helmets off, freeing their faces from the protection of the metal cages.

"Come at me, bro," Morrison yelled.

Kenny raised an eyebrow. This dude had seen way too many hockey movies with cheesy fight lines.

Every skater on the ice crowded around them as the refs hung back, waiting to see if they needed to step in. Glancing down at his already bruised knuckles, Kenny remembered what Kyle had once taught him. Don't fight someone bigger, someone smaller, or someone with a chip on his shoulder. Too many hockey players had dulled their skills fighting senseless battles on the ice. Breaking hands and fingers so many times they lost the ability to puck-handle at a high level. For as much of an asshole as pretty much the entire world thought Kenny was, he did care about one thing: his future in hockey. It was all that got him out of bed some mornings.

He shook his head. "You're not worth it." He turned to skate toward the bench.

"I knew you were too much of a fairy to fight," Morrison yelled after him.

Kenny froze, his back still to the rest of the guys on the ice. Ever since the photo came out, he'd prepared for the remarks he knew would come once hockey season started. It wasn't exactly a welcoming or diverse sport. There were no openly gay professional hockey players, and in the high school ranks, it tended to be mostly open to wealthy white kids who didn't accept people different from them.

But there was a difference between preparing for the words and actually hearing them.

"Say it again." He turned so abruptly his skate created a rut in the ice. "Go ahead. I dare you."

Morrison approached, dropping his voice and lifting his chin. "Fairy."

He barely got the word out before Kenny lunged, tackling him to the ice. Morrison's head hit the cold surface with a crack, but he didn't stop struggling until two refs pulled Kenny off him. Kenny yanked his arms out of their grip and wiped blood from his lip. His breath came rapidly as he stared at the boy who still lay on his back.

It was only then Kenny noticed the rest of the scene. A line brawl broke out with Killer hauling guys down to the ice, a dangerous look in his eyes.

The refs blew their whistles, and all ten boys on the ice stopped as if they hadn't noticed the chaos they'd created.

A ref skated toward Kenny. "I'm throwing you out."

"Perfect," Kenny spat. First game of the season and already a game misconduct penalty. But he didn't care. Before this year, he'd have said hockey was the most important thing in his life. Now, everything confused him. He walked down the hall toward the locker room, slamming the door open. A trainer followed him.

As Kenny sat on the bench in front of his locker, he hung his head. The trainer dabbed a damp towel across his busted lip. "You don't need stitches."

Kenny only grunted and bent to untie the laces of his skates. The trainer left, giving him the blissful solitude he wanted.

Running a hand through his sweaty, brown hair, Kenny wished he could turn back the clock to before he'd realized, as a fifteen-year-old boy, just how different he was.

Footsteps sounded in the hall before the door swung open, and Kyle walked in with a scowl on his face. "What was that?"

Kenny only shook his head, still too keyed up to answer. He'd known Kyle for years and could handle anything the ex-NHLer threw at him. He was supposed to advise him on all things related to the business of hockey. It was why Kenny accepted Boston College's offer over others. Kyle said it was a good path to the NHL after the draft.

"Answer me, boy." Kyle stopped in front of him, glaring down at the top of Kenny's head.

"I got carried away."

"Carried away? You think NHL scouts watching want to see you pummel some kid, risking injury to those skilled hands of yours?"

"Just leave me alone, Kyle. I'm not in the mood."

Kyle blew out a breath. "You know I care about you as if you were my own, right?"

The sad thing was, he did. Kyle was more of a father than Kenny's own dad. He'd certainly been to more of his games over the years, and he represented the path Kenny wanted to take—hockey. His father only wanted him to consider a career in politics.

Kyle sighed. "All right, nothing I say will help you with whatever is going on in that head of yours, I get that. Go take a shower. I'm heading out. Dinner tomorrow before I fly back to New York?"

"Sure."

He squeezed Kenny's shoulder before leaving him to the quiet locker room once more.

After removing his pads and sweat-soaked clothes, Kenny walked into the bathroom and stepped into the shower. A blast of cold water hit him before it warmed, but Kenny barely felt it. He'd been called a lot of things in his life. Ken doll was a favorite because of his resemblance to the little plastic man with all-American good looks. Short brown hair. Golden eyes. Tanned skin.

He could probably have any girl in the school.

Some people called him Mr. Montgomery, mocking the importance of his father.

Fairy… that was a new, but not unexpected name.

Placing both hands on the wall of the shower, he let the water stream down his spine and examined the bruised knuckles of his left hand…his shooting hand. Coach was going to kill him.

Commotion came from the locker room. The game must have ended. Kenny turned off the water, ready to face the music. He wrapped a towel around his waist and joined his raucous teammates. Smiles lit their faces, and some kind of country music blared from the speakers.

"Ugh," Will, the team's best defender, complained. "Whose turn was it to choose the music today?"

Killer pulled his shoulder pads over his head and threw them at Will. "Don't be an asshole. Beckett Anderson is awesome."

Kenny knew he'd recognized the voice. He wanted to dislike Becks, but the man had talent. "What's the verdict?" He guessed the team won by the joyous atmosphere but needed to hear it.

Will snapped him with a towel. "Well, after you got thrown out, Killer was angry. And we all know what anger does to him. He didn't let a single puck through. St. Mary's was all over us. I've never seen a sequence quite like that from him."

A man of few words, Killian only grunted and turned to his locker.

Will continued. "Then yours truly fired a slapper from the left dot, and that was all she wrote." He took a bow, not realizing Coach Ryan stood behind him.

"Take a seat, boy."

Will scrambled to sit.

"You should all thank Killer for saving this game." His hard eyes found Kenny. "And you..." He shook his head. "I want you back out on the ice right now."

"Coach?"

"Your teammates were out there for a full sixty minutes. You will be too."

Kenny didn't bring up the fact that he'd already showered or that it was only the first game back and his legs were already killing him. No one argued with Coach Ryan. "Yes, Coach." He sighed as he pulled on dry workout clothes and laced up his skates.

Will clapped him on the back before going to take his well-deserved shower. The rest of their teammates offered little in the way of comfort for their top centerman. Before this summer, they'd been like a family, but since the picture of "the kiss" came out, Kenny hadn't known how to act around them.

But Kenny had wasted too much time worrying about what everyone else thought of him. He stepped onto the ice. The Zamboni had yet to clean the rutted surface.

"Suicides," Coach said, following him. "Start at the blue line."

Kenny sucked in a breath, inhaling the cold air he'd come to associate with home. The stands finished clearing out, leaving Kenny alone with his coach. In the silence, he could almost forget about the game that happened only minutes ago.

It was his senior year but the first year Kenny lived in the dorms rather than his parents' large house in Twin Rivers. He'd been one of the few commuters. Since that changed, he'd found himself wandering campus late at night, sometimes ending up inside the arena that brought him peace. When everything else in his life was torn to shreds, this, hockey, was his constant, the only thing he could count on.

As he started his suicides, he focused on the wind rushing in and out of his lungs and the burning in his legs. He pushed himself as much as he could, hoping it was good enough.

When he got the chance to glance at the bench, Coach was gone. He'd left Kenny to do as many suicides as he saw fit. Not for the first time, Kenny marveled in his coach's trust of his players.

Kenny didn't trust anyone.

He skated until his legs gave out beneath him at center ice. The Defiance Academy logo sat underneath him, a knight meant to protect its charges. That was what the school was for. Politicians, diplomats, and other important people sent their children to this school to keep them out of the public eye, to keep them protected.

Kenny lay back, enjoying the feel of the cold ice on the back of his head. He closed his eyes, soaking in the peace he never found anywhere else. He'd never been more sure of anything. Hockey was in his blood. It owned him, heart and soul. He couldn't imagine doing anything else.

But what if the game betrayed him? What if it pushed him out simply because of something he hadn't chosen for himself?

Sometimes, the fear of being who he was overcame the relief at finally not having to hide anymore.

"Mr. Montgomery," someone called from the Zamboni tunnel.

Kenny lifted his head, finding Frank, the elderly man who led the arena's maintenance team. "Hey, Frank. I'm in your way, aren't I?"

"I can give you a few more minutes, kid. Don't worry about it."

"No." Kenny got to his feet. "It's okay. Ice is all yours, man." He nodded a goodbye to Frank before stepping from the ice and walking toward the locker room once more. One of the trainers waited for him, protein bar in hand.

Kenny took it. "Thanks."

"You good now, son?"

Pulling off his skates, Kenny nodded, giving the only answer people wanted to hear. They didn't want a sob story or anything resembling the truth.

But what was the truth?

No, Kenny was not okay.

He didn't bother showering or changing his clothes before stepping into his tennis shoes and hiking his hockey bag onto his shoulder. With a wave at the trainer, he walked out.

A ding sounded from his bag, and he pulled his cell free of the side pocket.

Kyle: You're going to be okay, kid.

He didn't respond because another text came in.

Nicky: Saw a clip of the fight on YouTube. You good?

He wanted to hate Nicky. He and his superstar boyfriend were the reason Kenny was outed in the media after all. But for so long, Nicky had been the only person who knew Kenny's secret, and there was something bonding in that no matter how their relationship ended.

Besides, Nicky was the only person who might understand.

Walking into his dorm, Kenny peered into Will's open room. Seeing his roommate already passed out, Kenny crossed the sitting room to drop his bag in his room before entering the bathroom.

After taking a quick shower and pulling on a pair of sweats, Kenny flopped onto his bed and pulled up the video Nicky mentioned. You couldn't hear what Morrison said, but the word wasn't hard to make out on his lips.

Kenny regretted the anger he saw flash across his face as

Morrison's head snapped back. It didn't take much searching to find out Morrison went through concussion protocol and would miss St. Mary's next game.

Kenny opened Nicky's message again.

Kenny: I didn't mean to hurt him.

Nicky: I know. It gets better. I promise.

Kenny didn't respond, because he wasn't so sure he believed Nicky's words.

He scrolled through the contacts in his phone, stopping at his dad's number. Would he answer? He'd spoken to his parents once in the last two months. Neither mentioned the picture, but they'd informed him he'd be living in the dorms this year.

He didn't understand why he couldn't live in their Twin Rivers house. It wasn't like they were ever there, spending all their time in Washington DC instead.

Mustering up the courage, he pressed his thumb over his dad's name. It rang once before going to voicemail.

"Hey, Dad," he said. "I was just… If you and Mom are going to be in town anytime soon, I'd like to see you. Please… I… Yeah, just call me. Your son. This is Kenny. Um… Bye."

Throwing his phone onto the bedside table, he sat back against his headboard and closed his eyes.

His dad didn't return the call.

Chapter 2

Asher

"We could work at my house." Asher Brooks watched his classmates stare at him blankly, and he realized how dumb that sounded. "I mean, I have a studio we could use if, you know, we need a place to work."

"That's cool. Thanks, Ash." His best friend, Harper, was his savior. "Let's meet at Asher's place next week to come up with a plan for our company. Everyone, think about company names and branding ideas. We'll need a kick-ass logo by the end of the month, so let's all come up with two good ideas and some sketches before we meet."

"Sure, Asher's place sounds good," Nichole said, grabbing her things to make a quick escape.

"Whatever." Ethan left to follow Nichole.

"Have I mentioned I hate group projects?" Asher pulled his hoodie up over his head to hide his telltale natural locks courtesy of his African American father and Caucasian mother.

"Hiding again?" Harper followed him down the wide hallways of Sidwell Friends School—the most elite private high school in DC.

"It's easier." Asher shoved through the double doors of the ultra modern building into the quad teeming with other Sidwell students heading home for the day.

"Later," Harper called as she waited for her driver in the long line of sleek black town cars making their way up the main drive to the school.

"Let's go, Valor." The tall suit lurking behind him closed the space between them.

"What did I say about codenames, Danny?" Asher's shoulders slumped at the snickering coming from a group of seniors nearby.

"Right, not at school, sorry. Let's go, Asher." He shoved Asher toward the waiting limousine. "And it's Special Agent Fuller or Dan. Only my mother gets to call me Danny." He held the door open for Asher and slid in beside him after checking their surroundings. "Why so glum about the art project?" Dan asked, nodding to the chauffeur to leave along the rear routes reserved for certain students and their drivers.

"The art part is a no-brainer. I just don't like group projects." Asher stared out the window.

"At least you have Harper on your team. But it wouldn't kill you to make friends with the other two since you invited them to your house."

"I don't know, it might." Asher fiddled with his phone in his lap.

"You have invites to several art shows next month. If you want to show at any of them, we need to know this week so we can get protocol in place."

"I'll let you know." Asher loved creating art. From painting, sculpting, and digital art to photography, he loved it all—and he liked to think he was pretty good. But the attention he got for his art wasn't about his art at all, and that made him second-guess his talent. When the whole world kissed your ass because of who your parents were, things like real friends and honest opinions didn't mean much.

Asher's phone buzzed—something it didn't do often.

Mom: Stop by the office when you get home from school.

Ash: Almost there, anything I should worry about?

She didn't respond. She was busy, and he was used to it. "Drop me off at the office, will ya?" He slid his earbuds in to drown out Dan's constant droning.

He didn't wait for one of his babysitters to open the door before he hopped out of the limo and entered the building. Asher set off down the wide, shiny hallway to meet his mother, leaving Super Agent Danny to field all the attention-seekers eager to kiss Asher's butt.

"Hey, Asher, my man." Some dude in a suit tried to high-five him as he walked past.

He just nodded and kept walking, focusing on the beat of the music only he could hear. He paused outside the white paneled door, waiting for permission to enter.

"Hi, sweetheart," his mother called from her perch on the sofa where she preferred to work.

Over the last ten years, Asher had entered the Oval Office thousands of times. He was so young when his dad first landed the top job in the West Wing that the reverence most people held for this room was completely lost on him.

"We've talked about the hoodie, son." His mom frowned at him. "Don't cover your beautiful hair."

With his natural Afro hair, coupled with hints of his mother's blond coloring, most people recognized Asher by his hair alone. He shoved his hoodie back and snagged the earbuds out of his ears.

"What's up, guys?" He shot a look at his dad behind the Resolute Desk, his feet propped up on top of the antique desk. "You supposed to be there?"

"Come sit, Asher. Let's talk about your birthday." His mom patted the sofa cushion beside her.

"If the word party comes out of your mouth, I'm bolting for the door." Asher took the seat by his mother and propped his feet on the coffee table.

"Feet on the floor, son."

"Seriously? What about Dad?" He pointed at his father's shoes scuffing the priceless furniture.

A knock at the door interrupted them. "A word?" Senator Montgomery stepped into the room before anyone could respond. "The bill you asked for review, Madam President." He placed a large binder on the table in front of Asher's mom.

"Thank you, Preston," his mom said without looking up.

"Bennett, always a pleasure." Preston Montgomery cast a look of disdain at the former president seated behind the Resolute Desk. "I believe you served your time behind that desk." The senator tried to make a joke of it, but the wildly conservative Ohio senator wasn't overly fond of the more liberal First Family.

"Eight years." Asher's dad didn't budge from his seat. "It kind of grows on you after all that time. This is my thinking spot."

"Well, boys, I'm the president now," Asher's mom said, "so I don't mind if my husband keeps my seat warm." Her winning smile had them all relaxed. She knew how to work a room. It was the reason she was elected eight years after her husband first took the Oval Office. The people loved her, so it looked like Asher and his older sister would be the first First Kids to call the White House home for sixteen years.

"Please let me know if I can answer any questions for you, Madam President." Senator Montgomery turned to leave.

"Oh, I do have one question, Senator." She turned her smile on Asher.

Ah crap, I know that smile. It was her shut up and don't argue with what I'm about to say smile.

"Asher has a birthday coming up, and we'd be honored if you and your family would attend the party we haven't told him about yet. It's been so long since we've seen your son, Kenny, around here."

Asher winced at the mention of his one-time friend who turned out to be a colossal jerk. They were friends way back before either of their parents were in the national limelight. And even after Asher's dad was elected President of the United States, he and Kenny spent a lot of time together. But when Asher came out to Kenny at thirteen, he discovered his friend wasn't such a great friend after all. He seemed fine with it at first, but in the weeks after, Kenny pulled away from him until he finally figured out Kenny's conservative parents didn't want him hanging out with a gay kid. After that, Kenny just got mean, spouting some of the same anti-gay garbage his parents did. Asher hadn't had many friends since then. When you were a seventeen-year-old gay kid living in the White House, it was kinda hard to meet people.

"Sure, that would be great, Senator Montgomery. I'd love to see Kenny again." Asher spewed the words his parents expected him to say, trying to hide his smile. He shouldn't find Kenny's current situation funny at all. It was just ironic that the kid who refused to be friends with him because he was gay ended up plastered all over the media in a picture, lip locked with Beckett Anderson's boyfriend.

"Thank you, Madame President. Kenny's at school back in Twin Rivers, but I'm afraid he's not allowed to attend any parties right now. We've had some discipline issues with him recently, as I'm sure you can understand." He cast a glance at Asher.

Uh-oh, abort, abort! The senator hit his mom's hot button and probably knew it too. President Nora Brooks narrowed her eyes at the senator and his insinuation that Kenny needed to be disciplined for the simple crime of being different.

"Come now, Senator, Kenny's one of the most well-behaved kids in the political arena today. You and Victoria should be proud. We insist, please invite your family on our behalf. We're looking forward to seeing you all there."

"Of course, ma'am. We wouldn't miss it." He gave a curt nod at Asher and his father before he left.

"What did I say about a party, Mom?" Asher leaned back, propping his foot over his knee.

"Oh, so sue me, I want to have a party for my son. I'm such a *terrible* mother."

"Something tells me I'd lose that lawsuit." Asher threw his head back against the sofa cushions and groaned. "Do we have to make it a State affair? Can we just invite a few people?"

"No. We're inviting everyone we know who has kids your age. You need to meet more people and make new friends."

"I have Harper."

"And we love Harper, but you need boyfriends, darling."

"Make her stop talking." He shot a glare at his father.

"I don't perform miracles, son. And your mother is right, you're like a lone little fish in a sad little bowl here in Washington. You have, like, fifteen people in your class, and I'm willing to bet most of them are assholes—though that's off the record and doesn't leave this room. We want you to meet some real people. More like Harper, but you know ... boyfriend material."

"Oh my God, you guys are trying to get me a boyfriend for my birthday? I think I hate you." Asher stood, slinging his messenger bag over his shoulder. "Just try to contain yourselves with the party planning, please. And if you expect me to show up, I'm going to need a few people on the guest list I actually like."

"Of course, sweetheart, it's your party. Um, who else do you want to invite besides Harper?"

"I have other friends, Mom." He rolled his eyes. "Invite Becks Anderson and his boyfriend Nicky St. Germaine."

"Oh, the singer and what's-his-name's son?"

"Grayson St. Germaine," his dad supplied. "One of the finest NFL players in history."

"Yeah, them."

"You've kept in contact?" His mom looked like she was about to threaten him with hugs, his cue to leave.

"Yep, so I've got homework now." He darted for the door to the Rose Garden. "I guess, just tell me where to show up and when." He jogged across the immaculate lawn to the residence, ignoring the people he passed along the way. Super Danny followed on his heels, his constant shadow. Asher charged up the red-carpeted stairs to his bedroom on the third floor. The only people allowed in his room were his parents and, occasionally, the secret service. Asher's room was his escape. One of the few places in the White House where the tension that was always with him finally eased. Asher grabbed his phone to text Becks and Nicky, but he already had a group text from them.

Becks: Party at the White House!

Nicky: We can't wait to see you. Happy Birthday, and thanks for inviting us.

Ash: Wow, word gets out fast, I just told her to invite you guys like ten minutes ago.

Becks: FLOTUS works fast, bro, she called us a few minutes ago. I almost peed my pants.

Nicky: Babe, she's not FLOTUS anymore, she's POTUS now.

Becks: You know I just pretend to know what that means, right?

Asher grinned, watching two of his closest friends argue with each other. They were sickeningly sweet, but Asher was secretly jealous of their relationship. He wanted that with someone, but at seventeen, behind the sterile walls of his world guarded by a flock of secret service agents, Asher had never been kissed, much less had a relationship with anyone.

Ash: I need you two to keep me sane, you know I hate these stuffy official events.

Nicky: We're here for you, Ash.

Becks: It's sweet that your parents want to play matchmaker.

Nicky: You probably weren't supposed to say that, honey.

Becks: Oops.

Ash: I'm going to kill them.

Becks: Whatever, we'll come. I'll sing. We'll dance, and if there are cute boys there, even better.

Ash: Love you guys.

Asher tossed his phone on the desk. Laying back on his bed, he stared up at the ceiling wondering how many other president's children felt trapped in this mansion that felt more like a prison than a home.

Chapter 3

Kenny

Didn't someone say senior year was supposed to be the time of a high schooler's life? It got easier, they'd always told him.

Lies. Kenny scribbled the last of his algebra notes, writing down their homework assignment for the weekend, just as the final bell rang. To his right, Diego Reyes rested his head on his desk, making of mockery of the fact that he was even in this class. Kenny kicked Diego's desk, jerking the tall boy upright.

A year ago, Kenny might have given Diego grief for being the ultimate nerd, but then he'd learned what it felt like to have a label plastered across his forehead for the world to see. Now, when he looked at the guy, all he saw was the asshole Kenneth Montgomery once was.

It had taken a month this year for Diego to even meet his eyes. Kenny hadn't apologized for how he'd treated him. That wouldn't do any good, anyway. But the tension between them fell away, and Kenny hoped maybe they could end up being friends of a sort. He was short on friends these days, and Diego looked like he could use one.

Diego pulled his black-framed glasses from his face and wiped them on his shirt. "I fell asleep again, didn't I?"

Kenny laughed. "Dude, why are you even in this class? Shouldn't you be in like trig or calc instead?"

"I am." He shrugged and replaced his glasses. "Algebra's just an easy grade."

"Why do you need an easy A?" Kenny paused. "And how does the school let a math genius take plain-old algebra?"

"They kind of do whatever I ask them to." He seemed a little embarrassed by the admission. "And I told them I needed the refresher. I haven't been in an algebra class since junior high."

That was when Kenny remembered the Reyes family was one of the big donors to Defiance Academy. They owned a tech company in Silicon Valley, making apps for the financial industry. And if there was one thing that controlled the academy, it was money. Kenny had benefited from that mind-set as well.

Slinging his bag over his shoulder, Kenny stood and followed Diego from the classroom. The two couldn't look more different, Diego with his slim dark looks—inky hair, black stubble coating his chin, and deep brown eyes—and Kenny with his athletic build and boy-next-door style.

Yet, they came from similar backgrounds. Their wealthy parents shipped them to boarding school to keep them out of the way. It was the story bonding most of the students walking the halls of the prestigious, ivy-covered buildings.

Diego was quiet for a long moment. "I need an easy class in my schedule. I...don't exactly have a lot of time to study. Or sleep."

Kenny filtered through what he knew of the guy. He wasn't an athlete. What could take all his time?

They pushed through the front door of the building, stepping into the chilly late Fall air. The quad stretched between academic buildings. At the end of the school day, it teemed with students.

Commotion came from Cambridge Hall just across the quad from where they stood. Kenny noticed cameramen before anything else. In some settings, it wouldn't have been unusual, but the Defiance Academy campus sat behind tall walls to protect the high-profile students from such an event.

Kenny wasn't watching where he was going and slammed into someone, gripping their arms to keep them from going down. That was how he found himself face to face with Beckett Anderson.

Ripping his hands away as if the country star burned him, he stepped back.

Becks lifted the sunglasses shielding his eyes from view, pushing them into his hair as he slid his eyes up Kenny. "Hey, Ken doll."

"Ken doll?" Diego glanced at Kenny. "I didn't know you had a doll?"

A grin slid across Becks' face as he turned to Diego. "I like you. Let me give you a bit of advice though." He hooked his thumb toward Kenny. "This is not a guy you want to be friends with."

With that, Becks sauntered away, making a beeline for his sister, standing with her arms crossed over her chest and a permanent scowl etched on her face.

Wylder Anderson did not look happy to see her brother.

Diego released a nervous laugh. "Who's that guy?"

"Do you live under a rock or something?" Kenny sent him a questioning look. How could this guy not have seen the fiasco that was Kenny's media circus of a summer? The one where a kiss with Beckett's boyfriend turned Kenny's closet inside out.

"Pretty much." Diego shrugged. "I don't pay attention to much that goes on at this school. Is he like a sports guy?"

"Are you asking if he's a jock?" Kenny wanted to laugh. This kid was clueless. "Becks doesn't go here, thank God." He couldn't imagine having to face Beckett Anderson every day. Kenny had been in love with Nicky, and he'd screwed it up with his stupid fear.

The girl he'd dumped Nicky for hadn't even lasted long. Penny graduated last year, and it was a relief to have her gone. Sure, Kenny was attracted to both boys and girls, but only one boy had ever made him feel something.

With a wave to Diego, Kenny walked toward the cameras, unable to stop his curiosity. Why was Becks on campus? Did he bring Nicky? Scanning the faces, Kenny couldn't find the one he wanted to see. He'd gotten over Nicky, or at least, he'd tried to.

But something about him still had Kenny curious about the man he chose over him. Someone handed Becks a guitar and told him to sit on the Cambridge steps—the oldest building on the main campus. They placed three girls near him, each more beautiful than the last.

"And action," a well-dressed man in a suit called.

Becks strummed his guitar and looked to the camera. "I sent my sister to Defiance Academy because they could take care of her, teach her, mold her into the kind of woman our future needs. This place isn't like other schools. It's special."

"Cut!"

Kenny couldn't hold in his laughter. The country superstar was doing a commercial for Defiance Academy? Just the thought of that was ridiculous.

Not to mention, their entire setup was cheesy as hell.

His laughter drew Beckett's attention. "Got a problem, Ken doll?" Becks had been calling him that since he hurt Nicky. It was a crack at what most people saw as Kenny's biggest flaw. Perfection. Even the questions about his sexuality hadn't dented the image of the fair-skinned, blue-eyed, well-spoken, future politician.

"Actually, yeah. That sucked."

Becks raised an eyebrow while the director scowled.

Getting to his feet, Becks handed off his guitar and approached Kenny. "Tell me, Montgomery, what do you suggest we do?"

Kenny scratched the back of his head, thinking. "Do you know how many hockey players we've sent to the NHL in the past ten years?" He didn't wait for anyone to answer. "Nineteen, with a handful more playing in the AHL or Europe. That program is our biggest recruiting tool. When we're on the ice, the arena is more alive than any part of this campus. If you want to show the world the heartbeat of this school, you have to step out onto the ice." He cocked his head. "How are your skating moves?"

"This was a terrible idea." Becks gripped the wall for support as he skated forward.

Wylder laughed from the safety of the team bench. "No, this is gold. If you insist on embarrassing me with this commercial, at least let me get some enjoyment out of it."

Kenny did a quick lap around the smooth surface. Coach watched from the tunnel. He'd been skeptical about using the arena for the commercial, but the camera crew had been given full access to use any part of campus they deemed necessary.

Killian appeared at the mouth of the tunnel in full pads. "This better be quick."

He'd come when Kenny called him, begging him to show up. If the commercial was about the school, it needed to feature some of the best parts, and Killer would make sure they were in for a battle.

Kenny skated backward toward Becks. "You're going to have to let go of the wall, eventually."

"I will." Becks sucked in a breath. "Someday."

Kenny shook his head and crossed the ice to retrieve two sticks from where he'd left them on the bench.

Wylder met his eye. "How much do I have to pay you to see Becks checked into the boards? Oh! Or he could lose a tooth. He's way too pretty."

Kenny laughed. Only an hour ago, he'd probably have wished for the same thing. But seeing Becks struggling on the ice, unwilling to admit he couldn't do this, softened Kenny's opinion a bit. He could see what Nicky liked about the guy. There was a certain charm. And he sure as hell looked good. Well, not right that moment inching along the wall.

Kenny shook his head and drifted to his side, handing him a stick. "This may help your balance."

"Okay." Becks took the stick. "I can do this." He closed his eyes —not something Kenny would have advised—and pushed away from the wall. For a moment, he stood upright, his free hand thrown to the side.

Kenny met his panicked eyes a second before Becks' feet flew out from under him, and his butt slammed into the ice. His stick slid toward the goal, stopping as it hit the post.

Even the ever-intense Killian couldn't contain his grin. "Dude, that was epic."

Kenny looked up into the lens of the camera trained on them, noticing the red light. They'd gotten it all on camera. "Can I get a copy of that?" Suppressing another laugh, Kenny extended a hand down. Becks took it reluctantly.

"Why am I out here again?" he groaned as he got to his feet, not letting go of Kenny's arm.

"Because you wanted to prove something to me." The moment he'd said it, he knew it was true. Kenny was Nicky's past. Whatever future Nicky now had with Becks, it didn't negate that.

"Anyone ever tell you you're a douchebag?"

"All the time." Kenny shrugged. "It's part of the charm." When he noticed the camera still on, he slid his hand out of Becks'. He'd learned that lesson. No matter if the video would only be used to promote the school, even if any Kenny and Becks' interactions were cut out, Kenny wouldn't risk another incident like the kiss with Nicky. The world wouldn't forget that, but in time, maybe, it wouldn't be such a big deal.

If he conformed to what they wanted from him.

Killian skated forward. "All right, country boy, enough with the flopping around. Let's get this over with."

A man Kenny didn't recognize skated onto the ice.

Becks took his guitar from him with a nod of thanks. He handed the stick off to Kenny and slid the guitar strap over his head. "Okay, your job is to make sure I don't fall and smash this baby."

Kenny's brow creased. "Beckett..." He stopped himself. This wasn't his commercial. Whatever the director wanted, he could have. He'd already given in to Kenny's suggestion they do this on the ice.

Kenny took Becks' arm and followed his direction to center ice, leaving him standing directly in the center of the school logo.

The director told him to get out of the way and motioned for the camera to start rolling again. Becks strummed his guitar, repeating the same lines as before and then starting in on his most popular song, "Love Me."

Kenny stayed on the ice with Becks and Killian for another hour, helping Becks pretend to shoot pucks at Killer. He didn't know why he was there. Becks wasn't his friend, and probably never would be, but the commercial took his mind off the fact that his dad still hadn't returned his call and that most of his friends didn't know how to talk to him anymore.

Coach suspended him for a game after his fighting incident. The Knights lost, and Kenny felt it was all his fault. So, he'd come back and scored a hat trick the next night and netted points in the two games since. Still, it didn't erase the way his teammates walked on eggshells around him.

Kenny and Becks skated off the ice together and walked to the locker room to remove their skates. Becks gripped his shoulder. "Look, I know there's history and shit, but thanks, man. Today was a lot more fun than I'd thought it was going to be."

Kenny shrugged him off. "Sure."

"If you ever want to, you know, hang with me and Nicky when I'm not on tour, give us a buzz."

Kenny only shrugged again. He wondered if Becks knew he sometimes texted Nicky. Would he care? Who was Kenny kidding? He couldn't be friends with those two. Not if he didn't want a media storm to descend on him once more.

If that happened, his parents might never speak to him again.

By the time Kenny made it back to the dorm, Will was already out doing whatever he did on Friday nights, and weariness overcame Kenny. It was the weekend, and all he wanted to do was collapse face-first into his bed. No one ever told him being stared at all day was so exhausting.

And the thing was—they weren't staring because he'd been caught on camera kissing a dude. At least, not only that. For the first two months of school, he'd suffered under their gazes and whispered words not because a boy couldn't like other boys but because one in particular boy couldn't. Who was that boy? The son of the conservative senator.

The entire situation made Kenny a curiosity for his classmates.

Then throw in that the boy he kissed was dating the country singer every high schooler in the US currently idolized.

Yep, the only way Kenny would get away from the expectations was to graduate and leave all these people behind.

But there were some people he'd never be free of. His phone rang, and he slid it from his pocket. "Kyle." He sighed. "What's up?"

"You sound exhausted, Kenny. Don't forget to get enough sleep. There'll be scouts at pretty much every game from here on out as teams prepare for the draft."

"I know. We've only talked about this a million times."

"I'm just excited for you, kid."

And he knew that was the truth. Kyle wanted Kenny to succeed. "Thanks, man. Was there a reason you were calling?"

"Just checking in. You don't have a game this weekend, but I hope you'll be ready for the next one. No more shenanigans. Let your talent speak for you, not your anger. Whatever they say to you, the best way to get back at them is to beat them."

"Yeah, yeah. I know. You sound like Coach."

"We're all rooting for you." Kyle liked to include Kenny's parents in the royal "we," but Kenny knew they barely noticed what he did.

As he pushed open the door to his dorm, his mother turned to face him, a strained smile on her face.

"Kyle, I need to go." He hung up and threw his phone onto his bed.

"Kenneth." His mother stepped forward, putting a hand on each of his shoulders and kissing his cheek. "Was that Kyle?" Something lit in her eyes. "How is he?"

"Um... Okay." He glanced around his pristine room, making sure nothing was out of place. They'd drilled the need for order into him from a young age.

"Dear." Her smile dropped. "Um is a nonsense filler word. What have we taught you?"

He sighed. "To always speak with purpose. Never say anything I don't mean. Only use words that emphasize my point." He rattled off their lessons in speech etiquette like the robot they'd hoped he'd be. As the only child of his ambitious parents, their desire for a lasting political legacy rested on his shoulders.

His mom patted his cheek. "Good job, darling." Her eyes scanned his face, moving over the workout clothes he'd worn on the ice. For a moment, he wondered what she saw.

"Kenneth, we've talked about this. You insist on playing that game, but outside of the stadium—"

"Arena, Mom."

She waved away his correction. "When you leave the building, you need to look presentable. You never know who will see you."

He had to keep himself from rolling his eyes. She wouldn't have taken that well. But who was going to see him on a high school campus? Most of his classmates lived in sweats or jeans.

She tsked and dug into her purse, pulling free an envelope. "This is for you."

Kenny took it and found an invitation inside. As he read the words, his eyes widened. Asher Brooks was having a birthday party. Yes, Kenny knew it was pathetic his mother was delivering birthday invitations to him. But this was a party he definitely didn't want to attend.

Because Asher Brooks happened to be the president's son. As in—President of the United States. As in—the boy Kenny wanted nothing to do with. They'd grown up together in the same political circles and even been friends once. That last time he'd seen him, they hadn't even spoken. Asher showed up in Twin Rivers to help Becks win Nicky back. Somehow, the three of them had become close friends.

Kenny looked to his mother. "Asher won't want me there."

"Well, it's a good thing he doesn't get a say."

"It's his birthday, Mom."

"Son." She calmed her voice like she was speaking to a child. "Everyone will be at this event. The president is sparing no expense. The Montgomerys must present a united front...especially after your...indiscretions."

He wanted to laugh at that. Indiscretions? That was what she called being outed in the media? What she was really telling him was they needed to show all their fancy friends their son was "normal" and it had all been one big misunderstanding.

"Fine, Mom." He sighed, knowing there was no winning with her, especially when she probably looked at his hockey schedule to make sure he couldn't lie and say he had a game. "I'll go."

She smiled. "Good boy. I'm headed back to Washington tomorrow, but I'll have a driver pick you up next Friday afternoon. You'll fly to Washington for the party Saturday night. I've already chosen a suit for you, and it will be waiting at our townhouse in DC when you get there." She turned her wrist to check the time. "I really must be going. Goodbye, dear." She walked away.

Kenny nudged his door shut with his foot and dropped his backpack near the desk. He flopped onto his bed and stared at the plaster ceiling. "I'm fine, Mom. Thanks for asking. It's been a little rough lately, but nothing I can't handle." He rolled onto his side. "I'm just glad you care."

She'd never hear those words. His first contact with either of his parents in months, and she'd only come because they needed him in Washington.

For Asher's party.

He couldn't help wondering what Ash thought of him now. Asher told the world he was gay when he was thirteen. He'd been

Kenny's best friend despite being the president's son. But Kenny's parents stopped allowing them to spend time together. They retreated into their conservative circles, doing anything necessary to thwart the president and the gay-loving First Family.

And Kenny hadn't fought them on it. He hadn't been there for Asher. Instead, he'd abandoned him.

How was Kenny supposed to look Asher in the eye now that his secret was out? How was he supposed to breathe in a room full of people who were wondering if his kiss with a boy was forced upon him—as his parents told people—or if he was one of 'those' boys, the kind they thought deserved no rights?

He rolled onto his stomach and buried his head in his pillow. If he had a way out of the party, he'd take it.

If he had a way out of the political world he'd been born in to... Well, he'd take that too.

Chapter 4

Asher

Asher slouched down in the worn leather chair, enjoying the last few minutes of peace he would get until his big birthday bash was over. It was tradition. Since he was eight years old, whenever his presence was required at events of State, he withdrew from the chaos in the final hours before the event. Everyone knew to leave him alone in his "secret" hiding spot behind the Usher's Office. From there, he could watch people arrive, but he didn't actually have to deal with them until the last possible moment.

After several painful hours with his stylists, trying to make him look cooler than he actually was, he was ready for a break. Sitting in his too-tight pants with his hair styled so it stuck out in loose curls all over his head, he felt ridiculous. Most people thought the president's son was a trendsetting fashion icon, but the reality was far from the truth. His stylists were the trendsetters. They stocked his closet and routinely selected outfits for him to wear to school. Asher tended to stick to jeans, T-shirts, and sunglasses, but they picked those too, so he ended up looking like someone who had a clue about fashion.

Asher tapped the Netflix icon on his phone and settled back to binge-watch one of his favorite shows. Sipping a hot vanilla latte and picking at the special cupcake the executive pastry chef had left for him, he knew he was spoiled rotten. And ungrateful. But if someone had actually asked Asher what he wanted for his birthday, he would have said a family dinner without interruptions or phones or secret service. Just Asher, Mom, Dad, his sister, Caroline, and maybe a pizza. But no one bothered to ask him.

"Damn it." Asher licked icing off his fingers, eyeing the spot of red, white, and blue on his black too-tight tuxedo shirt.

"I knew I'd find you in your secret spot." His sister's voice rang out behind him.

"It's not actually a secret when everyone knows about it." Asher brushed at the spot with a napkin.

"You're making it worse. Sit." She dipped a linen napkin into the pitcher of ice water the kitchen staff left for him. "Did you save me half of your cupcake?" She dabbed at the spot on his shirt.

"Of course. That's part of the tradition."

Caroline stood back and eyed his shirt. "Your jacket should hide it, so I guess you'll do." She took the seat beside him, stealing more than just her half of the cupcake.

"You look nice." His sister wore a high-fashion couture ball gown by some Italian fashion designer neither of them could pronounce. Layers of black and gray tulle fell to her feet in an ombre effect.

"I feel like this dress is wearing me." She fussed with the bodice. Caroline was just as uncomfortable in fancy clothes as her brother.

"It suits you. And it's not over the top. I, on the other hand, look ridiculous." He held his hands wide, glancing down at his shirt.

Caroline tried to hide her smile. "A little bit hipster with a hint of badass. It looks good, little brother. So not you, but it looks good."

"I look like an Elton John impersonator, and not in the good way." He stood, shrugging into the white embroidered jacket, also too tight. "Too flashy?" He tugged on his black-and-white bow tie and ran his fingertips over the embroidered lapel covered in a black-and-white rose motif. "I don't think I can pull this off."

"You happen to look adorable, Asher. Now, escort your big sister to this shindig of yours, and save me a dance for later."

"Where's your boyfriend?"

"I happen to like him too much to subject him to this nonsense. I learned a long time ago these birthday parties aren't actually for us."

"I just wish this town didn't pretend they cared what we do." Asher sighed, offering his sister his arm. "Let's go greet my guests —you know, all the people we don't know bringing all the gifts we can't keep." As the president's son, any gifts he received tonight were considered gifts of State and would go to the National Archives. He could purchase his own gifts from the archives if he really wanted them, but he'd likely never even see most of them. He'd asked his parents to request donations to his LGBTQ charity in lieu of gifts, but most visiting dignitaries would donate and bring a gift—not to be outdone by the other partygoers.

"Wait, we can't just walk into the hall with the other guests." Caroline pulled him back. "This is your birthday bash, we have to make an entrance." She dragged him up the back stairs to the second floor, down the long hall to the grand staircase. "You ready?"

"As ready as I'm going to get." Asher plastered on his fake smile, and they made their way down the red-carpeted steps to the entrance hall where their parents waited to greet their guests. Asher and Caroline would have to wait with their parents in the receiving line, the most tedious part of State affairs.

"Don't you two look dashing." Their mother turned her smile

on her children. Dressed in a strapless, blue-and-white ball gown, she was as beautiful as ever. "Happy birthday, sweetheart." She pulled Asher into her arms and whispered, "Just get through the night, and your real birthday present will come in the morning."

"Thanks, Mom." He took his place beside his father, waiting to greet the Speaker of the House.

"Happy birthday, Asher, you're looking handsome this evening." The Speaker's wife shook his hand, moving along to make way for the Chief of Staff and her family. Everyone made a point to introduce their children—the same kids he'd met a hundred times before.

"Happy birthday, Asher," the National Security director said. "You remember my son, Nate?"

"Of course, Nate, how's it going?" Asher forced another smile.

"Could be a lot better, Ash," Nate said when his father turned his attention on the president. "Thanks for throwing yourself a birthday party on the same night my girlfriend's parents are out of town." Nate clapped him on the shoulder and moved on.

Asher turned back to the receiving line, hoping to see the end in sight. No such luck, but he did catch a glimpse of some outrageous hand waving that could only belong Beckett Anderson. He and Nicky stood behind a few other celebrities the White House invited. Asher waited patiently to greet each person, but he was anxious to spend some time with his friends. Harper was already inside dancing.

"Stop fidgeting." His dad elbowed him. "You can leave with Becks and Nicky."

"Thanks, Dad." Asher breathed a sigh of relief, but a pair of dark eyes caught his attention. Preston Montgomery stood just behind Becks and Nicky, a disgusted look on his face. But Asher's eyes went right to his son, Kenny. Kenny looked like everyone else their age—wishing he were anywhere else but here. He hadn't seen Kenny in a couple of years and those years had been kind to him. Nearly a foot taller and toned from his dedication to hockey, Kenny Montgomery was all grown up and looking hot.

"Lovely to see you again, Madam President." Becks bowed his head and kissed her hand like she was the queen of England.

"You too, Becks." Asher rolled his eyes when his mom blushed at Becks' attention. The guy could charm anyone. Except, apparently, the Ohio senator behind him.

"There's our guy," Becks roared. "The birthday boy." He swept Asher up in a big bear hug, kissing both his cheeks.

"I missed you guys." Asher turned to greet Nicky, the more subdued of the couple.

"You two are just the cutest couple in the world," Asher's mom gushed after hugging Nicky. "I'm so glad you could make it. Asher doesn't have enough gay friends," she whispered.

"I'm not gay, but my boyfriend is." Becks took Nicky's hand, grinning from ear to ear at his favorite joke.

"What does he mean?" Asher's dad leaned in to ask.

"Dad, Becks is pan." Asher begged him to be cool.

"As in Peter Pan? That makes perfect sense." A smile tugged at his lips.

"Pansexual, Dad." Asher shook his head. "Becks is attracted to the person, not their gender. But Nicky is gay and is only attracted to men."

"Okay, I'm down with that." The former president nodded.

"Ugh, can I please go now?" Asher begged. Kenny and his parents were next, and he didn't want to deal with any of them.

"Can we move this pride festival along?" Senator Montgomery said in an unconvincing teasing tone.

"Preston." Asher's father reached for the senator's hand, gripping it harder than necessary. "Glad you could make it."

"Asher." Kenny nodded, refusing to take his hand.

"Good to see you," Asher said, looping his arms through Becks' and Nicky's arms.

Asher glanced at his father and gave another nod before escorting his guests to the dance floor.

He could still feel Kenny's eyes on him. "Guess some things never change."

Chapter 5

Kenny

If Kenny could have been anywhere else, he would have disappeared. Instead, he found himself standing next to his father in front of the President of the United States. He watched Asher walk away with Beckett Anderson and Nicky, surprising envy snaking through his gut.

They weren't supposed to be Asher's friends. He wasn't quite sure how they'd met, but he'd known Nicky for years, though not nearly as long as he'd known Asher.

And he wasn't the only one watching them. Kenny's father smoothed out the hatred on his face before turning to the president and clasping her hand. "Thank you for having us."

As they chatted, Asher's father—the former president—smiled at Kenny. "It's been a while, kid." He extended a hand.

Kenny took it stiffly. "Yes, thanks for inviting me."

"You're always welcome in our home, Kenneth. There was a time we couldn't get you to leave."

Kenny dropped his hand and glanced at the long line behind him. "I should probably let more important people talk to you." Really, he just wanted to get away from the man who'd always treated him with more kindness than his own father.

The current and former presidents both smiled at him once more in that easy way of theirs. Kenny followed his father as he cut his way through the crowded ballroom, caring little for the people having to skitter out of his way.

Behind him, his mother held her head high, offering tight smiles to those they passed.

Senator Johnson stepped in front of them. "Preston," his voice boomed. "You've been avoiding my calls."

"Eric." Kenny's father put a hand on the Alabama senator's arm. "Not tonight. Come to my office tomorrow if you'd like to talk."

"I've been trying to talk to you for months."

Preston ignored the words. "Have you met my son? Kenneth is a politician in the making."

Kenny hid his wince as he used the bored expression he'd perfected over the years. One of his father's first lessons about politics was to never let a politician feel that you cared too much about what they were saying. That was how they gained leverage over you.

Senator Johnson offered him a wary smile. "Oh, yes, I'm sorry for what your boy has been through, Preston. Terrible business."

"What I've been through?" Kenny glanced from his father to Senator Johnson.

Anger sparked in the senator's eyes. "They have no respect for normal Americans."

As soon as the word normal left his mouth, Kenny knew exactly what they were talking about—the kiss with Nicky, the picture in the media.

"Attacking you like that." The Alabama senator shook his head.

Kenny suddenly couldn't breathe. Nicky attack him? He flicked his eyes to his father. He knew the ridiculous story his parents concocted to explain the kiss, but he couldn't believe they were actually using it. That anyone would believe sweet, kind Nicky would try to force himself on Kenny.

An arm slid through his. "Senators, I'm sorry, but there's an emergency, and I need Kenny's help." He met his savior's eye, and Caroline winked.

The senators barely spared them another glance as Caroline pulled Kenny away.

"Thank you." He pushed out a breath.

She laughed. "You looked like they were pulling your fingernails off one by one."

"Graphic much?" She wasn't wrong. Few friends of Kenny's ever got to experience the full assholishness of Preston and Victoria Montgomery. But Kenny, Caroline, and Asher had grown up in the same circle of politics most of their lives. When they were kids, the three of them would sneak away from events like this and spend time together any chance they got.

Before they grew up and everything became so complicated.

"Was I wrong?" She peered up at him with wide amber eyes.

"No." He pulled her tighter against his side. "Thank you."

"Come on. I want to dance."

He let her pull him toward the dance floor. A string quartet played a dull song Kenny knew Asher would never have chosen.

Dancing was one of the lessons insisted upon in the Montgomery household. Their lives were designed so they never looked out of place. Kenny wanted to laugh. If the guys on the hockey team could see him now.

As they danced, Caroline studied him. "When was the last time I saw you?"

"It's been a while."

"Years."

He shrugged.

She pursed her lips. "You stopped coming around."

The moment Kenny started at Defiance Academy his freshman year, he'd set his sights on hockey and little else. His parents all but wrote him off, only calling on him for the occasional event where they needed to look like the perfect parents. It had its benefits. He'd been able to forget about all things Washington, but he'd also lost contact with good friends like Caroline.

We don't want you associating with the Brooks children. Those were his mother's words in the days following Asher's epic closet burning. *We have our beliefs, son, and we expect you to fight for them.*

"I didn't have a choice," he finally admitted.

"I figured. How have you been?"

Her question was more loaded than she knew. How had he been? Well, his closet had become a black hole he couldn't escape from. His parents were dicks. And oh yeah, the entire world saw the image of him kissing Nicky—and now, people were accusing Nicky of taking advantage of him?

"I've been good." The lie tasted sour on his tongue.

Caroline laughed, softly at first. It grew in volume until she couldn't contain it any longer. "That is such a Kenny Montgomery thing to say. You are not good. I know your parents, remember? And I've seen the tabloids. If you were going to kiss someone, wouldn't it have been smarter to choose someone who didn't have paparazzi constantly following him around?"

Kenny sighed. "Probably."

Her laughter died away, but her eyes didn't leave his face. "Nicky wasn't random, was he? Not just some experiment?"

"How the hell can you tell that?"

"I may not know you lately, Kenny, but I can still read you."

He hadn't admitted what was behind the kiss to anyone. Only Nicky and his friends knew the truth. But the Brooks siblings had always elicited an insane amount of trust. Asher wouldn't even look at him, but Caroline was there, and it had been so long since Kenny had anyone to confide in.

Leaning in, he spoke low enough so only she could hear. "I sort of dated him for two years."

She let out a squeal. "You dated Beckett Anderson's boyfriend?"

Not the reaction he was expecting from telling one of his oldest friends he'd dated a guy. As if on cue, the string music cut off, and Becks stepped onto the stage, a microphone in one hand. "I promised Asher I'd perform a few songs to provide some entertainment." His cheeks reddened as he glanced at the quartet. "Not that you guys aren't entertaining. Just kind of boring, yeah?"

A grin spread across Caroline's face. "I may be a bit in love with Becks."

"You and the rest of the world."

Becks started singing, which only reminded Kenny why everyone loved him.

"Is that jealousy I detect?"

"What? No."

She squeezed his arm. "I'm glad you told me." Her arms slid around his waist, and she pulled him closer for a hug.

He wrapped his arms around her. "You don't think I'm a terrible person?"

"For what?"

"I've spent years supporting my parent's anti-gay stance."

"Terrible person? No. Confused? Definitely."

He'd spent most of his life in a constant state of confusion, wanting things he knew he shouldn't. Hated himself for things he couldn't control.

"People are staring at us," Caroline whispered.

"It's because of me. I've felt their eyes on me since the moment I arrived."

"Well, for once, it's nice not to be on the receiving end of their judgments." She went quiet for a moment. "Want to mess with them?"

"What do you have in mind?"

"Well, I'll have quite a bit of explaining to do to my boyfriend, but he'd be the first person wanting me to give them something else to talk about."

"I don't understand."

She rose up on her toes, fitting her mouth over his. The kiss wasn't heated. There was no tongue. Just two friends who were in this together. She pulled away and smiled. "The first daughter and the maybe-gay senator's son sharing a lip lock? Scandalous."

"Not gay. I'm bi, so I still enjoyed that." He grinned.

"Okay, well, we won't tell my boyfriend that part." Her laughter cut off when a figure walked toward them.

Preston Montgomery's imposing frame towered over Caroline, matching Kenny in height. "Son," he growled. "You're making a scene."

He didn't know what got into him, but defiance took hold. "Actually, Father, you're the one currently making the scene." He gestured to the politicians and dignitaries who'd stopped talking to stare at them.

Preston gripped Kenny's arm. Kenny winced in pain but acted otherwise unaffected, schooling his features.

His father leaned in and dropped his voice. "You are not to associate with the Brooks children. They will corrupt you, Kenneth."

A laugh burst out of Caroline, and she clapped a hand over her mouth. Kenny's father didn't even spare her a glance as he kept his hard eyes trained on his son.

"I expect more out of you, son. You have a big future ahead if you don't associate with the wrong people."

All defiance drained out of him at that, replaced with pure exhaustion. He didn't see the same future his father did. One of politics and scheming. All Kenny ever wanted was to play hockey and to live on his own terms.

Turning to Caroline, he offered her a sad smile. "My father has some people he'd like me to talk to."

He didn't say I'll talk to you later or see you soon because he didn't know if that would be true. Once upon a time, all the kids surrounding the power in Washington could exist in the same place together. Now, as they grew up, sides had to be chosen. A line was drawn down the middle of the aisle based on beliefs, political views, and policies. And children followed in the footsteps of their parents—at least until they found their own voice.

Kenny trailed his father through a long line of greetings. Senators on the "right side" of the issues smiled and shook hands. Some offered false sympathy for what Kenny went through. Their teenage children stood alongside their parents like the drone Kenny never wanted to become.

Did it ever change?

Out of the corner of his eye, he saw Nicky standing off to the side trying to get Kenny's attention. Even after everything that happened between them, they were still sort of friends. Nicky was the only person who truly knew Kenny.

Kenny waved him away as he eyed the conservative men and women standing with his father, the same men and women who considered Kenny's kiss with Nicky an assault.

But Nicky didn't get the hint. He walked toward them, toward his own doom without realizing it. And all Kenny could do was stand frozen, seeing the truck that was about to hit Nicky but unable to stop it.

Kenny's mother joined them, and it took her a moment to

realize Nicky was there. A tense beat of silence stretched between them as Victoria Montgomery lifted her head.

"Hey, Ken." Nicky stuck his hands in the pockets of his slacks and lifted his shoulders in an "aw shucks" gesture Kenny had always loved. Nicky was the ultimate boy next door. Handsome in an unassuming way and too good for the likes of Kenny Montgomery.

"Nicky," Kenny choked out. "You shouldn't—" A heavy hand landed on his shoulder.

"You have a lot of nerve, kid." Kenny's father took a step toward Nicky. "Coming to the White House like this."

Nicky narrowed his eyes. "I was invited."

Kenny's mom stepped in, her voice going up a notch. "Ah yes, by the First Son. You gays have to stick together, huh?"

What little hope Kenny had that his parents would ever understand shriveled inside him. He searched frantically for a way out, wanting to be anywhere else. Partygoers in the vicinity stared at the Ohio senator and his wife, who were supposedly defending their son's honor.

But Kenny had no honor. If he did, he'd stop this before it went any further. Instead, he became a kid again, punished for the slightest disobedience. Since then, he'd learned it was best to excel at his parents' lessons. One of which was to never let anything affect you emotionally.

If only that worked.

Nicky grit his teeth. "Yes, us gays do stick together so bigoted assholes like you can't tear us down."

"You don't know me, young man. But I know you. I know your kind. You take whatever you think belongs to you as if your desires are something we should all celebrate."

Nicky looked to Kenny in sympathy, as if he finally understood why Kenny took the actions he had in their closeted relationship—why he never fully gave himself to Nicky.

But Kenny didn't want sympathy. He needed Nicky to hate him for his mother's words, to despise him for his inaction.

Victoria Montgomery wasn't finished. "Your lifestyle is unnatural. I won't let you bring my son down with you."

"Mom…" Kenny couldn't get another word out.

His mother didn't even look at him. "My son is a good boy. And you attacked him."

Gasps rang out around them. Kenny wanted to yell at everyone present. Nicky didn't attack him. If anything, it was the other way around. Kenny had gone to Nicky's house, hoping to get back together. He'd initiated the kiss beside the pool—just as he'd initiated a thousand kisses with Nicky before. How was he to know the paparazzi were lurking around the St. Germaine property?

And still, Kenny's lips remained clamped shut. Sweat dotted across his brow. He'd never truly feared his parents, not until then. Nicky didn't deserve this, but who would be there for him? Becks was still up on stage, oblivious to the verbal beating his boyfriend suffered. And Kenny… well, he was a coward.

A tear slid down Kenny's cheek. His mother finally noticed him. She raised her voice when she addressed Nicky again. "Look at my son. You've destroyed him. You're a vile human being."

Nicky's eyes watered as he took in the crowd. Kenny wanted to go to him, to tell him he was sorry. But his legs wouldn't move.

"You're going to pay for what you've done to my son."

Chapter 6

Asher

"I'm sorry, Mrs. Montgomery." Asher stepped between Nicky and the woman bullying him. "Correct me if I'm wrong, but it sounds like you're threatening one of my guests." Asher's heart thudded in his chest. He should not be doing this, but someone had to step in and put these assholes in their place.

"Your *guest* has a history of harassing my son." Victoria Montgomery's face turned red with rage.

"Kenny seems fine to me. A bit embarrassed by his mother, maybe, but I'm embarrassed by my parents all the time. What kid isn't, am I right?" He tried to make light of the situation. "But seriously, I know Nicky St. Germaine pretty well, and he wouldn't hurt a fly."

"He assaulted my—"

"I know what the tabloids claim and I've heard the rumors. Everyone here has, *ma'am.* And everyone here also knows that ninety-nine percent of what they publish is garbage."

"Are you calling my son a liar?"

"Definitely not. I don't recall Kenny ever saying a mean word about Nicky, but that's not the point here, is it? You've verbally attacked one of my closest friends, who happens to be gay, like me

—and we all know how you and your husband feel about that. You don't have to like us, but you should give us the common courtesy of treating us like human beings." Asher took Nicky's hand in his. "Whatever happened between Nicky and Kenny is between them. Respectfully, Mrs. Montgomery, it's none of your damn business." Asher turned, dragging a stunned Nicky behind him.

"You didn't have to do that," Nicky whispered, "but thank you."

"I don't have very many friends, so the ones I do have are really important to me." Asher cast a nervous glance at the bystanders. "But I probably just made it worse." He'd seen more than a few phones out during the scene he'd just caused with the senator and Mrs. Montgomery. No doubt it was already making its way onto social media.

"Well, it's not like either one of us hasn't been there before. But Kenny can't take another stint in the media circus. It's really getting to him."

"You're defending him? He's telling people you assaulted him." Asher couldn't see how Nicky could be so kindhearted.

"There's a lot more to it than that. Kenny's struggling to find his way, and his parents don't make that easy. He needs friends he can count on."

"You're a good guy, Nicky." Asher dropped his hand, aware of all the eyes on them. If he were totally honest with himself, he had a bit of a crush on Nicky. What he wouldn't give to find someone like him. A nice guy with a good heart and no drama.

"Hi, Nicky," Asher's dad approached them.

"Mr. President, sir." Nicky's cheeks flushed pink. "It's wonderful to see you again."

"Please call me Bennett, all of Asher's friends do." Asher choked back a laugh. Harper was the only one who called his parents by their given names.

"Of course, er...Mr. Bennett, sir." Nicky's hand trembled as he shook the former president's hand.

"That'll do, I suppose." Asher's dad laughed. "I apologize for Senator and Mrs. Montgomery. There's no excuse for their behavior." He laid a comforting hand on Nicky's shoulder. "You're our guest, and you shouldn't be subjected to that kind of hate—anywhere in this country, least of all the White House."

"It's okay, Mr. Bennett. I'm used to dealing with jerks." Nicky tried to shrug it off. He'd certainly dealt with his fair share of media attention and the slander that inevitably came along with it as Beckett Anderson's boyfriend.

"No, it's not okay, son. It's never okay for someone to treat another human being with such hatred. We should be setting a better example for your generation." The former president sighed.

"We'll get there one day, sir." Nicky cast a glance back at the hate-filled senator who was supposed to represent him and the state of Ohio.

"It shouldn't be this hard to teach people not to hate," Asher added. "Grown-ass adults should know better."

"Couldn't have said it better myself," Bennett said. "Mind if I have a word with my son?" He turned to Nicky. "I believe Beckett will be off stage soon, and he might need some—"

"Adult supervision," Nicky supplied with a grin. "I'll catch you later, Ash." Nicky turned to leave.

"Sorry, Dad, I know—"

His father held up a hand to stop his apology. "I get it, Ash. Your friend was in trouble, and no one was there to defend him. As a father, I could not be more proud of you for standing up for Nicky. But we're a political family, son. Your mother is the president of the United States, and our behavior reflects on her. Next time, alert one of the secret service agents to the situation and let them handle it."

"Right, right." Asher nodded. He knew this speech by heart. He'd heard a version of it his whole life. He couldn't remember a time when one of his parents wasn't the president or running for president. Asher didn't know a world where he was free to just be himself. He wondered if anyone realized he had no idea what it was like not to live under a microscope with secret service agents guarding his every move and every little thing he said and did ending up in the media.

"It's okay. I'll smooth things over with Senator and Mrs. Montgomery. You just go enjoy your birthday and be more careful about what you say next time." Asher's father walked away, leaving his son feeling even worse than he had before.

Would he ever know a life outside the presidency? Outside of Washington and politics? Asher scanned the crowd around him, looking for a friendly face. There were lots of them, but none he cared to approach. "My birthday party and I know like four people here."

"Ugh, I know that look." Harper handed him a champagne glass filled with sparkling water. "I wear that look myself at these things. Come on, chug that and let's dance."

"I don't want to dance." Asher knew he was sulking, but he didn't care.

"Your boy, Beckett, is almost done performing. We have to dance. It's, like, impolite not to dance when your friend is singing at your birthday party."

"Fine." Asher guzzled the sparkling water that turned out not to be sparkling water at all. "Dad will kill me if he saw that."

"It was *water*." She gave him a wink. "That's all Papa POTUS needs to know."

Asher let her drag him on to the dance floor where everyone watched them, cheering for the birthday boy who would literally rather be anywhere else than in the spotlight.

"There he is, ladies and gentlemen," Beckett said in his exaggerated announcer's voice. "The man of the hour himself, Asher Brooks! I'm singing 'Happy Birthday' for you before I leave this stage, kid, so don't go anywhere. Harper, sit on him if you have to."

"I'm your girl, Becks!" Harper shouted, holding Asher's hand in a death grip.

"This one's for you, Valor." Becks shot him a wink as he started up Asher's favorite song, "It Is What It Is." It was a fun, upbeat song with such complex guitar playing, few could pull it off, but Becks made it look easy.

Asher was normally a wallflower, preferring to stick to the shadows by himself, but there was one thing he loved about these events, and that was dancing. On a crowded dance floor, he didn't have to worry about people watching him or studying his every move. He didn't have to worry as much if he ended up in a video on someone's social media feed because he was actually a pretty good dancer. And Harper was even better.

People called them the perfect couple despite the fact Asher was gay. With her short curly hair in a wild mess, threaded with feathers and subtle blue highlights, she was a fashion icon herself. Her dress was modestly short but brightly colored with a flouncy skirt and chunky jewelry. She dressed like no one else, funky with a hard edge but always fashionable. There were fashion bloggers who stalked her for tips. He supposed his stylists dressed him to compliment her style since they spent a great deal of time together and that made people want to see them together. He loved Harper and was happy to have her in his life. He just wanted more than a best friend.

"Loosen up, Ash." Harper moved with him to the beat of the music. "It's your birthday, try to have some fun for once. It's not every day we get serenaded by Beckett Anderson."

"We?" He laughed at the star-struck look on her face. "You're right." Asher smiled, and for the first time that night, he relaxed and enjoyed himself. Part of it was the dancing, part of it was having Becks on stage, and part of it was likely the champagne he'd chugged. It wasn't his first time drinking, but champagne tended to hit him hard, and he'd always promised his parents he wouldn't be seen drinking openly at these events—at least not until he was twenty-one. Asher really hoped by then these parties wouldn't be such a big part of his life anymore.

"That was fun!" Harper clapped when the dance was over and Beckett prepared to finish his set. "You know I love you right?" She took his hand, slipping a small giftwrapped present into his hands. "Do NOT turn this in as a gift of State. It doesn't qualify because it's something stupid from your bestie."

"Thanks, Harp." He threw his arms around her as they stood with everyone else near the stage. As Becks sang "Happy Birthday" a cappella, Harper whispered to him, "I'm going to head out early and let you hang out with Becks and Nicky for a change."

"You don't have to do that. They'd love to meet you."

"And I will. Next time. Go hang with your people. You have Harper time every other day of the year."

"Harper time?" Asher smiled, watching the way Becks worked the crowd with just his voice.

"Yes, and you'll have me back all to yourself soon. Go try to enjoy your birthday."

"Love you." Asher hugged her tightly.

"Love you too, you sad little mess." She gave him a playful shove as she slipped away through the crowd.

"Happy birthday, Ash," Becks called from the stage. "We love you, kid." Becks cheered with the crowd, wishing him the happiest of birthdays. Asher shoved his hands in his pockets and pasted on his fake-confident smile for the crowd.

He waved and smiled, leading the audience in a cry for an encore from Beckett.

As Becks started up with his band for one more song, Asher managed to slip away, seeking a moment of solitude. He was going to explode if he didn't get two seconds to himself soon.

He appreciated Harper's gesture, letting him have the rest of the night with Nicky and Becks since he didn't get to see them as often as he'd like. But at the same time, she was his buffer against the stares.

Asher walked past the bar, grabbing a bottle of champagne on his way toward the balcony. It was his eighteenth birthday, if he couldn't have his Prince Charming and a party of his own choosing, then he at least deserved some alone time with his thoughts and a little liquid courage to get him through the rest of the night. He was beginning to think his Prince Charming was lost somewhere, refusing to ask for directions.

Chapter 7

Kenny

The cold November air slapped Kenny in the face as soon as he stumbled onto the promenade balcony that wrapped around this end of the White House. Below, secret service agents patrolled the perfectly manicured grounds.

Tapping the open champagne bottle he'd snagged from a table near the door against his leg, Kenny stepped up to the railing, disgust washing over him. No, not disgust for who he was. At least this time.

Disgust for what he'd done—or hadn't done. Nicky's shocked face would be forever burned into his brain. Why couldn't he be a better friend, a better man?

Why did he let his parents control every aspect of his life?

Because he'd never known another way.

"You're spineless, Kenneth Montgomery." He let his own words break the silence of the night. It wasn't the first time Kenny let his sense of self-preservation get the better of him. He'd treated Nicky like a horrible secret for the entire two years they'd dated before finally dumping him for a girl—at least that was what Kenny made him believe.

Lifting the bottle to his mouth, Kenny took a swig, letting the dry champagne burn his throat. He needed more, anything to make him stop feeling like such a failure. He failed his parents by being something they hated. He failed Nicky by freezing instead of defending him.

And he failed himself for refusing to accept such a gigantic part of himself.

After another gulp of too-expensive-for-gulping champagne, Kenny lifted his hand to his forehead, forming an L with his thumb and index finger. That's what he was.

"What are you doing?" A familiar voice interrupted the silence of his sanctuary.

Kenny quickly dropped his hand and lifted the bottle against his lips instead of answering Asher.

Asher stepped up beside him and held out his own bottle of champagne with a laugh. "Great minds think alike?"

Kenny only shrugged. Once, he'd confided in Asher Brooks about everything. The president's son was the only person who knew how hard living in Preston and Victoria Montgomery's house really was. But that was before. Before the First Son came out as gay, sparking a nationwide debate many had thought long dead.

Before Kenny chose the wrong side in that debate.

Before their friendship became a political casualty.

"I don't for a second think you consider me to have a great mind." It was the kind of joke Kenny would have once laughed at. Instead, he said it dryly with no humor, only truth.

Asher rolled his eyes. "Look, I just came out here to get away from the masses."

"You mean like my mother?" Her words to Nicky still rang in his ears.

"And every other person who looks at me like something is wrong with me. Sorry, Ken, but you're the lesser of two evils right now, so I'm not leaving." He blew out a breath. "Besides, this is my balcony."

"You own a balcony?"

"Shut up."

"You shut up."

One corner of Asher's mouth tilted up. "Real mature."

Kenny shrugged and took another drink, enjoying the warmth spreading through him. "What's going on in there?"

"Dinner will be served once Becks finishes his last encore."

"And they won't miss the birthday boy?"

Asher ran his free hand through his natural hair. "My parents probably will, but no one else really cares what I do."

"Are you serious right now?"

"What?"

"Everyone cares what you do. It's why your face is constantly plastered across the tabloids."

"Seems you and I are the same in that."

Kenny wiped the back of his hand across his mouth. "Excuse me?"

Asher studied him for a moment. "Seems like the paps like you just as much as me these days. Conservative senator's son caught in a lip lock with another dude. Bet your dad hated that."

"Why are you talking to me, Ash? We aren't friends."

Asher rubbed the back of his neck and bit his lip. "Want to get out of here?"

It was on the tip of Kenny's tongue to say no. Asher had every reason to hate Kenny, and it only made Kenny feel worse. He flicked his eyes to the door. On the other side, the sycophants and narcissists of Washington were sitting down to eat.

"Yeah." Kenny took another drink. "Where can we go?"

"Follow me."

They slipped into the back of the banquet hall, and Asher

motioned to a secret service agent Kenny recognized as Danny. He'd been guarding Ash since he was young.

"Danny." Asher eyed his agent. "We're getting out of here, and I don't want you to argue."

"It's your party, kid." Danny folded his arms across his chest.

"I'm aware. Either we're sneaking away without you or I allow you to do your job if you tell no one else."

Danny sighed, sounding for a moment like a tired parent. "Fine. This better not be dangerous, Asher." His gaze caught on the bottles of champagne they both carried. "And you better not get me fired."

"We won't. Promise." He nodded to Kenny. "I'll be right back. I need to find Becks."

Asher wound around the tables, leaving Kenny with the broad-shouldered Danny. Danny watched him suspiciously. Once, Danny had been like a friend too, always right alongside them, protecting them. But the coldness Kenny had expected in Asher was evident in his agent's eyes.

Asher returned only a moment later. "Becks and Nicky will come when they can."

Great, Kenny thought to himself. *Just what I need.* Even all the way in Washington, he couldn't get away from those two.

Asher waved him forward. The president lifted her eyes to them as they made their way to the front doors. Her disappointment was evident on her face, but so was her resignation. She wouldn't stop her son.

Kenny made a cursory glance, making sure his father didn't spot him. Finding him nowhere, he followed Asher into the hall.

"You bring a coat?" Asher asked.

Kenny shook his head. He'd only worn his suit jacket. "Where are we going?" He hadn't really needed to ask. As soon as Asher asked about a coat, he knew. Asher had lived in the White House since he was seven years old and his father won the presidency. His parents became the first couple to hold the office back to back.

Kenny spent a lot of time roaming the storied halls, but there'd been one place the boys loved more than any other.

Asher shot him a wink and picked up speed. Secret service agents paid them no mind as they slipped into the West Wing, crossing the expansive line of offices before pushing open the door to the outside.

On the southern side of the West Wing sat the White House pool surrounded by rows of trees screening it from view. Cabanas lined the concrete all the way to the pool house.

"Little cold for a swim," Danny remarked.

Asher ignored him as he entered the pool house, returning with a bottle of whiskey and two glasses. "Better than champagne. My mom keeps a stash in the pool house."

Kenny stared at him, seeing how different he was from the boy he used to be. "You're telling me the president comes out to the pool to drink in secret?"

A smile cracked Asher's lips. "It's not how it sounds. There's no privacy in the White House. Even in the residence, we have people constantly around. My parents come here to get some time together without everyone constantly watching them."

Already buzzed from the champagne, Kenny dropped onto a chair in one of the cabanas, stretching his legs out in front of him. He'd always liked the president despite his mother's feelings about the "liberal witch" as she called her.

Asher sat next to him while Danny gave them space.

Taking the shot of whiskey Asher held out for him, Kenny studied the dark liquid as if it held all the answers he needed. He threw it back, letting the liquid burn his throat. Despite appearances, Kenny wasn't much of a drinker. Most of his weekends were taken up by training, and he'd been so focused on his game for the past few years, he'd forgotten to have any sort of fun.

Not that he would call sitting with his ex-friend fun. Awkward silence settled over them until Asher coughed and sputtered as he took a shot. He pounded on his chest, trying to breathe.

Kenny couldn't help but laugh. "You okay over there?"

"No," Asher wheezed, shaking his head. "I'm not much of a drinker."

"Then what are we doing out here?"

"I don't know." He leaned his head back on the chair. "We don't do this, Ken. We don't talk."

"I know."

"But you're the one here." He sighed. "Half the people at my own birthday party think I'm some scourge on this country. And the other half think I'm an idol, someone to look up to because I'm just so damn brave."

Kenny didn't know what to say to that. He hadn't spent much time around Asher in recent years, but he'd followed him in the news, and yes, he'd idolized him. But the tired look in Asher's eyes told him that wasn't something he should admit. As the president's son, he was under intense scrutiny, yet he lived his life openly, never apologizing for who he was.

Kenny envied that in him. "You must hate me."

Asher met his gaze. "I do. I really do."

Bending forward, Kenny rested his arms on his knees and averted his eyes, not wanting to show Asher just how much that affected him. At the same time, he wanted the hatred, needed it. It made sense to him.

Asher blew out a breath. "You have done some pretty awful things. It hurt when you abandoned me when I told the world I was gay. It was okay, though, because I realized you were just an asshole and I didn't need you in my life. But Nicky? Tonight, I saw your mother try to break one of my friends—a guy who was only in that position because of some stupid picture I don't even want to ask you about."

He ran a hand over his hair as the silver light from the moon caught in his shining eyes. "You didn't do anything, Ken. I saw the look on your face. I know there's something more going on, but I refuse to believe Nicky attacked you like your parents claim. Contrary to popular belief, us penis-loving men don't go around preying on straight dudes."

"Why aren't you yelling?" Kenny reached for the whiskey and poured himself another shot.

"What?"

"Yell at me. Rant about how I'm some bigoted asshole, no different from my mother. Go on. You know you want to."

"Would that make you feel better, Kenny?"

"Yes."

Asher got to his feet. "I'm not in the business of making you feel better." He walked out from under the cabana, stopping at the edge of the pool.

Kenny took another shot before following him, just hoping it stopped the disgust swirling inside him. Not disgust for Asher or anyone else. Disgust for the man he was becoming.

"Get mad," Kenny yelled. "Why aren't you more mad?" He stopped a few paces away, the whiskey emboldening him.

"No. I wish you had the balls to stand up to your parents, but they have controlled every aspect of your life. I know them, remember? And I used to know you. In a weird way, I understand why you do the things you do."

"I don't want you to understand. I don't deserve it."

"No. You don't."

"Then punch me. Please."

"No."

Anger rose in Kenny, and he didn't know what he was doing until he'd closed the space between them and lunged for Asher, shoving him toward the dark water.

Kenny hit the heated water seconds after Asher. His slacks dragged him down. He kicked his legs as hard as he could to breach the surface and found Asher near the far wall, sputtering and choking out water.

"You're an ass." Asher shook sopping hair out of his eyes.

The water doused the flames of Kenny's anger. "I'm sorry. I shouldn't have pushed you."

"You think?"

"I just don't understand how you can even look at me or be around me. I'm kind of awful."

Asher sighed. "You're not awful. We both live in this world of politics where you have to take a side on everything. There's very little room for the shades of gray between positions."

Kenny wiped water from his eyes and kicked across the pool toward Asher. "You sound like such a politician."

"In a way, I am. As the president's son, I can't ever say the wrong thing."

"I know how that is." Kenny reached for the pool edge and hung on, facing Asher. "Don't you ever just wish you could say what you really think?"

"Sometimes, but I don't know what I really think."

"Me either." Kenny studied his old friend in the dark. The years had changed him, that was for sure. Gone was the gangly kid with skinny legs and buzzed hair. He'd let his natural, curly hair grow out into what some people would call an Afro, but that didn't seem like the right term. He was still kind of skinny, lacking the muscles Kenny developed through his hockey training, but it suited him.

Intelligent eyes met Kenny's. He'd met few people in his life who were as smart as Asher. Not book smart. More like life smart.

"I'm not brave like you, Ash." He dropped his voice. What would Asher do if Kenny admitted to him that he'd dated Nicky for two years in secret before their infamous kiss got out? Instead of voicing the truths he feared, Kenny went another direction. "My parents... I don't know how to stand up to them."

"One moment at a time. One word, one action. Then you move onto the next. If you don't want to be this guy, then don't. Break their control or you'll always be ashamed of yourself."

"I never said I was ashamed."

"Aren't you? You can't tell me while you stood there frozen that you didn't want to tell your mother just what you thought of her."

"Do you think Nicky is okay?"

Asher nodded. "He has Becks. Those two are—"

"Disgustingly cute."

"Yeah." Asher grinned, and the act lit up his entire face. "They really are. They're so sweet together it makes me want to puke."

"Yet you invited them to your party. I was surprised. I didn't even know you kept in touch with them."

"How well do you know them?" The question touched on dangerous territory.

"The three of us grew up in the same town."

Asher nodded as if that was the only explanation he needed. "I guess I knew that. You and Nicky are friends or used to be? You don't have to tell me." He peeled his suit coat down his arms and flung the soaked jacket onto the concrete apron. "You could have at least let me take that off before throwing me into the pool. You're lucky it's heated, because if I froze to death, I'd haunt your ass."

"You weren't going to freeze. Do you know how many stories there are of first ladies swimming every day, even in winter?"

Asher lowered his gaze to Kenny's, ignoring his useless fact. "I wasn't kidding, you know."

"About what?"

"You need to break your parents' control. Be your own man, Ken."

Kenny hadn't realized how close they'd gotten until the steam from their breath mingled between them. Asher didn't even seem to notice as he kept on talking.

"You aren't this guy. The one who fights to take people's freedoms away or lets hatred guide what he does."

Asher didn't know Kenny anymore. He didn't see the man he'd become. In the two years of dating Nicky, Kenny treated him like something to be embarrassed about. He'd broken his heart in the end and then tried to get him back once it was clear he'd moved on.

Who does that?

"I used to think I knew you." Steam rose around them, curling in the cold air.

Kenny dipped his head back, needing to let the water warm his freezing hair. When he tilted his face back down to look at Asher, his old friend watched him closely.

"You did know me." Kenny edged closer.

"Why did you abandon me when I came out?" The vulnerability in his voice caused Kenny's heart to squeeze. He hadn't realized just how hurt Asher was by his actions. "After the news broke, I tried getting in touch with you. My parents used to tell me you just had to get used to the new version of me. But I wasn't a new version, Ken. I was the same kid I'd always been."

"I was scared." Kenny swallowed heavily.

"Of what? That you'd be gay by association? That I had some

kind of disease that would rub off on you?" Tears sprang to his eyes.

When Kenny didn't respond, Asher backed up. "What were you scared of, Kenny?"

Maybe it was the alcohol making him brave. Or maybe he was just so damn tired of not having what he wanted. He inched forward along the wall.

"What are you doing?" Asher asked, his voice shaking.

"Breaking my parents' control." Kenny reached out, wrapping his hand around the back of Asher's head.

Kenny had kissed boys many times before. He used to love kissing Nicky for hours. Acting on his desires wasn't anything new to him. But this wasn't just any boy. It was Asher, and he deserved so much better than the guy who'd crushed him.

Yet, in that moment, Kenny didn't care. He fit his cold lips over Asher's, waiting for him to respond.

But that moment never came. Asher's body went rigid in Kenny's arms, and his lips clamped shut.

"Kenny." Asher said his name on a breath, pushing him away just far enough so a sliver of space stood between them. His eyes flicked between Kenny's. "That's not what I meant when I said you had to break your parents' control."

Kenny pushed away from him, swimming toward the opposite ledge. He was an idiot. For once, he'd let himself act on something he wanted. Asher was right there in front of him, looking way too good with his wet hair hanging around his face and silver light reflecting in his amber eyes.

And Asher thought it was an act, a ploy to piss off his father.

"Kenny," Asher called after him. "Why would you do that if not for your father?"

"You know what, Ash? I don't know." He hauled himself out of the pool. "Must have just been a stupid impulse. Forget about it, okay?"

Asher was quiet for a moment. "Ken…"

"I said forget about it."

"Yeah. Okay."

Danny appeared at the edge of the trees looking frazzled. "Asher, your friends are harassing me to let them back here."

"Who is it?" Asher, refusing to look at Kenny, focused on his secret service agent instead.

"Beckett and Nicky."

An indulgent smile spread across Asher's face and Kenny wished he was the one who'd put it there. "Let them in."

"Thank God." Danny rubbed his chin. "If I have to listen to Beckett chatter on about nonsense for one more moment…" He grumbled to himself and turned to walk back where he'd left them.

Kenny walked into the pool house to retrieve a towel. After wringing out the bottom of his shirt, he wrapped it around himself, trying to still his shivering as a gust of chilly air struck him.

Becks sauntered toward the pool like he owned the place. "We swimming? Hell yeah." He threw his suit coat on the ground, before taking a running start, and leaped into the air, ending in an epic belly flop.

"Ouch." Nicky laughed as he watched his boyfriend surface and shake off the pain. He turned to Kenny, scanning his wet clothes.

All Kenny wanted to do was leave the White House and forget about the night entirely. But Nicky's gaze held him in place. There was a time where he'd have done anything to pull Nicky into a closet or a back room and kiss the smirk from his lips.

But now, he shrank under the scrutiny.

Nicky rubbed his eyes as if not believing the next words out of his own mouth. "You must be freezing. Take off your shirt, and I'll give you my jacket."

"You'll give me your jacket?"

"Just do it, Kenny."

He unbuttoned his dress shirt and slid it from his shoulders before taking Nicky's offered coat. It fit him tight across the shoulders but started providing his body with some of the heat it had lost.

"For what it's worth," Kenny began, looking to the stars overhead. "I'm sorry."

"It's not worth very much."

Crossing his arms over his chest, he lowered his gaze to his probably-ruined shoes. "I know."

"But I'll take it."

"What?" Their gazes connected, and Kenny saw the kid he'd known, the one he hadn't let himself love.

"We both know what happened with that kiss. I didn't attack you. You kissed me. We also both know that you were a confused asshole the entire time we dated. But…you didn't ask for the media attention that surrounded me at the time. If I hadn't been the paparazzi's favorite punching bag because of my relationship with Becks, you'd never have been dragged into the mess. No one should be outed against their will. I don't hold it against you that you can't tell your parents yet."

He shrugged. "It's your story to tell, Ken. No one else's. But you've got to stop being an ass."

"I know."

"Does Asher know? The truth, I mean."

Kenny sighed but said nothing.

"I'll take that as a no. Just…if you're going to be friends with him, be careful."

"I'm not friends with him." Not anymore, at least. One night didn't change years of separation.

"Okay. That's your choice too. But when Becks was struggling, Ash was there for him. He's probably the best kind of friend to have. I know what you're going to say, though. You don't need anyone. Kenny Montgomery never has."

Kenny shrugged. "I can't change who I am."

"No." He gave him a pointed look. "You can't. But you can change how you feel about who you are." Putting a hand on Kenny's shoulder, Nicky turned his attention to the pool where Becks and Asher had started wrestling, dragging each other under the water. "Excuse me. I have to go make sure my boyfriend doesn't kill the president's son." He shot him a smile before canon-balling into the water.

Kenny gave them all one final look before walking past Danny and crossing the south lawn. He nodded to secret service agents once he reached the back entrance into the West Wing. A middle-aged woman stopped him and insisted on escorting him back to the party. He agreed, knowing he wasn't supposed to wander the White House on his own.

As soon as he stepped into the ballroom, his father rushed toward him, red creeping up his neck. "Where have you been, Kenneth?"

What could he say? Drinking with the president's son? Trying to kiss a boy who didn't want to kiss him back?

"You're soaking wet." His mother joined them and guided him from the room, away from the curious glances burning into them.

"I fell in the pool." Kenny shrugged.

His father leaned in. "Have you been drinking? Your breath reeks of whiskey."

Once again, he only shrugged.

His mother wrapped a tight grip around his arm. "Where is your shirt, Kenneth? We're leaving. You're an embarrassment."

His dad, never one to take Kenny's side over his mom's, nodded. "My colleagues asked about you, but you'd disappeared. And you show back up dripping wet and smelling of booze."

"And don't think Asher Brooks' absence has been missed. Were you with the gay kid?" His mom's perpetual scowl deepened.

They reached the front walk where a car waited to take them to their DC townhome.

His mother continued to blather on about Asher not being their type of people, and Kenny couldn't take it anymore.

"Stop it!" he yelled.

The driver opened the back door of the car, but Kenny refused to slide in, not until he'd said everything he needed to say.

"Kenneth." His father's grip tightened. "Watch your tone."

"Why do you hate them so much?"

"I don't hate anyone."

"Bullshit. Do they frighten you?"

"Don't be stupid, son."

"Well, guess what—" Kenny never got to finish his statement because bile rose in his throat, and he hunched forward, spilling the contents of his stomach onto his father's thousand-dollar shoes.

Chapter 8

Asher

"Dump water on him."

"Nope, he will come up swinging. Dad has the scars to prove it."

"It's like trying to wake the dead. Are you guys sure he's all right?"

"How much did he drink last night?"

"I'm going to pull his hair."

"Touch the hair and die, Beckett," Asher mumbled from under his covers. His head throbbed, and his tongue stuck to the roof of his mouth.

"Wake up, birthday boy." Beckett and Nicky bounced on his bed.

Asher sat up, shoving the covers off his head as his stomach heaved. "I'm going to be sick."

"Drink this, little brother, it's a magic hangover cure." His sister shoved a cold bottle of water in his hands.

"Water?" He rolled his eyes at her. "Really?"

"Really. The alcohol dehydrates you, so you rehydrate, and you feel better."

Asher brought the bottle to his lips and as the water passed his parched lips, he wasn't sure he'd ever tasted anything as wonderful as ice-cold water. It helped, but he still felt like puking. "What the hell happened last night? And why are you all so cheery?"

"I only had a few drinks," Caroline said, "but I don't think I was cool enough to get invited to your pool party. Besides, I think my stylists would murder me if I jumped in the pool wearing couture."

"I don't drink." Nicky smiled.

"I had a few beers." Becks shrugged. "You gotta be careful with champagne, kid. It's all fuzzy and sweet, but it'll get you hammered. Especially that expensive stuff."

"Ugh, I don't normally drink more than a few sips." Asher didn't really like the effects of alcohol. He didn't like losing his inhibitions when the least little thing he did could cause repercussions for his parents. But last night, he was looking for an escape, and he'd found it, but he wasn't proud of it.

"Knock, knock," Danny's voice drifted in from the hall.

"What is happening right now?" Asher frowned at the series of dining carts the kitchen staff wheeled into his room.

"Your birthday breakfast is served." Nicky sat pretzel style on the edge of the bed.

"Food?" Asher's stomach heaved again. "I can't handle whatever's on that cart." The thought of eggs and bacon and all the heavy breakfast foods the kitchen likely sent up was more than he could stomach. He covered his mouth and reached for his bottle of water when Becks made a show of unveiling his breakfast feast.

He laughed before he could get the bottle to his lips. "Cereal?" He grinned when he saw every assortment of sugary and healthy cereals displayed on the carts. "I am way more excited about this cereal buffet than I should be." He crept out of his bed, aware of his rumpled T-shirt and too-big basketball shorts. His hair probably looked awful too, but he didn't care.

"It's pretty sad they don't let you eat cereal, man," Becks said around a mouthful of Lucky Charms. "That's like a staple in our house."

"We'd probably starve without it," Nicky added.

"Oh, you guys are living together now?" Asher asked as he made the first of many bowls of cereal he planned to eat this morning. This was so much better than a fancy party with people he didn't know.

"No, when Becks says 'our house' he means the apartment I share with my brother and Nari. Becks lives across the hall when he's home from the tour, but there's never any food there. He would die if we didn't feed him."

"It's only funny because it's true." Becks nodded gravely. "Pass me the Froot Loops."

"Don't you want fresh milk, man?" Asher frowned at him. "You cannot mix your Lucky Charms milk with your Froot Loops milk. That's just Cereal 101."

"I like to live dangerously."

"You guys are too adorable for words, aren't you?" Caroline said.

"Yes, ma'am." Becks tipped his imaginary cowboy hat at her.

"I'm going to leave you boys to your cereal and cartoons." Caroline stood to leave. "And, Ash"—she paused at the door—"you've got about an hour before Mom and Dad descend on you with their birthday presents."

"Thanks, sis." Asher poured himself a bowl of Count Chocula, his favorite. He didn't think they even made it anymore.

"Where's the remote," Becks asked.

"Dresser." Asher nodded across the room.

"Becks, that's rude, babe." Nicky elbowed him in the ribs.

"Hey, the lady said there would be cartoons." Becks sat back against the headboard, sandwiching Asher between himself and Nicky.

"Now, *this* is a good birthday." Asher smiled at his two friends, sitting on his bed eating cereal and watching cartoons like they were five.

"I hear lots of laughter coming from this room." Asher's mom peeked inside her son's room.

"Good morning, Madam President." Becks scrambled from his spot on the bed and gave her a formal bow. "Always a pleasure, ma'am."

"Is he always so silly?" She actually giggled, her cheeks blushing.

"Pretty much," Nicky said. "But thank you for having us, Madame President."

"You can call me Nora when it's just us." She winked. "And I'm so glad you two could make it. I hear there was one hell of a party at my pool house last night."

"Sorry about that, ma'am," Becks said in that charming way of his. "But the boy deserved a real party for his birthday—not that your party wasn't cool too."

Nicky hid his face behind his hands, and Asher just laughed.

The president threw her head back and laughed with her son. "We do know how to throw the dullest parties here in Washington, don't we? We knew something was going on when all the college and high school kids disappeared at dinner and the staff was scrambling to keep you guys warm and dry outside the heated pool."

"I thought about ditching the banquet when I saw three of the staff rolling heat lamps out toward the West Wing," Asher's dad added as he came in to join them. "I knew there was probably a much better party wherever you all disappeared to."

"Sorry, Mom," Asher said, scratching the back of his head. "It just kind of happened. I hope we didn't end up on the news for it."

"Oh, but we did." Becks laughed, pulling his phone from his pocket. Clearing his throat, he read, "The White House turned into the House of Beckett last night when the singing sensation Beckett Anderson—that's me—serenaded his biggest fan, First Kid Asher Brooks—that's you—on the night of his eighteenth birthday bash. White House sources say the State affair turned into an impromptu pool party on this cold October night when the birthday boy and his closest friends opted for a late-night swim in the heated pool, in lieu of the formal banquet dinner his mother—none other than the POTUS herself—had planned for them inside."

"Sorry, kid, it seems I took the headlines from last night." Becks shook his head with regret.

"Don't listen to him," Nicky said. "He just looked for the one article that mentioned him more than you."

"No bad press then?" Asher eyed his parents.

"None you need to worry about, kiddo."

"Well, Nick-Nick, we need to get going." Becks tugged his boyfriend against his side. "Our flight leaves at noon, and I *think* our man, Ash has somewhere to be."

"Nah, I don't have plans. Wish you guys could stay a little longer."

"Maybe next time." Becks grabbed his hand and gave him a man hug, complete with a back slap. "I have to get back to the tour, and Nicky has school."

"You should come visit Nashville sometime," Nicky said,

offering Asher a much more understated hug. "It's boring with this guy on the road all the time."

"Yeah, I'll try to make it out there sometime soon." Asher tried not to show too much enthusiasm, but he so rarely got to leave Washington he'd jump at any chance to get out of this town—if that meant he got to see his friends too, then even better. Hell, he'd go see Kenny if it got him out of politics for a day. But the thought of Kenny brought memories of last night crashing back into his mind. Memories he'd rather forget.

"Text us when you get back." Becks called over his shoulder as he and Nicky left his room.

"Back?" Asher frowned.

"Hush, babe, you'll ruin the surprise." He heard Nicky's patient voice down the hall.

"Where am I going?" Asher looked at his parents.

"Get dressed, we're going to Camp David for a few days." His mom shoved him toward his closet.

"Really?" Camp David was his favorite place on the planet. It was the closest thing to a normal home he'd ever experienced, and Asher loved it.

"I'll see you in the helicopter, birthday boy." She left to go make her final arrangements for the trip.

"Like, how many days? Two?" he asked, hoping for at least three.

"Four," his dad said.

"Don't joke. Four days?" They never got to stay that long unless it was a pre-planned vacation that took months of organizing schedules to manage.

"Four whole days, and we're leaving in, like, twenty minutes so you better hurry up and do something with that hangover hair."

"I need to pack!" Asher lunged for his closet.

"Your sister packed for you last night while you were having a pool party. Meet us on the south lawn when you're ready."

"Thanks, Dad."

"Happy birthday, son. I'm proud of you."

"For what?" Asher glanced back at his father.

"Just for being you, Ash."

"Do you really need eight pairs of Target jeans, son?" Asher's mom asked, looking ridiculous in her disguise. Their stylists had helped them conceal their identities before they left Camp David this morning to sneak off to Target for some guilty pleasure shopping. He wouldn't recognize his mom if he hadn't seen her transformation into a green-eyed redhead with his own eyes.

"You have no idea how much I need these in my life." Asher clutched the stack of comfortably loose jeans to his chest. "I'll have to hide them from Carlie, or she'll throw them away. She insists on putting me in tight skinny jeans."

"She's your stylist, it's her job to make you look nice, Ash. And she does her job well. But if you're getting comfortable jeans, I'm getting T-shirts while we're here. I'll meet you in the bakery, and we'll pick out a cake for dessert, and then we'll go to that burger place you like to order dinner."

Asher smiled as the President of the United States turned her shopping cart around and headed to the women's department at the local Target in Thurmont, Maryland.

Of course, the secret service was everywhere, but they blended in with the other shoppers and kept a close eye on them. It probably wasn't the best idea to go incognito, but it was one of his favorite things to do with his mom. This was just the first time they'd attempted it since she became president.

Asher took off for the toy department to look for board games. He had his eye on a new *Settlers of Catan* expansion pack, but he wouldn't admit that to anyone outside his family. He was supposed to be this cool, gay, fashion icon, but in reality, he was just a quiet kid who spent most of his time alone.

Asher often wondered what kind of person he would have been if he hadn't grown up under the microscope of the White House.

"Get the *Seafarers* pack, it's the best," an unfamiliar voice said. "*Traders and Barbarians* is too fussy."

It was a jarring sensation to be approached by a stranger in Asher's world. It caught him off guard for a moment. "Uh, thanks, man," Asher said, reaching to make sure his hair was still tucked inside his hat. It would only be a matter of seconds before Danny and his minions swooped in to steer the boy away from him. He could see them coming now, closing in the circle around him, but Danny intercepted them, letting Asher have his privacy for a moment longer.

"You can start playing *Seafarers* pretty much right away." The boy reached for the blue box, oblivious of the security situation going on around him. "This set up is the best." He pointed to the huge map on the back of the box. "You can pick up the new rules as you go. *Traders and Barbarians* has cool stuff too, but it's not really a pick up and play kind of expansion you'd want to introduce on game night."

"Yeah, my mom would get frustrated with too many new rules," Asher said, taking the box from the super cute but dorky guy beside him.

"Your mom?" The boy laughed, and Asher's heart sank. Even among the gaming nerds of the world, it was so not cool to spend game night hanging out with your mom.

"Yeah, well, she insists on family game night every couple of months."

"Your mom sounds cool. My mom forgot how to have fun years ago. She lost that ability the same place she lost her sense of humor."

Asher relaxed. "I'd rather play with my friends. They aren't as vicious as she is." He laughed, wondering if Becks and Nicky were the board game types. Harper was, for sure. Maybe he could plan an actual game night with friends—now that he had more than one.

"Well, hope you enjoy it." He gave Asher a wink and walked away with a set of gaming dice and a pack of some kind of trading cards. *I could definitely be into cute gaming geeks.* He placed the expansion pack in his cart and set off to meet his mother in the bakery. She was likely still picking out T-shirts, so he stopped by the electronic department on the way, feeling about as normal as Asher Brooks had ever been.

Asher reached for his phone in the darkness, unable to sleep. Again. Barely three days ago, he'd received his first kiss...ever. It was a train wreck, but he couldn't stop thinking about it. Or what it meant when the one who'd done the kissing wasn't even gay. Was Kenny trying to mock him? Or had it actually meant something to him? Was there some truth to what the media said about him?

Asher scrolled through Kenny's Instagram profile...not for the first time. He didn't know why he bothered. His feed was full of hockey stuff and the occasional image of Kenny at Defiance Academy. It looked like he was living on campus now even though the school was in the same town where his parents lived. Kenny's parents spent a lot of time in Washington these days. Had they just stuck their kid in boarding school to keep him out of trouble and away from the spotlight? As much of an ass as Kenny Montgomery was, Asher felt kind of sorry for him.

Asher almost scrolled past a picture of himself with Kenny from years ago. They were at Kenny's house in Twin Rivers during his father's second campaign. They must have been about twelve at the time. It was a good memory. Asher tapped on the heart button below the image without thinking.

"No! Undo, undo!" He tapped at the screen only to unclick and reclick the heart again. "Stop spazzing, Ash." He dropped his phone on the bed in front of him before he could do any more damage. Calmly, he unclicked the heart button. It was early in the morning, so would Kenny even see it? Did he have push notifications on? If you unliked a photo right away, did the app take back the push notification? "Crap." He sat back against his headboard.

"One failed sort of half-kiss, and now he knows I'm stalking him." Asher beat his head against the upholstered headboard. "It couldn't have been a recent post I liked. No, it had to be something so far back in his profile it's practically a fossil."

He grabbed his phone and scrolled through his contacts. He still had Kenny's number as long as it hadn't changed. "One little text could clear this up." He started typing.

Asher: Hey, Kenny. It was good to see you again …

"That's so stupid, Ash." He erased the text and started over. Several times. How did you tell someone you didn't mean to like their post and not sound like a total loser?

Asher: Hey, so I found this old picture of us from ...

"Just stop while you're ahead." Asher deleted the text but the phone fumbled out of his hand and slid between the headboard and the mattress, landing on the floor under the bed. He leaped off the bed and scrambled to reach his phone.

"Oh my God, what did you *just* do, you idiot!" Asher lay on the floor and stared at the screen, his stomach coming to rest somewhere between his lungs. He'd sent a text. And not a good one. "How am I so bad at this?" Staring back at him wasn't a "Hey, how you doing?" text. He could live with that. Instead, he'd sent Kenny a boxing glove emoji. A nonsensical, accidental drive-by boxing emoji.

"Knock, knock." Knuckles drummed against his door just before his father stepped inside his room. "Oh, good you're up."

"Yeah, I'm up." Asher continued to stare at his phone screen unsure what he should do. Then three little dots started bouncing beneath his stupid text, and Asher clicked the screen off. He couldn't handle a response from Kenny at six a.m.

"What are you doing on the floor, Ash?" His dad frowned down at him.

"Oh, I dropped my phone under the bed." Asher stood up, eager to crawl under the covers and forget about the idiocy he'd just committed.

"I thought we'd go for a hike this morning. Get outdoors with nature and smell the fresh air."

"Outside, huh?" Asher looked through his window at the light dusting of snow over the grounds. "It's cold out there."

"Get your boots on and grab a coat. I'll show you my favorite spot at Camp David."

"All right, I suppose some exercise won't kill me." Asher trudged to his closet to change into his warmest clothes, grateful for the new jeans he had stashed there. At least a hike would get Kenny off his mind.

"Son." His dad placed his hands on his hips when Asher met him in the front yard of the lodge.

"Father?" Asher quipped back.

"You look like I suggested we trek through the Alaskan tundra."

Asher shrugged under his many layers of warmth. "I don't like cold. You know this about me." He followed his father down to the closest hiking trail, secret service bringing up the rear at a distance.

Halfway up the trail, his dad took an overgrown pathway to the right with a steep incline.

"I discovered this trail the first time I came to Camp David before I was president. Back when I was governor of New York and you were just a little guy."

"I'm not so sure this is a trail, Dad." Asher swept some leafless branches aside.

"It's a deer path."

"You know, the actual trails here are clean and trimmed back so you can, like, walk without killing yourself."

"The way I see it, the deer know these woods better than we do, so we should check out the sites they like to visit. We just might see something amazing."

As much as he liked to complain about being outside, Asher was in good shape and kept up with his athletic father without too much of a struggle. After about a mile of some serious hiking, they came to a clearing.

"Oh wow." Asher stopped short at the sight of a gurgling creek bed fed by a waterfall just a stone's throw away. "I didn't know this was here."

"I come here a lot," his dad said, taking a seat on top of a massive boulder near the water's edge. "Why don't you have a seat in my office, son." He patted the rock beside him.

"Oh, no. I know what that means." Asher climbed up beside his father, drawing his knees up to his chest. "Lecture time."

"No lecture, I promise." He draped his arm around his son. "It's called parenting."

"Parent away, I'm all ears." Asher liked to mess with his dad, but he secretly loved their talks.

"You're eighteen."

"For three whole days now," Asher agreed.

"And you're a senior."

"Yup, so this is a college talk, huh?"

"Eh, let's call it a life talk." His dad drew out a knife and picked up a piece of fallen branch. He liked to whittle when he talked. He was pretty good with a knife, so Asher supposed that was where he got his interest in art. "Granddad is better at this than I am," he said, as if reading Asher's thoughts. "That's where you get your talent from."

"Granddad can turn nothing into the most amazing woodwork, and he makes it look so easy." Asher would love to have half his talent.

"You do the same with your digital art, and, I swear, you can draw anything and make it look so damn easy." He shook his head, a proud smile on his face. "What do you want to be when you grow up, Ash?"

The question was a frequent one his parents liked to discuss. His patented head shake and shrug used to work, but he'd felt the clock ticking on that expiration date for a long time.

"A lawyer, I guess." Asher focused on the waterfall rather than meet his father's eyes. He wasn't sure how to answer the question when he really had no idea what he wanted in most aspects of his life. How was he supposed to have an answer when he'd spent most of his life in a holding pattern, waiting for his parents to finish running the country?

"Why do you say that?" His dad finished scraping all the bark off the chunk of wood.

"Politics is kind of the family business." He shrugged. "It's in the blood, and law school is how you get there."

"True, a degree in law could offer you many options for your future, but you do know your mother and I have never expected you to pursue a career in politics unless that's what you really want."

He sort of knew that. They'd hammered that lesson home with Caroline, but in the end, she chose politics anyway. Asher would probably do the same. "It's kind of all I know. A familiar career path, you know?"

"Sure, I get that. It feels safe to stay in the family bubble, right?"

"Yeah, I guess."

"You know, Caroline has a gift for the law. She'll make a great lawyer or even a politician one day. And she loves it. It was the right choice for her." He squinted into the afternoon sky before he went back to shaping the piece of wood in his hands. One end narrowed to a point, like a knife handle. One of his specialties.

"Like I said, it's in the blood." Asher watched the form in his father's hands continue to take shape. He loved watching his dad work, wondering what it would be and if he could guess when it was still an inconsequential lump of wood.

"In her blood, yes. She's so much like your mom. And you." He nudged Asher playfully. "You look like your mother but you're more like me."

Asher's mom always told him he got the best of both his parents. His mother's looks and his father's temperament.

"Did you know I almost majored in history?" He focused on the form in his hands. It now had two narrow ends with a wide middle. Not a knife handle.

"No, didn't you always dream of being a Supreme Court judge?"

"The papers like to tell that story. It's true, but it wasn't until I was at NYU and took my very first political science class that I decided I wanted a future in the judicial system. Before that, I wanted to be a teacher. And back then, politics wasn't even on my radar, much less the presidency."

"So what you're saying is I don't have to decide right now?"

"Yes and no. You need to have a plan, Ash."

"Right. In this family, we have plans." Asher sighed, deciding the figure in his dad's hands was going to be a bird with a wide wingspan.

"You're lucky, son. You have a political legacy that would offer you so many opportunities if you chose a career in politics. And you're smart too. You have the right disposition. You're quiet and you think things through before you speak. A valuable asset many of our contemporaries lack. You'd make a fine lawyer or politician. But that's not why you're so lucky. Unlike most of us, you have a God-given talent, Asher. One I know you haven't fully realized yet, but make no mistake, son, you are an artist in every sense of the word. You have so many options. Take some time to explore them, and don't let anyone tell you what direction to take. Not me, your mother, or sister, and certainly not the media or half the fools in Washington who would try to pressure you to follow in footsteps you might not want to follow."

Asher took a deep breath, feeling an enormous weight lift from his shoulders. "Thanks, Dad. That means…more than you could know. I've thought a lot about a career in art. I just don't know if it's a wise decision. There are lots of talented, unemployed artists out there trying to vie for the few creative jobs available. And freelance work is killing their livelihoods. It just feels like a risk."

"I understand that." His father carved tiny feathers into the bird's wings. "You know, in the political arena, you have a lot to say about the issues. You're well informed, and you also have one thing no one else has."

"What's that?"

"You have more experience in the White House than most people, and you're only eighteen. By the time your mother's done with her job, you could have sixteen years on your résumé. That's a highly unique accolade, son." He brushed the wood shavings off his lap and set to work on the beak. "You know all the major political players across the globe. You've had a front row seat to the shaping of the future of this country. You have so much knowledge up here." He tapped the bird's wing against Asher's head.

"So…you're saying the political track is probably the better use of my skills and experience."

"No. Not necessarily." He held out his left hand holding the bird Asher was pretty sure was going to be an eagle. "On the one hand, you're a brilliant artist. And on the other"—he held out his other hand holding the knife—"you have more than a decade of political issues, lawmaking, and legislature stored in that head of yours. Now, think about this." He turned the bird over to scrape some of the excess wood away from the wings. "Put those hands together, and what do you have, Asher?"

He frowned at his dad, not following his reasoning. "Politics and art?" And then it clicked. "A political artist?" He blew out a breath, his cheeks puffing out. "That's a tall order, Dad. That kind of artist has to be bold and brave enough to say what needs to be heard. They have to be willing to put it all out there and damn the consequences."

"You did your mother's campaign posters. That was a step in the right direction."

"That was just a stunt. A way to show the world the kind of

mom she is. That she would use her kid's art for something so important."

"I know it's difficult to believe when people tell you your art is amazing. You've had your butt kissed for ten years—and thank God that hasn't given you a big head. But I promise you, there is *no* way your mother's campaign manager would have allowed her to use your artwork if it wasn't better than good."

"I don't know, Dad. I don't know if I have that much to say with my art."

"You're young. You have years of college ahead of you. You have so many life experiences to have before you'll really find your voice. And don't feel special, Ash. Every eighteen-year-old high school senior is petrified of making this choice. You're in good company. But no matter what career path you choose, I will be proud of you." He placed the completed eagle in Asher's hands. "It's time to soar like an eagle, son."

Chapter 9

Kenny

Coach was trying to kill them. At least, that was what Kenny assumed as he finished the bag skate. The rest of his team followed, none quite as fast as their superstar center. But at six in the morning, who could blame them?

Kenny never wanted the attention, but that was what would get him to the NHL. His speed. His hockey sense.

If only those smarts extended over other parts of his life. He hadn't been able to stop thinking about Asher's party. When they were alone at the pool, it had started to feel like it used to, like they were friends.

If he were honest with himself, Kenny had friends. A lot of them. His teammates would give him an epic pummeling if he said he didn't. If he wanted a girlfriend, all he'd have to do was ask the first girl he saw. But there was a certain shallowness to the word friends. Anyone could claim the connection whether they really cared or not. It didn't mean anything.

A few years ago, Kenny had someone who was more than a friend. No, not in the romantic sense. Not then. But Asher had been special. Brother wasn't the right word. He'd just been

Kenny's person. In their political circles, every mistake, every flaw was magnified, even in kids. It was never like that with Asher.

But now…

Be your own man, Ken.

He'd tried. He was trying.

Coach Ryan blew his whistle, signaling the end of practice. Around him, Kenny's teammates bent over, trying to catch their breath. A few sprawled on the ice.

Kenny's legs burned, but he ignored the pain as he skated to the tunnel and stepped off the ice. A trainer handed him his blade guards, and he snapped them in place before walking toward the locker room. Inside, he sat in his stall and pushed sweaty hair from his forehead. The rest of the guys trickled in slowly, collapsing onto the benches in front of their stalls to remove their skates.

Kenny took a long drink from his water bottle and bent to untie his laces.

Will sat down heavily beside him. "Don't you ever get tired?"

He shrugged but didn't respond.

Will bumped his shoulder. "Come on, man. Tell us the secret to being Kenny Montgomery."

"Work." Kenny grunted. Work and secrets, but he wouldn't say the last part. Though, his problem was that few things were secrets in his world.

Coach strolled in, surveying the room. "All right, gentlemen, listen up." His eyes fell to his clipboard. "The fall festival in Twin Rivers is in two weeks. Normally, this is an event the academy stays out of because Twin Rivers High puts it on. But they've had a number of people drop out and are short on booths. I told them my boys would be more than happy to do their civic duty and create a few."

A collective groan rang out, but Coach raised a hand. "This is not up for discussion. You boys have yet to play like a team this season. We've had problems with fighting and people leaving campus—which is strictly off-limits mid-season."

Kenny never thought he'd find out about last weekend. His coach was one of the few people who didn't give him extra privileges because of who his father was. But he wasn't the only one leaving campus on the weekends, and Coach punished the entire team with early morning skates.

"Maybe if our team leader actually led us..."

Kenny wasn't sure who said it, but no one argued the words. Last season, Kenny gave impassioned speeches and made sure his team strived to be the best. He didn't want anything holding him back from the NHL. But since the summer, he'd been distracted.

Having to help with the festival was his fault, and they all knew it.

Coach sighed. "We will not assign blame to anyone. Instead, look at this like an opportunity. Academy kids rarely get the chance to interact with Twin Rivers High kids."

For good reason. The public school kids didn't like them. They saw their pressed uniforms and high walls as symbols of some kind of elitism.

Coach continued by rattling off names, assigning pairs to come up with booth ideas in two days' time. Kenny's head snapped up when he heard his name.

"You're with Killian."

He met the goalie's eyes. They'd never been close, in part because Killer didn't talk much and in part because Kenny was pretty sure Killian thought he was an asshole.

"Hit the showers, boys."

They filed into the shower stalls. Kenny was the first one out. He shoved his sweaty workout clothes into his bag and pulled on a pair of low-slung sweats and a hoodie.

As he yanked on his shoes, his phone dinged. Asher's name flashed across the screen as Kenny unlocked it. The text message was short.

Ash: 👊

"What the hell?" Kenny stared at it harder as if that would make words appear explaining the message. Was Asher saying he wanted to punch him? Was it about the kiss? Oh man, it was, wasn't it? Kenny scrubbed a hand across his face. He'd tried to forget about his moment of stupidity since it happened—with no such luck.

And now Asher was pissed at him. Why was he only just telling him now? And why did Kenny care so much? They weren't friends. It wasn't like they ever saw each other. It shouldn't matter if Asher wanted to punch him.

Besides, Kenny deserved it.

"Talking to your girlfriend?" Will tried to glance over his shoulder. "Who is Ash? She cute?"

In Kenny's mind, he told Will that "Yes, Ash was cute, but he was also a dude." In his mind, he spilled his feelings to his friend.

Instead, he did what he always did. Laughed. Joked. Acted like girls were the only thing on his mind. "Yeah, man. She's cute."

Will clapped him on the back and turned to get dressed.

When Kenny first realized he was something other than straight, he knew he still liked girls. For so long, he planned a future where he'd just live a normal life with them. But what was normal? What if the only person who'd made him second-guess that plan in a long time appealed to the other side of his sexuality?

Being bisexual didn't mean he had more options. Only more confusion.

And the one person he could have talked to about it hated him.

He deserved it. He'd treated Asher horribly when they were younger. It was an attempt to win his father's approval back when he still thought that was worth something.

After staring at the emoji for a moment longer, Kenny typed a question mark before deleting it and sliding his phone into his pocket. Killian stood by the door, waiting to talk to him.

"Got plans this morning?"

Kenny hiked his bag higher on his shoulder. "Nah. I was just going to crash."

"Good, then we're working on booth ideas." He turned and walked out without another word.

Kenny raised a brow. "Guess I'm following you then." Goalies always had more intensity than skaters, but Killian tended to take that to an entirely new level.

He didn't speak as he walked across the quad separating the arena from the academic buildings. Kenny followed him down the path that wound up a hill and down to the dorm buildings. The only sound between them was the crunch of leaves beneath their feet.

Killian flashed his keycard in front of the scanner, and the doors clicked open. Noise from the dining hall reached them. Other sports teams finished early practices and flooded the food lines. Playing a sport for Defiance Academy was serious business. Early practices, extra training, basically no life.

"You hungry?" Kenny asked.

"No."

"Well, okay, then." Kenny wasn't particularly hungry either. Not with Asher on the brain—and his stupid glove emoji that held way too much meaning.

Killian lived a floor below Kenny. When he pushed open his door, a familiar face looked up from his computer.

Diego's eyes widened when he saw Killian. "You're back."

"It's my room." He walked past Diego, crossed the room, and dropped his bag at the foot of his bed.

Diego pushed thick glasses up his nose and arched a dark brow at his roommate's rudeness. He must have been used to it though. He only shook his head and turned tired eyes on Kenny. "Can you, uh, shut the door? There's too much noise coming in."

Only a few people lingered in the hall, and it was fairly quiet, but Kenny did as he was asked before rounding Diego's overly large computer. Unintelligible code scrawled across the screen. "What are you doing?" He'd known the kid was smart, but this looked like next-level stuff.

Diego clicked his screen off. "Nothing." Red crept up his neck. "Just…uh…nothing."

"We going to do this or what?" Killian asked.

"What are you guys doing?" Diego turned his chair to face them.

Killian flopped onto the edge of his bed. "Some stupid fall festival thing."

Kenny perched on the desk chair beside Killer's bed. "We have to come up with a booth idea."

"That sounds like fun." Diego's eyes brightened.

"More like torture." Kenny pulled a notebook out of his bag.

Diego stood. "I'll, uh, get out of your hair." He pulled open a drawer and removed his laptop before sliding it into a bag. Slipping the strap over his head, he left without sparing them another glance.

"Your roommate is odd, isn't he?" Kenny cracked a smile. He liked Diego. The guy reminded him of a more awkward version of Nicky.

Killian did a weird, almost laugh thing. "Doesn't begin to describe him. His parents are tech gods in Silicon Valley. He's always fiddling with some kind of computer code and refuses to ever tell me what he's doing. He makes all these calls and speaks like some businessman. Sometimes, I don't think he remembers he's only a teenager."

It was the most Killian had ever said to Kenny at once. Before he could respond, his phone dinged. He contemplated ignoring it. He didn't need Asher sending him something worse than the glove emoji. What would it be this time? A knife? Maybe just a splat?

But Asher's name didn't appear on the screen.

Nicky: Dude, you have all the luck. How did I get dragged into the media again, and you aren't even mentioned?

Then he sent a link.

Kenny only hesitate a moment before clicking it. An article about Asher's birthday party appeared. Most of it was an uninteresting account of who'd come to celebrate, but then halfway down was a picture and a sectioned labeled "The Real Party."

In the picture, Asher, Becks, and Nicky wrestled in the pool fully clothed. The article spoke of Asher abandoning his important guests to frolic with his superstar friends, but Kenny didn't care what they said. For once, Asher looked happy. He didn't wear the strained smile he used for the media or public appearances.

Nor was there confusion clouding his eyes like when he looked at Kenny.

This picture was the real Asher. And Kenny wasn't part of it. Nicky was right; he was glad he didn't have the media attention, but it only made him realize he didn't have friends like that.

And it was his fault.

He'd pushed Asher away and even kept Nicky at arm's length.

"If your phone is so interesting, I could just do this myself." Killian leaned back and crossed his arms.

It took Kenny a moment to realize what he was talking about. "No. I'm sorry." He set his phone down. "It was just a friend."

"My friends don't typically make me frown like that." He leaned his head back to stare at the ceiling. "But whatever. Let's just get this over with."

"We could do a kissing booth?" It wasn't a serious suggestion, but Kenny wanted to see how far he could push his intense teammate.

"And swap spit with a bunch of brainless idiots who need to pay people for kisses?" He shook his head. "Pass."

"We could bake a bunch of crap and sell it at a table."

Killian grunted. "Okay, Martha Stewart. Let's see if anyone will buy food from a hockey player who probably doesn't know brown sugar from white."

"Man, that's pathetic. How do you not know that?"

"Didn't say I was talking about me." Killian rolled his head to meet Kenny's eyes. "Unlike some people, I didn't grow up with people catering to my every whim."

Kenny snatched a pillow from the edge of the bed and chucked it at Killian. "I know what brown sugar is." It was his only retort. He'd never actually baked anything in his life. His mother didn't keep much sugar in the house, and their pristine kitchen had gone mostly unused except when his nannies cooked for him.

Unlike Asher's mom. Even as her political star rose, she was constantly baking. When she was the First Lady, the White House kitchen staff hadn't known how to handle her constant presence. She couldn't make a meal to save her life, but her cookies could save the world.

"What about one of those balloon pop things?" Kenny cranked up the ridiculousness. "You know, when people throw knives at a board to pop balloons and win prizes."

Killian sat up, his light hair falling into his incredulous eyes. "Dude, you want us to have kids throwing knives?"

Kenny smirked. "Entertainment."

"You're sick, man."

"What about a dunk tank?"

Interest finally lit in Killian's eyes, but it dimmed quickly. "That wouldn't be cheap."

The more Kenny thought about it, the more excited it made him. Sure, it would be freezing and uncomfortable but also kind of fun. He needed that. He needed fun. "Don't worry about the cost. I'll take care of it."

Killian scowled. "I can pay my own way."

"Don't worry about it. Come on, this will be great."

"There are a lot of people at this school who would do just about anything to knock Kenny Montgomery into a freezing pool of water."

"What about you? I'm not doing this alone."

"Fine. Dunk tank it is."

Kenny rubbed his hands together. This was going to be just the distraction he needed.

Chapter 10

Asher

Asher stared at the stupid boxing emoji. It just sat there, mocking him. And the blank screen below the emoji was even worse. Kenny had started to respond but never sent the message. Asher couldn't blame him. It didn't mean anything, but he couldn't take it back now.

Nicky: Why didn't you just delete the text?

Ash: Sure, that would have been the logical thing to do but that's asking too much from the universe. He saw it right away so it's not like that would have helped anyway.

Nicky: Well, it's not that bad.

Ash: It's bad.

Nicky: I'm trying here.

Ash: It's not working.

Nicky: It will blow over. He'll forget about it. Unless…

Nicky: Do you want him to forget about?

Asher wasn't sure how to answer that. Kenny was such an asshole, and he'd hurt Asher at a time when he'd really needed his best friend. There was no reason he should care. But he did.

Ash: I don't know.

Nicky: You have noticed he's hot, right?

Ash: Um, yeah, I have eyes, but what's the point?

Ash: And he's such a dick.

Nicky: It's his armor, Ash. He acts like that to keep people away.

Ash: It doesn't matter. He hates 'the gays' so IDK why I'm even stressing about that stupid text.

Nicky: Ash, I don't think you know him as well as you think you do. Maybe there's another side to him you aren't seeing. Just… don't write him off quite yet. You might find it's worth repairing your friendship with him at least.

Ash: Why are you always right?

Nicky: Becks would like to know the answer to that question too.

Ash: I have to go figure out how to explain I don't actually want to punch him. Not sure I'd even know how to punch him, much less come out of it without getting killed. He's huge. Love you guys. TTYL.

"Nice digs, Valor," Ethan said as Asher led the way up the main staircase to his suite on the third floor. He was already second-guessing his decision to invite his art group to work together at the White House. To him it was just home, the only one he really knew. He often forgot how others viewed "the residence."

"We can work in here." Asher ignored Ethan's biting sarcasm. "This used to be a sitting room adjoining my bedroom, but several years ago, we transformed it to an art studio."

"It's a great room, Ash," Nichole said, barely glancing around the room. "It's kind of a pain in the ass to come here though." She made herself at home at the white marble table at the center of the room, eyeing the huge iMac at Asher's desk under the windows overlooking the promenade deck.

"Sorry about that, I just thought—"

"Just thought it was a good chance to show off?" Ethan grabbed a seat next to Nichole. "We got that, bro."

"Shut your face," Harper growled. "Asher's the least pretentious person at our school."

"Whatever, Harper. It's fine." Asher sighed, taking a seat at the table beside her. "Let's just get to work. We only have a few weeks left on this project." Together, they had to create a branding identity for a real client. She was a high-end furniture designer who created textiles and furnishings with natural materials. If she liked what they presented, there was a chance she'd actually use it, which would be incredible for their portfolios. But that meant they really had to work together to create a cohesive design for a logo, letterhead, business cards, and a social media branding kit, complete with a custom designed font, a poster ad, and a mock-up of the boutique storefront. They'd already worked with the client to choose the location for her new boutique, but they'd agreed on little else.

"We should really decide on a logo today," Nichole said.

"And then we can each take a component of the branding kit and run with it based on the logo design," Asher agreed. Everyone spread their logo sketches on the long table.

"Let's pick one from each of our mock-ups and then do a pinup," Asher said. It took them longer than necessary, but they finally agreed on four of the eight possible designs.

"Now what, boss man?" Ethan rolled his eyes at the way Asher took the lead.

Asher didn't care at this point; he just wanted to get somewhere with the project. Asher didn't respond. He crossed the room to a sleek white wall strung with a gallery wire. He clipped each design to the wire so they could get a good look at them. He liked to do that with his own artwork so he could live with it for a while before making any major decisions.

"You know, these two have potential to merge." Nichole pointed to Asher's logo and one other he thought might be hers. Both were of a circle design.

"You're right, we could try layering them together."

"I'll boot up my laptop. Just send me your file, and I'll layer them together," she said.

"Let's try it this way first before you go to all that trouble." Asher carefully placed her logo over his and pinned them together before he hung them back on the wall.

"I can't really see—"

Asher flipped the switch on the white wall to backlight their drawings.

"Oh, that's nice." Nichole took a step forward to examine the drawings on transparent paper.

"That's kind of amazing," Harper said. "But it still needs something."

"Let's stay focused on the shape for now," Nichole said, "But you're right, it does need something to give it an extra punch. Something that shows the earthy, green-living aspect of what she does."

"What about this?" Ethan said from across the room. "Did you do these, Asher?" He pointed at a series of silk-screen images he did last year.

"Yeah." Asher's cheeks warmed at the impressed tone in Ethan's voice.

"This is silk screen, yeah?" Ethan took a closer look. "These are badass, man." He sounded like that was the last thing in the world he wanted to admit. "This sort of crackled, organic, leafy texture to the background would be amazing for the logo and it would bring in that earthy vibe we need without overworking the design. Do you have access to silk-screening equipment?"

As the president's son, he had access to anything he wanted, but he didn't want to tell Ethan that. "I'm sure I could find what we need."

"Silk-screening would definitely take it to the next level," Nichole agreed, staring in awe at Asher's work. "Who's the model? She's gorgeous."

"Harper," Asher said, scratching the back of his neck, embarrassed at the attention.

"Nice," Ethan murmured, casting Harper an appreciative glance that made her blush. "No doubt about it, Ash, you've got skills."

Coming from Ethan, that was probably the highest praise he'd ever received. The most honest too.

"You really think so?" Asher asked before he could stop himself.

"Well, I'm not going to kiss your ass about it, so don't push it. Just take the compliment, dude."

"Sorry." Asher sank back down to his seat. "When you live in the White House, you never know when people are honest or full of shit. My default is to assume everyone is full of shit, especially when it comes to my art."

"You know how it is, guys," Harper said. "We're all paranoid about our artwork, worrying if we're really good enough. Self-doubt is just the nature of what we do. It has to be ten times harder when you have absolutely no reason to believe *anyone* is being honest with you."

"Well, I'll be honest with you, Ash." Ethan said, sitting back with a shit-eating grin on his face. "I don't particularly like you, but that right there" He—he pointed at Asher's silk-screen prints —"that is gallery-worthy work."

"Thanks, man." Asher nodded. "So, um, back to our project. I think we've got the makings of a great logo. Nichole, why don't you take my sketches and my design file and keep working on it. I can give you some silk-screen backgrounds I haven't used yet, just to see if we really like that look for the logo."

"I'll have it ready in a few days," Nichole said.

"I'd like to play around with some of your silk-screen patterns and see what I can come up with for the business cards. I have an idea I want to run with," Ethan said.

"I'll set up a shared folder with some silk-screen stuff so feel free to use any of it for this project." Asher still had another silk-screen project he wanted to do, but he had tons of scraps the others could use for inspiration purposes.

"I've been working on some font sketches," Harper said, taking out a sheaf of tracing paper. "Typography is kind of my jam, so I'd like to run with one of these if you guys see anything you like."

"I love this one." Nichole pulled one of the sketches toward her. "The organic script style here would be perfect with our logo."

"I'd like to work on a mock-up of our poster," Asher said. "Just a general layout we can have ready to plug these items in as we finish them."

"Sounds good." Ethan stood. "We all have stuff to work on so I'm going to head out early."

"Sounds like I almost missed your meeting." Asher's mom stepped into the room.

Almost made it without a POTUS sighting. Asher's shoulders fell. "We were just finishing up, Mom." Ethan and Nichole shot out of their seats when they realized the president was in the room.

"Ma'am…er, Madam President, it's wonderful to meet you," Nichole said in a rush.

"Now, we'll have none of that in private. You can call me Mrs. Brooks when you're here in the residence. I hope you all had a good planning session." She eyed the room scattered with drawings and pencils.

Ethan scrambled to clean up the mess in front of him. "Sorry for the mess, ma'am."

"Oh, no worries, Asher will clean it up."

"What, no maid service for the First Kid?" Ethan snorted.

"Clearly, you've not met my parents," Asher said. "They're quick to point out *they* were elected to the presidency, not me. So I don't get all the perks that come with the job."

"Oh, don't think I don't know about your deal with Jenny, son. She does your laundry, and you let her daughter use your computer while she works."

"That's not...let's talk about that later." He gave his mom an indulgent smile.

"Yes, later, once I've forgotten again." She nudged Asher with her elbow. "I hope you kids had a productive meeting. I just wanted to stop by and make a mom appearance to make sure you have everything you need. Please feel free to come back anytime."

"We're good, Mom. You can go back to running the country now." Asher steered her toward the door.

"Oh, am I embarrassing you, Asher? Then my job here is done, bye." His mom waved as she left the room.

"Your mom is so cool," Nichole said with a dreamy expression on her face. Most girls worshiped his mother for the way she shattered the glass ceiling for women everywhere.

"Okay, so…do you guys want to meet here again in a few days?" Asher asked.

"Yeah, this room has everything we could possibly need for this project," Ethan said. "I'm a little jealous." His smile seemed more genuine and his tone had lost its asshole edge. They'd never be friends, but it seemed like Ethan had lost the chip on his shoulder. At least for now.

"Same time on Thursday, then."

"Do it, Ash." Harper insisted, staring over his shoulder at the invitation. "If you don't do it, I'm going to dress up like you and do it for you." She leaned over his shoulder and snatched the invitation out of his grasp.

"Harper. You know they're only inviting me to show my work because of who I am. They don't really care if I'm good or not."

"The Long View Gallery doesn't give a shit who your parents are, and even if they do, who cares?"

"I do."

"Why?" she demanded, turning her defiant eyes on him. "What does it matter what they think?"

"Because everyone will know I only got the opportunity because I'm Asher Brooks." He snatched the invitation back from her.

"So, that's what people will think at first. Then you do the show and wow them with your work and no one will ever question if you deserved the opportunity or not."

"I just...I want to make it own my own merit."

"News flash. You will always be Asher Brooks. People are always going to assume anything you achieve for yourself will be because of who you are. That's never going to go away. It's up to you to prove them wrong. So, you may as well start now. Do the show, Ash. The Long View is perfect for you. It's a real gallery, but it's not part of the political scene in this town."

"It will be if I show there," he muttered, wondering if that was why the gallery offered him a show. A way to increase their own prestige. But Harper was right; it was always going to be that way so why did it matter? The simple answer was it didn't. Not to anyone but him.

Asher stared at the three silk-screen prints on the wall in his bedroom. They were like the ones he'd done of Harper in his studio, but these included a male figure in shadow. He had several others that were part of the same collection. And several more were still in progress. He had enough for a show. Ethan's begrudging words rang in his mind: *"That is gallery-worthy work."* Ethan had no reason to pay him such a compliment. He could trust that. And an art show was just the distraction he needed.

"All right. I'll do it."

Chapter 11

Kenny

Yep, it was official. Kenny Montgomery and Killian James were idiots.

The fall festival began on Friday night—in November, only two weeks before Thanksgiving. The dunk tank was a great idea.

For anyone who didn't have to get into it.

But there stood Kenny. For once, being a senator's son couldn't save him. Having the popularity that came with hockey was no use.

He scanned the surrounding booths. His teammates barely put any effort into it. Some had crappy little games. Killian stepped up next to Kenny and pointed to where Will set up his baked goods table. Kenny didn't bother holding back his laughter.

The Twin Rivers High kids kept their distance like there was some invisible line in the middle of the festival. They'd had months to work on their booths so they put the academy ones to shame. Stands sold everything from caramel apples to cotton candy to corn dogs. In the center of the festival, a white gazebo housed a quartet of musicians.

Twin Rivers spared no expense. They never did. This festival did for Twin Rivers what the summer music festival did for the larger Cincinnati. It brought the people together. The late afternoon sun reflected off the river that provided the backdrop to the evening.

"Should we get started?" Killian lowered his hands to the belt of the terrycloth robe he wore over his swimsuit.

"You're up first, man." Kenny patted him on the back and took a step away.

Killian slid the robe down his arms, and Kenny almost doubled over laughing at the Speedo he wore. A crowd formed around the tank as people cheered for the enigmatic goaltender. He climbed onto the board hovering over the tank, his lithe frame making the act more graceful than Kenny would be.

Sun glinted off his pale skin as he pushed hair out of his face.

Diego appeared next to Kenny. "I-I can't believe he wore that."

"The guy is comfortable in his own skin, I guess." Kenny looked down at his long swim trunks that covered his muscular legs. "Who's up first?" A group of girls approached, giggling as their eyes flicked to Killian. He gave them a small wave.

For all the brooding Kenny knew him for, the guy sure knew how to play to the crowd. They'd have the most popular booth at the festival. A girl handed him her ticket and took the two balls. She hurled each at the lever, missing both times, and walked away with a slight slump to her shoulders.

"You good in there, Killer?" Kenny flashed him a grin.

Killian only flipped him off. Kids and adults they didn't recognize drifted by, some stopping for ill-fated attempts at knocking one of the elite academy boys into the freezing water.

"Can I give it a shot?" Diego asked.

Kenny only lifted a brow and extended the balls to him. Diego stepped up to the line, turning himself almost as if he was about to pitch to a hitter. He cranked his arm back and released. The ball hit the target, and all they heard was Killian's curse before he submerged into the water.

"Diego." Kenny put a hand on his shoulder. "You are my new favorite person. But you're also not allowed to throw when I'm in there."

He laughed as Killian emerged, water dripping down his torso, and realized for the first time in a while he was having fun. There was no overthinking, no worrying.

He looked down at his phone and flipped to Asher's text he never responded to. He wanted Asher to know he didn't need him, that Kenny was going to be okay. It wouldn't do to have Asher pity him.

Killian pulled himself from the tank and shook the water off like a dog. "Your turn, Ken doll."

Kenny ignored the nickname and stripped off his shirt. This was going to suck. He climbed onto the board and scooted his butt out to the edge, hanging his legs off. His feet sank into the icy water, sending a chill through him.

Random strangers tried and failed to dunk him. It wasn't until he heard a familiar voice he turned. Wylder Anderson held a ticket out to Killian and grinned when she took the balls. "I've been wanting to do this basically my entire life."

"Dunk someone in a tank?" Killian asked.

"No, dunk Kenny in a tank." She grinned wickedly as her eyes found him. "Dickhead totally deserves this." She pushed her dreadlocks over one shoulder and squared up to the target. As soon as she pulled her arm back, Kenny knew it would miss. He just didn't realize by how much.

"You have the worst aim of anyone yet today," Kenny taunted her. This girl was Becks Anderson's little sister and Nicky's best friend. She'd been a thorn in Kenny's side for years, and now even went to his school after getting kicked out of her own.

She pouted. "You're right. Little old me could never make the shot. Good thing I brought a friend." She reached behind her, her fingers latching on to Diego's arm. Ugh. Not again.

"No way." Kenny waved his arms at Killian. "She paid for the tickets. She throws the ball."

Killian only shrugged. Traitor.

Diego looked from Wylder to Kenny and back again, unsure of what to do. Kenny felt kind of sorry for the guy. Anyone who was friends with either of the Anderson siblings was put in uncomfortable situations basically daily.

Wylder cupped her hands around her mouth. "Diego. Diego. Diego." The crowd joined in until the boy in question had no choice. Not many people said no to Wylder.

Diego took the final ball and stepped up, readying himself just as he had before. Part of Kenny hoped Diego would take pity on him and go easier than he had on Killian. As Kenny glanced down into the ice-cold water, he knew he'd be meeting it momentarily.

Lifting his eyes, he fixed them on Wylder. "You're—" His words cut off as the board beneath him fell away, plunging him into the water. Ice snaked through his veins as his feet found the bottom, and he broke through the surface, sputtering and choking.

Wylder pulled herself onto the edge of the tank and grinned down. "You were saying something?"

Kenny splashed, and she jumped back with a shriek of laughter that quickly turned into a low cackle.

The color in her cheeks and the shine in her eyes spoke of a lightness she hadn't brought with her from Twin Rivers High to Defiance Academy. In their few classes together, Wylder was a silent participant, speaking to no one.

"Glad I could give you so much entertainment." Kenny pulled

himself from the water with a grunt, and Killian prepared to go in again.

Wylder snagged Killian's discarded robe and held it out to Kenny. Not caring about anything but the cold, Kenny shrugged it on and ran his hands up and down his arms, huddling under the heat lamp someone had the presence of mind to bring them.

Diego eyed him for a moment before taking over the ticket table. Ignoring Wylder, Kenny sat in one of the metal folding chairs at the table. Wylder disappeared as someone cheered, and Killian went into the water.

The next hour passed in a blur of freezing dips and still-cold moments in between. During a much-needed break, Killian sighed. "At least we don't have to do this all day tomorrow." The agreement with the team was they'd hold the dunk tank on the festival's first night, but the rest of the weekend would be theirs. Tomorrow night featured an important home game against Lincolnton.

Kenny watched Will at his booth nearby. His baked goods seemed to be a hit and all the two defenseman had to do was sit behind a table eating cookies. "Martha Stewart," Kenny grumbled. "I want to be Martha Stewart."

Killian shook his head. "Don't give up now, man."

"I can't feel my legs."

"This will help." Wylder set a foam cup in front of each of them along with bags of cookies that looked suspiciously similar to the ones Will was selling.

Kenny sniffed his drink.

"It's hot apple cider." Wylder sighed as she took a seat. "And no, I didn't poison it."

Kenny sipped it tentatively, groaning without shame when the heat hit his throat.

"This festival is boring." She twisted a blond dreadlock around her finger.

"I'm sorry this couldn't be more fun for you," Kenny deadpanned. "Let me find my little violin."

"Shut up."

An idea sparked in his mind. "You know…if you want to have fun…"

"Oh, no." She stood and backed away from him. "You couldn't get me in that tank if you paid me. It's freaking freezing. You'd have to be an idiot to willingly do it."

Kenny and Killian shared a look. They were the idiots of whom she spoke, and it wasn't exactly wrong. Making a silent agreement, they both turned toward Wylder. She stepped behind Diego as if he'd protect her.

"I dare you." Kenny met her gaze. If she was anything like her brother, she'd be a little crazy. It was a good thing he liked crazy. "Go on. If I can't hit the target, you don't have to go in the water. I'll only get one shot."

"A dare?" she challenged, walking closer. Her eyes narrowed, and she crossed her arms over her chest. "What do I get out of this?"

"What do you want?"

"You."

His brow furrowed. "Wylder… I like you, but…"

"Ugh, I don't want you like that, ya perv. Gross. You dated my best friend. That's like incest."

"I don't think incest means what you think it means." He suppressed a laugh.

"Here's the deal. I will go in your stupid dunk tank. I'll even let our surprise ringer, Diego, try to dunk me when you fail."

"I don't fail."

She smirked. "But I get a dare too."

"What do you want me to do?"

"I'm not telling you yet. I'll reveal my dare after I go in the tank. I want you to agree to it now. Whatever it is."

"Within reason."

"Within reason." She lifted her hand, but he hesitated to take it. "Unless you're scared. Does little Ken doll need to ask Daddy's permission first?"

He clasped her hand. "Deal."

With a grin, she released him. After taking off her coat and shoes, she climbed onto the platform as if the prospect of an icy drop didn't bother her at all. Steely eyes scrutinized the crowd that had formed as they solidified their dares.

"You're so screwed." Killian laughed. "That girl scares me."

Kenny watched her. She kicked her feet like she was splashing them in the water at the end of a dock on a summer day.

The girl who shunned the entire student body and was even more of a loner than Kenny also had the hardest will. She'd have made a great hockey player with her toughness.

And she was beautiful in a completely unique way. Of course, she looked too much like Becks for Kenny to ever go there, especially not with Asher on the brain. But he knew a lot of their classmates who would kill just for one look.

Will wandered over, a grin on his face. Kenny stepped in front of the crowd as if he could shield Wylder from their eyes. Maybe it was because she was Nicky's best friend, or maybe he saw a familiar loneliness in her.

Her eyes met his. "Go on then. See if you can do it."

A smile curved Kenny's lips. His fingers curled around the softball and he released a breath before throwing the ball.

It hit the target dead center. The board dropped, and Wylder fell into the water without a sound. Kenny waited for her to emerge, but she never came back up. He shared a look with

Killian before they both ran to the tank, Diego following behind.

"Wylder." Kenny reached into the water to pull her still form to the surface, panic clawing at him. Did she hit her head? He managed to take hold of her arm, but as he pulled her to the side, she sprang to life, splashing everyone who'd crowded nearby. She laughed as she gasped for breath.

Kenny yanked his arm back. "Not funny."

Beside him, Killian chuckled.

Wylder climbed from the tank. "What a balmy day. That swim was delightful. I don't know what babies said it was cold."

By this point, sunset had come and gone, replaced by stars overhead. More heat lamps lined the sidewalks, but it wasn't enough to help the idiots with the dunk tank. And yet, Wylder managed to keep herself from shivering.

Diego wrapped a towel around her, and she smiled at him gratefully before turning gleeful eyes on Kenny.

He groaned. "I'm not going to like this, am I?"

"You promised you'd go through with it."

"Not saying I won't."

"Good." She crossed her arms over her chest. "I want you to go in the tank."

"Okay…"

"Naked."

His mouth opened, but no words came out.

Killian and Diego rolled with laughter.

Wylder didn't even crack a smile. "You said you'd do whatever dare I came up with if I went in the tank."

One side of his mouth curled up. "That desperate to see me naked?"

Her face twisted in disgust. "Incest, remember? Maybe I'm just desperate to see you humiliated."

Who was this girl, and where had she been all his life? Everyone needed a Wylder Anderson. She stared him down like he was nothing.

And it made him feel like he was something for the first time in a while. So, he'd do it. He wouldn't back down from a dare. His smirk transformed into a grin and he draped an arm over her shoulders. "Wylds, trust me, I won't be humiliated if everyone sees me naked."

"Ew." She pushed away from him. "You disgust me."

"But I also think you kind of like me." He held his thumb and pointer finger up. "A little?"

"Nicky doesn't hate you." She looked away. "So, I figure you can't be the devil."

His grin widened. "Oh, I'm definitely the devil."

"Stop flirting with me." She dropped her voice to a whisper. "You don't have to make a show of it just so people don't think you're gay after the picture with Nicky."

Gay. Of course she thought he was gay, because there were only two options. And that was why he didn't do friends. They inevitably said something they couldn't possibly understand.

Turning away, he huffed out a breath. She circled around to face him. "Ken…you are gay, right? You weren't really hitting on me?" With the uncharacteristic vulnerability in her voice, he couldn't stay mad at her. Was she really worried about making him mad? The Wylder Anderson everyone at Defiance Academy knew didn't care about things like that.

"I'm…" He swallowed. "I'm…just going to do this dare so we can start packing up."

She rested her hand on his arms. "You don't have to, you know. I know most people just think I'm insane and ignore the things I say."

"I told you I'd go through with it, so I will." Forcing a grin on to his face, he removed Killian's robe and handed it to Wylder. When his hands started pushing down the waistband of his swimsuit, passersby stopped to see what was going on. They catcalled, but Kenny let their words roll off him as he stepped out of the trunks, bare-ass naked in the middle of Twin Rivers Fall Festival.

Silver light from the moon illuminated his skin as he walked with all the confidence he'd always pretended to have. He climbed up the steps and sat on the cool wood, crossing his legs to avoid the kind of view that his classmates didn't need in their minds.

He covered himself as best he could with his hands as he waited.

A long line formed, people drawn by the spectacle that was the naked senator's son. For a fleeting moment, he wondered if this would end up in the newspaper. His father would have a stroke.

But that moment passed, and all he remembered was that he'd actually had fun tonight. His eyes found the laughing Killian, Diego, and Wylder. For once, he wasn't left alone to brood. And it felt damn good.

He was so focused on that feeling, he didn't hear the ball hit the target. His stomach dropped as icy water encased him.

When he came up for air, music reached his ears as the quartet increased their volume. Wylder mimed a tiny violin as a smile split her face.

Kenny threw his head back to get the hair out of his face and glanced up at the stars overhead. A laugh burst free of him.

His moment ended when someone cleared their throat. Mrs. Donovan, the little old lady who taught English, scowled at them. "Mr. Montgomery, get out of the water right now."

"Uh, I don't think you want me to do that."

"I said now." She crossed her arms.

He shrugged and stood, revealing his state of undress.

Mrs. Donovan issued a curse they'd never heard come from

her mouth as Kenny tried to shield himself from the teacher's eyes.

Wylder held up Killian's robe, and he climbed down to take it, not breathing until he'd wrapped it securely around his body.

"Ms. Anderson." Mrs. Donovan sent her a scathing look. "I assume you had something to do with this? You made a promise when we let you into this school. No more trouble."

"It wasn't her idea." Kenny didn't know what he was doing, but he'd get in less trouble than Wylder. That was sure. "I orchestrated everything."

"You're telling me you wanted to sit up there…"

"Naked? Yeah. I did." He ran a hand through his sopping hair.

"Mr. Montgomery, you're a lucky kid. The school made a deal with the town. No reporters were allowed into the festival while our academy kids were working it. But your father will still get a call. I expect better behavior out of you." Her eyes fell on Wylder again. "And maybe reexamine the company you keep." With that, she turned and walked away.

Killian whistled. "How's it feel to know Mrs. D. ogled you, bro?"

"She did not ogle me."

Wylder punched his shoulder. Hard.

"Ow." He rubbed where she'd hit. "What was that for?"

"You rich kids. If she'd blamed me, I'd have at least a week's worth of dining hall cleanup duty or something. All you get is a call to daddy."

She was right. As long as it didn't end up in the press, his father didn't care what he did. He'd have to think about him at all for that.

Pressing his phone into his hand, Wylder leaned in. "You're not what you seem, Kenny. It took ovaries to do what you did."

"Ovaries?"

She nodded like it was the most serious thing in the world. "If people can use the term balls to describe strength, I can use ovaries." She turned away. "See ya later, Ken-Ken. I'm headed to the White House this weekend. I'll be sure to tell Asher you said hi." She shot him a wink as she walked away.

He almost laughed at the nickname, realizing just how similar she was to her superstar brother, but his stomach dropped with the mention of Asher.

The festival thinned out until it was only the people manning the booths. It didn't take long for Kenny and Killian to shut theirs down. The company they'd rented it from would pick it up Monday.

By the time Kenny got back to the dorms and took a scorching hot shower, he was ready to crash. He laid on his bed and unlocked his phone. Someone had changed his screensaver to a picture of him sitting on the board with no clothes. It didn't show anything sensitive, but he was obviously naked.

He shook his head. Wylder. Opening his photo album, he saw she took quite a few photos.

A text popped up.

Nicky: Wylder told me you had quite the night.

Kenny: Of course, she did.

Nicky: Thanks for hanging out with her. I think that's the first time she's admitted to having fun since transferring to the academy.

Kenny: For you, Nick, I'll put up with her.

Nicky would read between the lines. He always had. Kenny

had a good time too. He wasn't one to do anyone favors by spending time with them, and he didn't do anything he didn't want to do.

Flipping through his texts, he came to Asher's boxing glove. After all this time, the emoji just seemed ridiculous now. What had Asher meant to accomplish?

He wasn't getting off that easy.

If anyone knew how to fluster Ash, it was Kenny.

He pulled up one of the photos from the night. He sat on the board covering himself. Asher wouldn't be able to see anything, but if Kenny still knew him at all, he knew it was enough to get under his skin.

He hit send with a smile on his face.

Game on, Asher Brooks.

Two can play the confusing text game.

Chapter 12

Asher

"What the… What am I even looking at right now?" Asher gaped at Kenny's text message. *Is he...butt naked in a dunk tank? In November?*

"You look like you've seen something scandalous." Harper's grin widened as she sat up from her spot on the floor in her room. "Let me see."

"Nope." Asher shoved his phone in his back pocket. He was not about to discuss why Kenny Montgomery was sending him naked pictures. He was so not ready for that conversation even with his best friend. "It's nothing." He reached for his messenger bag. "I've got to get home. I have three new pieces to finish before the show, and I'm freaking out. We'll finish studying later."

"You've got a few days left before you have to deliver your work to the gallery. You'll do fine. Do not Asher out on me."

"Did you just use my name as a verb?" Asher's mouth slid into a half-grin.

"You know as well as I do that you're going to drive yourself insane until this thing is over. And I will probably have to talk you off a ledge at least three times between now and Friday night."

"Did I tell you they're taking some of my sculpture work too?"

Asher was excited for his first real show. After talking to the gallery owners, he was confident they were only interested in his art and not his connections or celebrity status. And once he'd finally agreed to do it, he threw himself into it, finding just the distraction he needed to get his mind off his spectacular failures in the art of texting. And now, the naked man had arrived on his phone to throw him completely for a loop. Again. *How do you even respond to unexpected sexy naked man pics?* What was the protocol for that?

"Yes." She beamed a proud smile at him. "I'm so excited you're finally doing this."

Asher let out a deep breath. "Me too. Thanks for browbeating me into it."

"Go be brilliant, and after your show we'll talk about whatever that was that had you blushing like a nun in a brothel."

Asher rolled his eyes and draped an arm around his bestie. "You're annoying, you know that, right?"

"But you love me." She gave him a playful shove.

"Yes, fortunately for you, I do." He peeked through the violent purple curtains at her bedroom window to make sure Super Danny was still waiting to take him home. "Later." Asher waved over his shoulder as he made his way down the white marble stairs of the nearly vacant mansion. Harper's parents were so rarely home she practically lived alone.

"Let's go, Valor," Danny said the moment Asher opened the front door. His eyes swept the lawn like would-be assassins routinely lay in wait for the president's son around every corner.

"I need to stop by the gallery before we head home." Asher slipped into the backseat of the town car. He wanted to see how the install was coming with the pieces he'd already delivered. The event would showcase a variety of young artists in the Washington area and Asher wanted to get a look at his fellow artist's work.

"You know we don't do unscheduled visits." Danny waved to the driver to take them home. "I don't know why you even ask."

"I've been there a dozen times lately. Do we really have to schedule every freaking moment of my life? This is important."

"And you have a scheduled visit there in two days. You can check on the install then when we've had time to do protocol."

"You know how I feel about that word, Dan."

"Just because you have stricken the word from my vocabulary doesn't mean it doesn't exist. We abide by *procedure,* no matter what. It's for your safety."

"Look at you, someone get you a thesaurus for your birthday?" Asher said dryly.

"You know—" Dan flashed an evil smirk. "—if your mom hadn't saved my life in the war in Afghanistan, I wouldn't even be here right now. And you, my little friend, would be stuck with some asshole former marine with a stick up his rear and no sense of humor. He—or she—probably wouldn't even play video games with you. So, be grateful your mother has friends in the Navy Seals because we're the cool ones."

"Keep telling yourself that, Super Dan." Asher buckled his seat belt, reluctantly accepting he wouldn't get to visit the gallery today. "Maybe one day it'll even come true."

"Stop fidgeting with your clothes, Ash. You look beautiful." Caroline pulled her sleek black sports car up to the valet booth in front of the Long View Gallery parking lot, deftly ignoring the motorcade escorting them. Their parents would arrive in a half hour to give Asher time to settle in before POTUS made an entrance.

Just for one night, Asher wanted to be himself. The kid with the art, just like the other artists showing at this event. Arriving with his sister helped him feel more like one of those kids.

"No well-timed comeback? You feeling all right, kiddo?"

"Just nerves, I guess."

"You've got this, Ash. You have more talent than you give yourself credit for. Believe me, I, of all people, know just how huge the shadow of the White House is and how stifling it is to live under it. But this is your moment in the sunshine. Enjoy it." She stepped out of the car looking like a fashion plate as she tossed the keys to the valet. Asher rushed to catch up with her.

A line of paparazzi stood flanking the entrance of the gallery. He'd known it was too much to hope they wouldn't catch wind of his event. He smiled and waved for the cameras and pretended he couldn't hear their questions.

Inside, the gallery had transformed from simple concrete floors and crumbling red brick walls to a richly appointed venue with leather couches and acrylic furniture scattered everywhere. Cater waiters moved about the room with hors d'oeuvres and champagne, and funky jazz music played in the background.

"Did you know about that?" Caroline asked, pointing to the banner placed in the doorway.

The Longview Gallery presents the budding artists of the Washington LGTBQ community. Tonight's event will feature debut artist, Asher Brooks, son of the President of the United States, Nora Brooks.

"Nope." Asher shoved his hands in his pockets as a wave of disappointment hit him. "No one told me I would be the poster child for the LGTBQ community tonight." That was why the gallery wanted him. Not for his art. It shouldn't surprise him. Ever since he came out, Asher's name became synonymous with "out and proud." Which he was, but he just wished people would see him for more than just his sexuality or who his parents were.

And judging by the familiar faces among the crowd, his parents had everything to do with the guest list. The eager audience looked like a who's who of Washington's inner circle, and Asher was their main attraction.

No one would arrive at this event for the art. It was exactly why he'd never wanted to do these shows before. The gallery owner had promised him this wouldn't happen, but he was a fool to think it wouldn't get out that the First Son was having his first art show.

"Don't freak out." Harper crossed the room with her hands held out, like she knew he was about to fall apart. "I've already made some heads roll. They got the message loud and clear."

"Did they care?" Caroline asked with a smirk.

"Not even a little bit." Harper sighed. "If they knew Ash at all or respected the sanctity of art, they wouldn't sell out like this."

"Whatever. It's what I expected all along." Asher shrugged. "They're just doing their jobs, trying to sell art."

"Have you ever thought about using a pen name?" A familiar voice said behind him.

"Nicky?" Asher turned, surprised to see his friend. "And Wylder too!" His mood lifted immediately. "I didn't know you guys were coming."

"Are you kidding? We wouldn't miss your first show. Becks sends his love, of course. He's still on tour and couldn't make it." Nicky's hug was just what he needed. His circle of friends was growing and that was all that mattered. The people who knew him best would appreciate his work. Beyond that, Asher no longer cared.

"I'm chalking this all up to experience." Asher gestured at the

LGBTQ signs and all the politicians around the room. "What's that about a pen name?" He laughed. "Do artists use those?"

"I don't know, but maybe you should," Wylder said. "I've thought about changing my name, and my brother's just a country star. I can't imagine what it's like for you, Ash."

It wasn't a half-bad idea. If he ever really wanted to make a go of it with his art, he couldn't do it as Asher Brooks.

"Guys, you have to see the full exhibit. It's amazing, and, Asher, your art looks phenomenal." Harper gestured for them to follow her. "Just ignore the diplomats and the politicians. They're here for the food and free booze."

The work on display was some of the best Asher had ever seen from young, untrained artists. There was no doubt his work was in good company, but most of his excitement for his first real show had dimmed when he arrived to discover the gallery had exploited his name and refrained from telling him what the show was about. There was nothing he wouldn't do for the LGBTQ community, but with things like this, he often wondered why it had to be an LGBTQ art show rather just an art show for talented young artists? Why did their sexuality need to be showcased front and center? Whose business was it?

Asher stood alone, admiring an abstract piece of a female form emerging from an ugly lump of clay. It was gritty and raw. Nothing like the beautiful sculpted forms he usually saw at shows like this. This was not a graceful feminine creature standing regally on her pedestal. This woman was angry, clawing her way out of the clay, determined to shake off the thing holding her back. This artist had a voice and she had something to say.

"Is that a good or bad frown?" someone nearby said.

Asher turned to see his secret service steering people away from him and his friends. Harper and Nicky stood across the room examining a rather odd sculpture of a gnome, and Wylder was snapping selfies in front of a painting that matched her dress.

A young woman stood beside Danny looking a little intimidated. "You know, I'm not actually a violent person. It's just my art that's angry." She cast nervous eyes up at the special agent.

"You're the artist?" Asher asked, begging Danny with his eyes not to cause a scene.

With a sigh, Danny let her approach Asher. "I don't like it when you go out," he muttered irritably.

"Don't listen to him, he's just cranky." Asher turned back to the piece. "This is going to haunt me."

"Ouch."

"No, sorry! I meant that in the best possible way. She is beautiful, strong, and fierce. But so honest and raw, I can feel her frustration. My mom would love this."

"I would die if your mom saw this."

"She'll be here soon. I'll make sure she sees it. She doesn't always get art, but she gets the struggle women go through just to be heard."

"I'm going to die." The girl's smile widened. "None of us had any idea you'd be here, showing with us. It's an honor to have my work alongside yours."

"Thank you, but the pleasure is all mine, er…what's your name?"

"Caitlin." She reached to shake his hand with stars in her eyes. "Your work is inspiring."

"Oh, I'm just here because I know people. You guys are the real talent." He steered them away from the growing crowd, checking out the other pieces as they walked.

"Don't sell yourself short, Asher. You may have gotten top billing tonight because of who you are, but that doesn't mean you don't deserve it. I'm here because I have nearly a half a million Instagram followers, and I sure as hell used my sphere of influence to score my place in this show, but I know my work speaks for itself."

"Thanks for that, Caitlin." Asher smiled. "You have no idea how much I needed to hear that."

"The LGBTQ community has to stick together." Caitlin stopped to admire his silk-screen triptychs. Each individual piece worked well on its own, but together, each set of three told a story.

"You don't feel like they're just exploiting that too?" Asher scratched the back of his neck, regretting the question as soon as it was out of his mouth. He'd been burned too many times in situations like this when he thought he was just talking to a like-minded teen only to find his words repeated on the news or social media networks. It wasn't worth trusting a stranger.

"Of course, they are." She shrugged. "We're hot right now, so they're just hopping on the bandwagon."

"Feels kind of weird that we get this amazing opportunity when a million other straight kids would die for it. Seems like it should be about the art."

"It is about the art, Asher. Our art as a community. No matter what we do, everything we create holds a piece of us. And each one of us here tonight has poured our blood, sweat, and tears into our work to tell our stories—stories that are all too familiar to the LGBTQ community." She turned to the triptych that had hung in his bedroom just a few days ago.

"Individually, these pieces look like three different young men. But as a whole, I can see they're the same person at different stages of his life. It's about this person learning to define himself on his own terms and coming out stronger because of it."

"I hadn't thought it was that obvious." Asher's cheeks flushed hot under the unforgiving gallery lights.

"It's not. Not to outsiders. But this is a journey we've all been on. That's why we're all here tonight, Asher. For us, it's about our voices. We all have something to say with our work, and opportunities like this don't come around that often for such young artists. Do not let anyone ruin this night for you."

"I swear you must be my guardian angel tonight." Asher shook his head, a half-smirk on his face. "Or my best friend, Harper, sent you over here with a script."

"No script, I swear." Caitlin threw up her hands in earnest. "Just someone who admires good work when I see it. Can I ask who your inspiration was?" She gestured back at the prints. "I don't think this was a personal story, right?"

"No, I'm lucky, my story is pretty simple. I had supportive parents, and it was all just so easy for me. This is for a close friend of mine. I watched him go through a pretty difficult time until he came into his own."

"Beckett Anderson?" Caitlin's voice went up an octave.

"Yeah, I see that wasn't too hard to guess either. I should try to be more secretive with my art."

"It seriously doesn't help that everyone knows everything about you. And I'm a huge fan."

"Becks is great. He's on the road right now, or he'd probably be here."

"Oh, yes, Beckett is wonderful, but I'm a total Nickophyte."

"You're a what now?" Asher couldn't help the grin that spread across his face.

"I adore Nicky St. Germaine, Beckett's boyfriend. Huge fan."

"Of Nicky's?"

"Oh, yes, I have been since their first kiss and all the hoopla that came after it. I'm so glad they ended up together."

"And there are more of you Nicko-what's-it's?"

"Nickophytes. His fan group on Instagram. He has more followers than Beckett."

"Really?" Asher's grin widened.

"Well, Beckett has YouTube followers in spades, so I'm not sure he's on Instagram all that much."

"Want to meet him?"

"I thought you said he's on the road?"

"Becks is, but Nicky's here. We should go find him."

"Oh my God. How's my hair?" Her hand fluttered to her face. "What am I saying? I like girls. But he's just so adorable."

"It's impossible not to love him. Oh, Nicky?" Asher waved at his friend sitting at a table with Harper and Wylder. "Meet my new friend, Caitlin." He half-dragged her into the VIP section.

"Wow. Nicky St. Germaine," Caitlin gushed, clutching her hands in front of her.

"Caitlin's a Nickophyte." Asher's face was going to split wide open if he grinned any harder.

Wylder spewed sparkling water out of her mouth trying not to laugh. "Wait, no, I wasn't ready. Say that again, Ash?"

"Turns out our Nick-Nick has a fan group."

Nicky's face was nearing a shade of maroon Asher wasn't sure was healthy. "You all right there, Nicky?" He patted his friend on the back, thoroughly enjoying this delightful revelation.

"Caitlin, so n-nice to meet you," Nicky said, standing to greet her.

"Would you mind?" She held up her phone for a selfie. She grinned, and Nicky did his best to live up to her expectations.

"Is this what it's like to be friends with me?" Asher leaned in toward Harper.

"Pretty much, yeah." She choked back a laugh. "But I don't think you're capable of turning that red. The poor kid's going to pass out if we don't get her away from him."

Fortunately for Nicky, the gallery owner came to find Caitlin to introduce her to a potential buyer.

"It was wonderful meeting you, Nicky. You too, Asher." She waved as she reluctantly left them.

"You enjoyed that, didn't you?" Nicky fanned his face.

"Immensely." Asher grabbed a bottle of water from a passing waiter and handed it to Nicky. "You might want to check your blood pressure."

"Oh just…you…shut up." Nicky pressed the cool bottle against his face.

"Oh, look, POTUS has arrived," Asher said. "Now, my night is complete." Asher watched his parents' arrival in a bluster of activity, camera flashes and glamorous smiles. His parents really were made for the spotlight.

"No politics tonight." Nora shook her head at the reporters. "Tonight I am a proud mamma here to support my talented son."

"You know you love her to pieces." Nicky jabbed him in the ribs.

"Of course. She's the best mom in the world. I'm just not a huge fan of her job." Asher left Nicky in the shadows and went to perform his duty in front of the cameras.

"It's about time you two made it." He smiled and turned toward the cameras. "Mom of the year, right here, ladies and gentlemen. I don't think our parents have ever missed a single important event. Right, Care?" As if on cue, his sister arrived to stand with him. They each knew their roles and played them flawlessly. They'd had years of practice smiling at the cameras and giving them what they wanted, so they'd go away and leave them in peace.

"Not a single one," Caroline said. "It probably helps that we both suck at sports."

"Okay, enough of that, you two," their dad said. "I'm dying to see the new pieces, son. Why don't you show us the exhibit?"

Asher gave his parents—and a few reporters—the grand tour of his work along with all the other artists showing alongside him. True to form, Caitlin fan-girled over his mom, but he couldn't blame her. His mom was pretty awesome, and she loved Caitlin's sculpture so much she bought it and sent Caitlin into a total freak-out.

After performing his obligations, Asher was ready to leave with his friends. It wasn't quite what he'd hoped for, but his first exhibit went well, and it was something to put on his college resume.

"It's just silk screen and digital crap. It's not even real art."

Asher's steps faltered and his shoulders slumped. *And there it is.* The two boys didn't see him standing behind the huge concrete pillar, but he heard all he needed.

"He's just here to draw in the crowd so the rest of us can get the attention of the real patrons. I actually sold several of my pieces tonight. Enough to pay for at least a year of art school, so I'm not complaining."

"It's just shitty print work taking the place of a real artist. We're all painters and sculptors. His crap is just fussy graphic design at best and has no place in a gallery like this."

He should have known better. He *did* know better, but his feet moved anyway. "I'm pretty sure Andy Warhol would disagree with you about print art. Silkscreen is a classic medium just like painting and sculpting and photography. You might want to take an art history class or two while you're in school, just to brush up on your knowledge."

"Hey, man, we didn't—"

"No worries, really. Have a good night." Asher turned and

walked away. He shouldn't care about what total strangers thought. But he did.

"Want to get out of here?" Asher asked Nicky and Wylder. "You're staying with us, right?"

"Your mom invited us just now," Wylder said.

"Let's go home and eat ice cream and *not* talk about art."

"Remind me again why we're watching a high school hockey game on your iPad?" Asher sat back against his headboard, scraping the bottom of his second bowl of cookie dough ice cream.

"I need you to explain this game to me so I can finally understand it. Kenny has been trying to teach me for years, but he gets frustrated before we get very far."

"You guys are that close?"

"Yeah. Sort of. This would help." He gestured at the screen. "I try to watch every game."

"But he's such an ass."

"He's not *that* bad once you get to know him," Wylder said, propping her fluffy pink slippered feet on the edge of his bed. "He's a dick, don't get me wrong, but that's just because he's … Kenny." She shrugged.

"Anything to get my mind off tonight." Asher sighed.

"It was a good show, Ash, don't let the other crap ruin it for you." Wylder stood to make her third bowl of ice cream. She'd vowed she was going to try every flavor the kitchen brought up, and she was halfway there.

"I know. And I appreciate it. I know I'm complaining about the most ridiculous things, but I just wish it could be about me and my art. Not my parents, their connections or my sexuality. I'm the LGBTQ Golden Boy, and I've never even been kissed. Well…

mostly never been kissed. I don't think a drunken half-kiss at a pool party counts."

"Pause. Who did you kiss?" Wylder set her bowl down and leaned forward.

"Wait, let's be half-decent friends here," Nicky said. "We're putting a pin in the whole "half-kiss" thing for one moment, but we're coming back to that."

"Oh my God, did you kiss Kenny?" Wylder's eyes sparkled with interest.

"Wylder, focus." Nicky rolled his eyes. "All right, Asher Brooks. It's time for some tough love. You've got first-world problems, my friend."

Asher laughed, reaching for a pint of chocolate peanut butter ice cream. He was going to be sick before this night was over. "I'm fully aware I'm being ridiculous, but I'm so sick of being the president's son. You know what it's like in the spotlight. They think they know you, but they're all just making shit up as they go."

"The media is the devil. I get this." Nicky finished his one bowl of plain strawberry ice cream and set it on the night stand beside Asher's bed. "But during my first stint in the spotlight, I *had* to learn to just let it be what it is. You have no control over what people say about you, but you do control your reaction to it. Rise above it, Ash. You'll be a lot happier with your life if you can let the haters hate."

"You do you, Asher," Wylder added. "The important people will stick around. All the others. They don't count. Now about that kiss that might or might not count?"

Asher threw his pillow at her.

"Seriously, how have you never been kissed?" She stared at him. "You're hot. You're like a teen icon. What gives?"

"I live in a tower surrounded by a moat, and my Prince

Charming is out there wandering around looking for me in all the wrong places."

"But seriously? How?" Nicky frowned at him. "You've been out for like five years. How has this not happened for you at some event somewhere?"

"I don't. Know. What. I'm. Doing." Asher stared them both down. "Seriously. That's it."

"But let's talk about Kenny in the pool and sort of kisses." Wylder crossed her arms over her chest. "Walk us through what happened before Nicky and Becks showed up and all the other kids ended up in the pool at your birthday party. Kenny was there with you alone, right?"

"How do you even know all this?"

"I follow the blogs and the important social news. Now, dish the story, or I'm going to get cranky."

"Fine." Asher shared the details of the weird non-kiss he experienced the night of his eighteenth birthday. "But it didn't mean anything. It happened so fast, and I wasn't sober. And I didn't kiss him back, so it doesn't count, right. Plus, he's straight, or at least, he's always claimed to be. I really don't know anymore. With the media circus a few months ago." He looked sideways at Nicky. "And ugh…the random kiss with you. He's probably just confused. I know that. He'll go back to his douchbag bigoted ways."

"I wanna tell him." Wylder sat back. "Can I tell him?"

"No." Nicky shot her a death glare.

"Tell me what?"

"Ugh, nothing. So what happened after the party? Did he text you or anything?"

"No. Well…I sorta texted him, accidentally."

"Accidentally?" Wylder frowned.

She laughed for at least five minutes after Asher told her the story of the random emoji text.

"Why didn't you delete it as soon as you sent it?"

"That's what I told him to do." Nicky grinned.

"Yeah, well, neither of you geniuses were there when it happened." Asher groaned, covering his face. It felt good to laugh about it with his friends.

"What did he say?" Wylder asked. "Did he respond?"

"He started to, but it took him nearly two weeks to figure out a response."

"Wait, he responded?" Nicky's ears perked up. "You didn't tell me that."

"It happened recently."

"What did he say?" Wylder asked again. She was getting far too much entertainment out of his humiliation.

"Nothing exactly." He fidgeted with his phone.

"He didn't?" Nicky gasped. "He's such an idiot."

"What? Ooh, did he send pics? Let me see!" Wylder jumped on the bed between them, her ice cream all but forgotten.

"You can't see anything." Asher's face grew hot as he thought about the picture. "But I have no idea how to respond."

"It was at the dunk tank wasn't it?" Wylder laughed. "I dared him to go in naked, so, of course, he did. I can't believe he sent you the picture I took. But then again, I kind of can."

"But, what does it mean?" Asher looked to his friends for answers. "What does it mean when a super conservative senator's maybe straight son sends you a naked man pic? Is there a rule book about how you're supposed to respond to these things?"

"Oh, I really wanna tell him, Nicky."

"Ignore her," Nicky insisted. "Why don't you try responding to his text with actual words and see if you can get a real conversation going? Then maybe you can come to terms with that kiss."

"It was a non-kiss. It doesn't count when it's over before you can figure out what's happening."

"Okay, but that non-kiss still means something."

"How can it? There is no way Kenny Montgomery is ever going to date a guy—even if he wanted to. I know his family. His father would ground him for life, and that's only if his mother didn't murder him first."

"I was in the same situation with Becks not even a year ago. I made the mistake of believing straight was the default. When we're born, we're supposed to be straight until we make the colossal decision to re-inform everyone in our lives that they've been wrong about us all along. For some, that conversation is the most terrifying thing you could imagine. My father had a hard time with it at first. You had it easy with your parents and a whole nation behind you. With people like Becks, it's not always easy to define themselves. Straight isn't the default, but neither is gay."

"Are you saying Kenny might have wanted that kiss? That he wasn't just drunk and reckless?" Asher wasn't sure what he thought about that.

"No, I'm just saying don't discredit him or assume you know what he was thinking or what he wants. There is a lot more to Kenny than he lets on, and it might be worth repairing your friendship to find that out for yourself."

"But *how* do I respond to the naked man text?" Asher knew he needed supervision if that was going to happen.

"I'll help you figure that out, if you can teach me how to follow Kenny's hockey games? He's tried to teach me, but he has zero patience for teaching.

"Deal. Next time there's a game, we'll watch it together over the phone, and I'll walk you through everything."

Chapter 13

Kenny

Playing in front of scouts wasn't anything new for Defiance Academy's star center. His family advisor, Kyle, showed up at a lot of games.

But the person who never came? Kenny's mom.

Yet, there she was. He thought he'd imagined it at first when his head crashed into the glass behind the net, and his eyes found her.

Wishful thinking, maybe.

But that would have required him to wish for it.

He tried to push her from his mind. They had a game to win. Defiance Academy was down two goals with three minutes left in the third. Killian tried to keep the team in the game, making save after save, but the defense hung him out to dry for each goal against.

He skated to the bench during the timeout, his face blazing red with anger. "What's wrong with you idiots? Play some damn hockey."

He wasn't wrong. Nothing seemed to be going right for the team.

Coach gave them a minute to collect themselves. He wasn't

one for impassioned speeches. Kenny scanned his teammates' faces. For many of the seniors, this would be their last season of hockey ever. Some would go on to play in college. A few might be lucky enough to hear their names called at the draft in June.

But the only ones who were said to be sure bets were Kenny and Killian.

After coach laid out a face-off play, the skaters moved back toward the left face-off dot. In the grand scheme of things, this game might not matter. No one would remember who made which plays. They'd move on to the next game.

But in the life of a potential NHL draft pick, every second on the ice counted.

Instead of following his wingers, Kenny skated to the goal. If this game could still be salvaged, one man had to be better than the rest.

"Do you have this, Killer?" He gripped the cage of Killian's mask.

"Of course, man."

"We can still win this." He glanced back over his shoulder to where the ref yelled his name. "You and me. Forget about everyone else on this ice. It's up to us. There are scouts here."

"There are always scouts."

Kenny grit his teeth. "Killian." He never used his actual name in a game. "I know you still have another year after this one, but I don't want to sit at the draft in June and look back at this season wondering if there was something more I could've done. You are I are the ones who are going to win this. Promise me you won't let a single puck hit the back of this net for the next three minutes."

Fire burned in the goalie's eyes. "Let's do this, Ken doll."

Kenny patted the side of his helmet and skated to where the refs and forwards waited impatiently. As he passed Will, he pointed. The puck was going to him.

Winning the face-off, Kenny slid the puck to Will before taking off down the ice, opening himself up for the stretch pass. The puck hit the blade of his stick, and he cradled it, deking around a defenseman and firing a shot into the top right corner of the net.

The horn blast reverberated in his ear. Turning toward Killian, he held up one finger. The team was still down.

Coach called for Kenny to change lines, but he shook his head. Even with heavy legs, he knew he couldn't leave this ice. There was a time he'd been a leader on this team. Maybe this was his chance to return to that.

New wingers joined him for the face-off. He didn't look at a single skater for the other team. This wasn't about them.

He won another face-off, getting the puck to one of his wingers. The guy passed it back, and Kenny skated in toward the net with an open shot lane.

If he hadn't been so focused on the puck, he'd have seen the huge defenseman coming. He'd have anticipated the pain. A body collided with his for an open-ice hit. The boy's shoulder rammed into Kenny's chin, throwing him back. He slammed into the ice. A sharp pain speared through his chest.

Play stopped, and a trainer ran onto the ice. Kenny's teammates hovered over him in worry. It wasn't until Kenny saw Killian he knew he had to get up. Together, they were supposed to save this game, to lead their team. Two unlikely boys.

"Lay still, son." The trainer tried to hold him down.

"No. I'm okay. I can play."

"You have to go through concussion protocol."

"After the game. Please. I didn't even hit my head." He looked to his coach for help. "We can win this. Let me show them I can lead this team. Coach…" His coach had been there for everything.

The stupid fights. Breaking the rules. He'd watched Kenny go from golden boy to confused and troubled kid.

"Fine." Coach motioned to a couple of Kenny's teammates. "Help him up."

The crowd erupted in cheers as Kenny stood and prepared for the penalty shot he'd earned. He pushed down the pain and shifted from skate to skate as he tapped his stick on the ice. His eyes met the opposing goalie's seconds before he started forward, gathering the puck, going from backhand to forehand in quick succession.

Before reaching the goal, he slowed almost to a stop. The goalie followed him, coming out of the net to track the puck. At the last second, Kenny released a burst of speed, pulling the goalie out of position before tucking the puck behind his left pad.

He couldn't remember ever hearing the arena so loud.

Defiance Academy tied the game.

Thirty seconds. That was how much time they had left to score to avoid overtime.

Kenny's teammates congratulated him with big hugs.

Will patted him on the back. "We need to get the puck to Ken."

"No. They'll be trying to cut off every play toward me. I'll draw them out of position. Someone else has to take the shot."

They all agreed, but Kenny wondered if they'd say yes to anything he told them at that point. Winning another face-off, he passed the puck back through his legs before sprinting up the ice. The two opposing defensemen followed him as he knew they would.

He cut toward the center of the ice as one of his wingers raced up the boards, passing to their other linemate in front of the net. The puck redirected into the net as the horn sounded, signaling the end of the game.

Kenny's teammates poured onto the ice, but he could barely

see them as black spots danced across his vision. He fell to his knees before everything disappeared.

Kenny jerked awake as someone held smelling salts under his nose. He sat up, taking in the trainer's room and the padded bed he lay on.

Coach Ryan stood next to the bed. "We want to get you checked for a concussion."

"Can it wait?" In that moment, he remembered his mom was at the game. She'd come to see him play. Whatever stood between them, that had to mean something.

Noise from the busy locker room filtered in. With a groan, he swung his legs over the side of the bed and stood.

Coach eyed him warily. "Fine, kid. But once everyone clears out, I'm taking you to the hospital."

His entire body hurt, so he wouldn't disagree with that.

As soon as he entered the locker room, voices cut off and dozens of eyes landed on him.

"He lives!" Will stepped up onto a bench. "Dude, you single-handedly won us that game. Well, you and Killer."

Kenny shook his head. "It wasn't just us. That was a team effort."

"You're not in the NHL yet, man. No one is making you say boring humble things."

Kenny laughed at that, the action sending a shock of pain through his head. Coach Ryan appeared behind him. "You're wanted outside the locker room, Montgomery."

Kenny pushed out into the corridor to where Anders Johansson leaned against the concrete wall. The former hockey star was now an amateur scout for the New York Islanders. He smiled when Kenny appeared.

"It's good to see you, Kenny." They'd met a few times already.

Kenny nodded. "You too, sir."

"This was quite the game. I was very impressed with how you put the team on your back. How's your head?"

"Fine." Despite the headache pounding in his skull.

"Even a lot of professionals would have been down longer than you after a hit like that. I hope you get yourself checked out."

"I will, sir."

"Good, good. I don't want to delay your treatment too long, but I just thought I should let you know I was here watching. You have doubters in my ranks, Mr. Montgomery."

"Doubters?"

"People who think you're more drama than your talent warrants. But my colleagues put too much emphasis on tabloid articles. Me, on the other hand, well, I always believe there's another side to any story. What I saw here tonight was special."

A hand landed on Kenny's shoulder, a grip he'd recognize anywhere. Kyle eyed Anders. "Anders, you know you're not supposed to talk to the boy without his advisor."

"That's not a real thing, Kyle. Maybe, loosen the reins a bit when you realize you have a special one here."

"Hello." Kenny closed his eyes, recognizing that voice. Could this get any worse? His mother went on. "I'm Kenneth's mother."

"Mrs. Montgomery." Mr. Johansson smiled. "Your son is very talented. The New York Islanders have our eye on him."

"New York?" Her brow furrowed. He knew what his mom thought of the city. She claimed it was nothing more than a hotbed for liberal immorality.

Luckily for him, she kept her mouth shut. Kenny would feel lucky no matter which NHL team drafted him. He could love living anywhere as long as his parents weren't there. His favorite team was the Blue Jackets, yet they were the only team he didn't want to play for because it was too close to home.

Mr. Johansson turned to him. "You've committed to Boston College next year, right?"

"He has." It was Kyle who answered. Apparently he was Kenny's mouthpiece.

"That's a very good hockey program. Many of our prospects have been through it." He stuck out his hand. "Good luck, Kenny."

Kenny shook his hand. "Thank you for coming, sir."

Mr. Johansson tapped the side of his head. "Get yourself checked out."

After he was gone, Kenny's mom dropped her fake smile. She didn't tell him why she was there or even mention the game at all. "I'm famished." She turned to Kyle. "Dinner?"

"Of course. I know just the place." He patted Kenny's shoulder. "Good game, kid. I'm proud of you." At least someone was.

As they walked away, Kenny sighed. Sure, he'd find his own way to the hospital. No problem. Who needed a mom to do things like that? Oh right, most teenagers.

She hadn't even asked if he was hurt.

Most of his teammates had cleared out by the time he returned to the locker room. He winced in pain as he showered and packed up his bag. He didn't want to bother Coach so he'd have to call a car to take him to the hospital, but all he wanted to do was go home and sleep.

As he stepped out onto the sidewalk outside the arena, he froze. Sitting on a bench nearby were Wylder and Killian. They jumped up when they saw him approach.

"How are you feeling?" Wylder's normal anger was nowhere to be found as she looked him over.

"Just kind of sore."

Killian took his bag. "Come on. You need to get checked out."

"Did you guys wait for me?"

Killian shrugged like it was no big deal.

"You went into a dunk tank naked for me last week." Wylder took his arm. "Least I can do is make sure you don't die."

He laughed. Was this what it felt like to have people who cared about him? His phone buzzed with texts, but he ignored them. If he looked at a screen, his head would only feel worse.

"I have a car on campus." Wylder hesitated. "But you can't make fun of me. It's kind of a crap heap."

"Wylds, you could drive a tricycle, and I wouldn't have the energy to laugh at you tonight."

When you were Kenneth Montgomery, son of the local senator, waiting in emergency rooms wasn't something you had to do. As soon as they arrived, a nurse took Kenny back to run some tests.

When he walked back to the waiting room two hours later, he expected Wylder and Killian to be long gone, but there Wylder sat with a frown on her face and Killian's head in her lap.

Wylder pushed Killian's head off and stood when she saw him.

Kenny shrugged. "No concussion. Just very bruised." Releasing a yelp, Wylder lunged at him, pulling him into a hug.

"Did you miss the bruised part?" He winced.

"Sorry." She pulled back. "Just glad you're okay. That hit was no joke."

"Wylder, does this mean we're friends?"

"No," she scoffed.

"I think it does."

"Definitely not. I hated you for too long."

He'd hated himself too. "But you don't anymore."

Her face twisted in disgust. "I don't want any friends at Defiance Academy."

"Sorry." He slid an arm over her shoulders. "I don't think you have a choice. Waiting in a hospital for me kind of solidifies your love for me."

"I don't love you."

"But you like me."

"No."

He pouted. "Maybe a little?"

"There's possibly an iota of like, but only because Nicky abandoned me for Nashville."

His eyes settled on a sleeping Killian. "Should we wake him up or leave him here?"

She laughed. "If I'm your friend, I think that means he is too."

Kenny had known Killian for years, but they'd never exactly gotten along. Killian had an intensity that scared most people away. Were they friends now?

By the time Kenny got back to his dorm, Will was fast asleep in his room. All Kenny wanted to do was crash, but his phone rang, and he couldn't ignore it any longer.

He knew who it was without even looking. "Hey, Nicky."

"Finally," Nicky huffed. "I've been trying to reach you since the game ended. I saw the hit."

"How'd you see it?"

"Defiance Academy streams the games online. Are you okay?"

"Doctor says I'm fine."

"Are you sure? It looked pretty bad. Asher and I were freaking out."

Kenny didn't know what to say to that. Asher watched his game?

"I bribed Asher into teaching me hockey so I can actually

understand half of what you say. We were Facetiming when it happened." Nicky sighed. "I'm glad you're okay."

He ignored the we part. "You're always worried." It felt good to have another person in his corner. Wylder, Killian, and now Nicky. It made the sting of his mom's dismissal lessen.

Nicky laughed. "Yeah, so now that I know you're okay, I have a question."

"I'm not going to like this, am I?"

"Don't be such a… Kenny. I checked your game schedule, you don't have one next Saturday, right?"

"No. We have one Friday. Why?"

"Becks is playing in Cincinnati. I was going to drive up, and I'm hoping you can come so I don't have to go alone."

Kenny sighed. "What about Wylder?"

"She's busy, and Avery has a school thing he can't get out of. Come on. Help me out."

"Coach doesn't like us leaving campus during the season."

"I know you, Ken. Since when does that stop you?" Desperation rang in Nicky's voice. Kenny knew Nicky hated facing Becks' screaming fans and rabid media at all, let alone by himself.

"Fine. I'll come."

"Yes! I promise you won't regret this. It's going to be so much fun."

"If you say so. Now, will you let me get some sleep?"

"Of course." Nicky laughed. "I imagine that pretty face needs extra beauty rest after the hit you took."

Kenny touched his face. It had been spared, unlike the rest of his body. "Yeah, yeah, go call your pretty boy boyfriend."

Nicky laughed. "Not when I'm tired. I need energy to counteract his weird. Night, Ken."

"Night, Nick."

He hung up and plugged his phone in by the bed before

relaxing into the mattress, wondering what he'd just agreed to. Nothing was ever simple with Nicky and Becks. They were always up to something.

But that was a problem for another day. Right now, he was just ready for this one to be over.

Chapter 14

Asher

"Try to be careful tonight." Danny gestured for Asher to follow him down the nearly deserted hall.

"I'm always careful." Asher glanced at the contingent of secret service agents accompanying him. There was no way anyone would get past them even if they wanted to. "Besides, there are like three hundred of you with me tonight. It'll be fine, Super Dan."

"You know, that was cute when you were seven. Not so much now, Mr. Funny Guy."

"If the cape fits." Asher shrugged.

"I still can't believe you talked your parents into this."

"I'm as surprised as you are. It wasn't even my idea. Nicky invited me to Beckett's concert, and I told him I'd ask. I didn't expect Mom and Dad to say yes. I'm starting to think they're worried I'm a loser."

"You're not a loser, kid." Danny rolled his eyes. "I just don't like you going to stuff like this alone."

"But I'm not alone. I have a million chaperones—and you, Super Agent Danny."

"You know what I mean." Dan opened the door that lead up to

the VIP private lounge. No one would even know the president's son was attending the concert. It was just going to be Nicky and Asher. Wylder and Harper were both busy this weekend, so it was just a party of two in Cincinnati. Becks would join them after the concert. Asher probably shouldn't be this excited, but he'd never been to a real concert. He'd only ever attended White House events, which were over the top, like everything else in Washington. This was his first normal concert, and he was way more excited than he should be. He just wished he could sit in the arena with everyone else.

"Have fun tonight, kid. You deserve this chance." Danny knocked on the door to the private lounge. Becks was already on stage. Asher had to arrive late so he could sneak in, so he'd already missed the opening act.

"What chance?" Asher frowned. "The concert, you mean?"

"Yeah, of course." Danny winked. "Have fun, but don't make me regret this—and don't make a habit of it either." He opened the door and greeted the agents who'd swept the room before Asher's arrival.

"All set, sir." The agent in charge nodded to Danny and gave Asher a salute.

"All right, kid, the room's all yours." Danny held the door open. "We'll be right out here if you guys need anything. Just remember, no one comes in or out until this thing is over."

"Yeah, fine, whatever." Asher caught a glimpse of Nicky leaning against the railing in front of the floor-to-ceiling windows. Black leather chairs sat just behind him in the dimly lit room. As the door shut behind him, Asher stepped across the plush gray carpet, Beck's voice loud in his ears. Pale blue theater lights lit the floor and the ceiling, casting an iridescent glow on the room.

Nicky flipped a switch on the wall to turn the sound down.

"Nicky, your boyfriend might be an idiot, but even I have to admit he's a talented one."

That was so not Nicky's voice.

"Kenny?" Asher took a step closer to the front of the room. The overhead lights brightened to reveal Kenny Montgomery leaning with his back against the gold trimmed railing.

"I should have known those guys weren't with arena security." Kenny's irritable laugh didn't give Asher the warm fuzzies.

"I was expecting Nicky." Asher crossed the room to check out the arena below. Once again, he'd give anything to be down there with everyone else and not trapped in this awkward cocoon with the very last person he'd expected to see tonight.

"Me too." Kenny turned back to the view below.

"I guess he'll be here soon?" Asher stood halfway across the room, trying to think of anything other than the naked picture of Kenny he still had saved on his phone.

"I think maybe we've been had."

"Why?" Why would Nicky set them up like this? It wasn't… couldn't be a setup, setup. Asher's heart kicked up a notch at the very idea this could be a blind date. *Nope, nope, not going there.*

"Nicky's…Nicky." Kenny sighed. "I suppose we should just enjoy the concert. There's a ton of food and drinks back there." Kenny pointed to the other side of the room Asher hadn't noticed yet.

Gold-and-black leather bar stools stood behind a counter where they could enjoy the food and drinks and still watch the concert. Behind that, a buffet waited for them.

"Sounds like a plan." Asher went to help himself. He really wasn't hungry, but he needed a minute to prepare himself for spending a whole evening with his former best friend turned asshole.

But Kenny seemed to have the same idea. When Asher turned

to get a drink, Kenny was right there, so close Asher almost dumped his plate of appetizers right on his clean white shirt. "Sorry." Asher took a step back to a safe distance.

"I forgot how much of a klutz you are." Kenny's mouth pulled into a half-smile, but Asher wasn't sure if it was mocking or… flirty. "The media shows you as this super cool fashion dude."

Asher laughed at that. "Yeah, well, you should know better than anyone that's all smoke a mirrors. I mean, people change. But not that much."

"So you're still you. That's good to know." Kenny popped a mini crab cake into his mouth. It was a perfect mouth, too.

Stop looking at his mouth, Ash. He walked back to the front of the room. "How much of the show have I missed?" He perched on the edge of a leather chair, positioned perfectly so he could see the stage.

"Not much. Becks just went on a few minutes before you got here." Kenny took the seat beside him.

"You're not his biggest fan, I take it?"

"Not especially, but I'm friends with Nicky, so I'm trying for his sake."

"Hello, Cincinnati!" Beckett's voice boomed through the arena after he finished his opening set. "It's good to be home, let me hear you roar!"

The crowd went wild. Asher stood up and clapped, but there was something underwhelming about sitting in a fish bowl in the middle of so much chaos.

"It's overrated down there. You're not missing anything."

"How do you know what I'm thinking?" Asher sat back down and pushed some of the food around his plate, too nervous to actually eat any of it.

Kenny leaned closer. "You forget, I know you, Asher Brooks.

And I remember how stifling the White House was for you. I can't imagine that's gotten any better."

"Definitely not."

"It always fires me up when I get to perform so close to my hometown." Becks continued to work the crowd. "Any of my Twin Rivers people in the audience tonight?"

Several areas of the arena went crazy with Twin Rivers fans. From the sound of it, the whole town showed up to see Beckett Anderson perform.

"I know I have lots of friends in the audience tonight. A couple of VIPs too." Becks cast his gaze up toward the VIP lounge.

Kenny groaned, setting his plate aside. "Don't do it, Becks."

"He's gonna do it, he can't help himself." Asher let out a real laugh, his insides finally relaxing at the look of utter embarrassment on Kenny's face.

"I've been sworn to secrecy," Becks continued. "You guys know my boyfriend, Nicky, right?"

The crowd went wild at the mention of Nicky's name.

"Wow, you sure you guys are here for me?" A face-splitting grin lit up Becks' face. "We've got quite a few Nickophytes in the house tonight."

The cheering made Asher wince, and for the first time that night, he was grateful he wasn't down there with the fans.

"That's right, of course, Nick-Nick's here with me. He's hiding, though. He doesn't think I know about his followers. He just forgets I'm the original Nickophyte."

He had the crowd eating out of his hands.

"If Nicky is here, then where the hell is he?" Kenny asked, looking over his shoulder like Nicky might be there right behind them.

"Nicky is working his butt off tonight behind the scenes,"

Becks continued. "He's playing matchmaker. Shhhh, I'm not supposed to tell."

"Matchmaker?" Asher glanced at Kenny. What *was* Nicky up to?

"Looks like we've been set up," Kenny said, propping his ankle up on his knee.

"So, to my good friends in an undisclosed VIP room in this arena, I better see some good old-fashioned smooching going on up there." He pointed right toward them. "I'll even set the mood for you." Becks reached for his guitar and began to play his next number.

"I love this song." Kenny scooted to the edge of his seat. "Just don't ever tell him I said that."

"Wait." Asher shook his head. "What is he even talking about? Nicky's trying to set us up? Like me and you…together? Like on a…date?" Asher tried to swallow, but he couldn't seem to remember how his throat worked.

"It appears that way." Kenny didn't look nearly as confused as Asher.

"But…you're not gay." *Or was he?* Asher thought about some of the things he'd seen in the tabloids about Kenny, but Asher tried really hard not to give them much attention. The tabloids were always dead wrong when it came to facts.

"No, I'm not, but where have you been, Ash?" Kenny laughed. "The cat's out of the bag. Has been for a while now, didn't you see the media shit storm about me?"

"I stopped paying attention to the media a long time ago. I'm a lot happier if I don't know what they say about me or anyone else I know."

"You must have had your head stuck in the sand all summer, then."

"I saw the photo, but all that crap about Nicky *assaulting* you? I know that's not true." There was some big hoopla about Nicky kissing Kenny, but it was so ludicrous Asher didn't give it a second thought.

"Asher, I dated Nicky for almost two years. He didn't tell you?"

"No." Asher sat back against the leather seat, wondering how he'd missed that.

"I wasn't out yet when we dated. I was still figuring things out for myself, and I didn't treat him very well. That last kiss that ended up on the gossip sites—I kissed him. It was stupid. I knew he was already falling for Becks, but I missed him. Since then, I've found out we make much better friends than boyfriends."

"Boyfriends? Wait, weren't you dating a congressman's daughter a while back? Penny something?"

"Yeah, I've dated Penny off and on for a while."

Asher's mind couldn't seem to put it together.

"Ash. I'm bi. I thought you knew. Or I thought you'd at least figured it out since I kissed you."

"Oh" was all Asher could think to say. "Oh." His eyes widened when he realized Kenny might have actually meant that kiss in the pool the night of his birthday party. And if he did, then this *was* a date.

Chapter 15

Kenny

Kenny had only seen Beckett Anderson in concert once before. At the beginning of the summer, Becks played a music festival. It was there he'd kissed Nicky for the first time—to save him from Kenny. Now, all these months later and Kenny sat beside the person he'd never expected to spend time with again.

It was almost as if they were kids again, enjoying music and crowds, with secret service lurking in the background.

Kenny eyed Danny, the agent who'd been with Asher since the president's son was running around climbing trees and scraping knees. Well, since Kenny was doing all of that. Asher had always been more of a watcher, preferring his books and his art. The two boys had little in common, yet they'd been the kind of friends that didn't come around often.

Glancing sideways at him, Kenny studied Asher. They liked to think they'd each changed, but really, they were the same scared kids. The only difference was back then they didn't know just how hard life was going to get for them.

Asher caught him watching, and his lips tugged down.

"Nicky said you watched my game last week." The words spilled out before Kenny could stop himself. He wanted to believe

Asher was interested in his life. As kids, it became a running joke how many peewee games of Kenny's Asher attended. Kenny's teammates gave him endless teasing about the constant presence of the secret service, but he hadn't cared. Not while his friend was there.

Red tinged Asher's cheeks and he ran a hand over the top of his head. "Yeah, uh, Nicky asked me to. Said something about needing the game explained to him."

"Which I've done a million times. That dude is hopeless."

Asher didn't smile at that. "You... That was a rough game."

"You mean the hit? I was fine."

Finally, one corner of Asher's lips tugged up. "You used to tell me that after every game. I never liked seeing you get hit. But this one looked bad, Ken. You scared the crap out of me."

Kenny met his gaze. "You were worried about me, Ash?"

"Yeah, I mean, who wouldn't be?"

"Careful. I might start believing you care."

Asher was silent for a long moment before speaking with low, measured words. "It wasn't me who didn't care."

Kenny looked away. Asher wasn't wrong. Back when their friendship ended, when Asher came out, Kenny tried not to care about him.

It never worked.

His gaze settled on Becks who'd ripped his shirt off in typical Becks fashion. "I can't believe Nicky is trying to set us up."

"Really? It's Nicky."

Kenny laughed, breaking the tension. "Think it was his idea or Becks'?"

"This has too much planning to be Becks' idea."

Settling back in his chair, Kenny let himself sink into the music he'd tried so hard to hate. At the music festival, he'd thought he'd finally made his choice. Gay or straight. Men or women. By hurting Nicky, he'd picked a team.

But now he sat next to a boy Nicky picked for him, one he'd kissed only a few weeks ago. What kind of universe was this?

He wasn't immune to Asher. The president's son was kind and talented and so damn cute it was impossible not to want to kiss him.

Plus, he was Ash. Sitting with him was like taking a step into a past where everything made sense.

"Do you remember when we led Danny on a chase through Columbus because we wanted tacos?"

Asher grinned. "We were at an event with my dad, and you found this taco place on your phone a couple streets over."

"We had to pay your sister to tell Danny we'd run to the bathroom, but he didn't believe her and went after us, catching up before we made it to the taco place."

"Then he bought us tacos because we'd used all the money we had to pay my sister."

Kenny laughed harder than he had in a long time. The secret service agents knew to be on their guard when Kenny was around because he'd had the habit of getting the First Son into trouble.

Asher went along with every one of Kenny's shenanigans. It was only then, with older eyes, Kenny realized why. "You trusted me."

"With my life."

Those words deflated Kenny. Asher had trusted him, and when things got hard, Kenny cut him off. "I'm sorry."

He didn't ask what Kenny was sorry for. Instead, he looked away. "We were kids, Ken. Sometimes I forget that. I've been out for so long, it's easy for me. My family supports me. Half the country loves me more because I'm gay. But you... I didn't know. I hated you because I thought you were another bigoted asshole straight guy. But you weren't. You were just…"

"Confused."

"Yeah."

"I'm still confused."

"I know."

They didn't talk for a while as Becks' music filled the silence. Kenny watched Asher rather than the prancing knucklehead on the stage. Could they get their friendship back? For years, Kenny had focused on hockey, telling himself casual friends were all he needed.

Then Nicky refused to stop caring about him. Then Killian and Wylder showed up at the hospital for him.

Now Asher…

He wasn't sure what to make of people caring what happened to him. His parents certainly didn't.

But something still bothered him. "Can I ask you a question?"

Asher nodded.

"Why did you want to punch me? Was it because of the kiss?"

Asher covered his face with his hands. "You mean the text?" His voice came out squeaky.

"Yeah, the boxing glove. I assumed it meant you wanted to clock me, but I gotta say, that's not really you."

Lowering his hands, Asher sighed. "I didn't mean to send it. I was…uh…staring at my phone trying to think of something to text you. And then I dropped my phone and accidentally sent it."

A slow smile spread across Kenny's face. "You were going to text me?" His smile widened into a full-blown grin. "You mean I sent you a naked dunk tank picture for no reason?"

"When is there ever a reason for that?"

"So, you looked at it."

"Of course, I did! You were sitting in a dunk tank naked."

"What'd you think?" Kenny cocked his head. He'd always been confident in his looks, and it was fun making Asher squirm.

"Um…" Red tinted Asher's skin from his neck to the tips of his ears.

Kenny couldn't help it. He reached out and touched the blushing skin. He swore Asher stopped breathing.

"How often did you stare at the picture, Ash?" Kenny no longer wore a smile as his eyes bored into Asher's.

"Every day since."

Those were the words he needed to snap him back to reality. A picture didn't matter. A kiss didn't matter. Asher did. Their friendship did.

Kenny withdrew his hand. "I'm glad Nicky set this up tonight."

"Me too. I've missed you, Ken."

He should have said he missed him too. He should have kissed him. But Kenny Montgomery couldn't kiss the president's son. Not again. Being with Asher meant finally cutting all bridges to his parents. It meant the country knowing what he'd always tried to hide.

And he definitely wasn't ready for that.

"Admit it," Asher sing-songed. "That concert was pretty great."

Kenny shrugged. There was no way he'd let anyone hear he didn't hate Becks' music.

Danny opened a door for them after showing a security guard their backstage passes. They entered a long hall teeming with people hoping to meet the country music star.

Whispers followed them as they pushed their way through. Asher Brooks, gay political icon, was on his way to hang out with

Beckett Anderson, sort of gay country music icon. It was an LGBTQ dream.

Nicky appeared at the end of the hall and waved them forward with a gigantic grin.

Kenny reached him. "You're in so much trouble."

Nicky shrugged with an "I don't know what you're talking about" look.

Asher only shook his head with a laugh.

"Come on." Nicky led them through another door to where band members lounged on white leather couches. At the end of the room was a final door. It stood open, and a very sweaty Beckett Anderson leaned in the doorway, laughing at something Nari said.

Nari broke away from him as their manager called her over.

Becks wiped his face on the shirt he held in his hand. Sweat glistened on his bare chest.

Nicky sighed and rolled his eyes. "He thinks he needs to live up to his hashtag basically all the time."

"SexyBecksy?" Kenny choked on a laugh.

"I swear, I spend half my time just trying to get him to keep his clothes on in public."

Asher stifled a laugh. "I don't know, Nick. I'd be totally okay if he never wore a shirt again."

"You wouldn't be if you had to deal with screaming girls constantly inflating his ego."

Becks grinned when he saw them. "Are you two now madly in love? It was all my idea, so you can thank me."

Nicky groaned. "Do you insist on being embarrassing, babe?"

Becks responded by grabbing Nicky and pulling him in for a bruising kiss. When he finally released him, Nicky stumbled back against the wall.

"Now, who wants to enter my lair?" Becks led them in to his dressing room where a wraparound couch sat in the corner.

Kenny jumped onto it, sinking into the plush leather. Asher sat next to him while Nicky perched on the arm.

Becks hopped onto the dressing table, letting his legs dangle over the side.

"Did you guys have fun?" Nicky asked.

Kenny shrugged, not wanting them to know he actually had. "It was okay except for the music."

Asher matched his frown. "Yeah. If you're going to try and set me up with someone I have zero desire to be around, at least let it be somewhere fun."

Becks crossed his arms. "So, it didn't work?"

Kenny almost laughed at the fact he didn't care they'd insulted his music, only that they weren't now hopelessly in love.

Nicky shook his head with a laugh. "It was a long shot. And, Becks, you didn't even know my plan until five minutes before the concert, so I don't know why you're so upset."

"Well…" Becks scratched the back of his neck. "It's just so sad. They were best friends, Nick-Nick. Asher comes out as gay, and his supposedly straight best friend can't deal. But that friend turns out to be bi. They should be made for each other."

He released a dramatic sigh. "And then the whole kiss thing."

"Becks," Nicky warned.

Becks went on as if he hadn't heard him, and he looked like he might cry. "Asher loses his kissing virginity to Kenny but assumes it was a drunken action by a straight dude. Then the hockey game where Ash was freaking out about the hit…" He sniffled. "It's just so…sad."

Nicky got up and walked to his boyfriend before slapping him upside the head.

"What was that for?"

"Stop talking, Beckett Anderson."

Kenny barely noticed their interaction because he was stuck on only a few of Becks' words. He turned to Asher. "That was your first kiss?"

Asher swallowed heavily and nodded. "I…yeah."

He didn't ask how because it made sense. Asher lived in an ivory tower. Kenny had been one of his only true friends.

Before he could truly process it, Kenny's phone dinged. Pulling it out, he saw Wylder's name and almost ignored it, but something inside him told him to open the message.

> **Wylder:** I know you're at the concert, but I wanted you to hear about this from me. I'm here if you want to talk.

Then she sent a link.

"Who is it?" Becks asked, nosy as ever.

"Your sister."

He hesitated a moment before opening the link. An article appeared, and the title stole the breath from his lungs.

> **Senator's wife caught in affair.**
>
> The wife of Ohio State Senator, Preston Montgomery, was photographed in an intimate embrace with Kyle Henderson. Mr. Henderson is the family advisor for the Montgomerys' only son as he plays his way to an NHL draft selection.

There were pictures of his mom and Kyle kissing outside a hotel.

"Ken," Asher whispered. "You okay?"

"No." It was the only word he could get out. Even when his parents failed him, Kyle had been there. He'd believed in Kenny at every step of his hockey career.

And now…how could Kenny even look at him? How could Kenny face his mother or even his father? Preston Montgomery was not an easy man to love, but he deserved better than this.

"What's going on?" Becks jumped from the dressing table and crossed the room to sit with them on the couch. Nicky followed suit until they all crowded Kenny, offering their support for something they didn't yet know.

"My mom." He held his phone to Nicky.

Nicky sucked in a breath. "Kyle, really?"

Asher read it next, and Kenny wondered what he was thinking. Their parents were political rivals, both families held up as the ideal by their sides.

The Montgomerys had never let people see their cracks.

But hiding wide fissures was nearly impossible in Washington.

Kenny couldn't move; he couldn't think. As his world crumbled at his feet, all he wanted to do was disappear.

But that was the thing about being a Montgomery. Disappearing was never an option.

Chapter 16

Asher

Asher couldn't stand the broken look on Kenny's face. Sure, he was arrogant and cocky, and kind of an asshole too, but in that moment, he just looked like a kid who needed a friend. And the last place Kenny needed to be was backstage at a Beckett Anderson concert.

"You know, I think we're going to leave." Asher motioned for Danny to do his thing and get them out of there.

"No, it's okay," Kenny mumbled. "I have my car here. I can drive myself back to school."

"We'll get your car back to school for you," Nicky said. "Go with Asher."

Asher took Kenny's arm and guided him toward the door to wait for Danny's team. "I know it's not enough, Ken, but I'm so sorry." Asher gave his arm a gentle squeeze before he dropped his hand.

Kenny nodded. "Thanks, Ash."

"Ready to go already?" Danny asked.

"Yeah." Asher nodded.

"You don't have to leave now if you want to stay and hang out," Kenny said.

"Don't listen to him, Danny, just get us to the car."

"You do know it's a madhouse out there? Girls are tearing each other's faces off trying to get a peek at Beckett. To be honest, I'm a little terrified."

"Let's just get it over with."

Two agents waited outside Becks' dressing room, and another two brought up the rear. Danny stood at Asher's side, glued to him like a barnacle on a boat. Another agent flanked Kenny's left.

"You come with a lot more baggage than you used to." Kenny attempted to joke.

"Yeah, well, I'm more popular than you, get used to it." Asher nudged him in the side, satisfied when he got a half-smirk in response.

"All right, let's move." Danny finally gave the go ahead. They moved quickly through the backstage area, but once outside the arena, they braved a gauntlet of screaming fans just hoping for a chance to see Beckett. Instead, they got the president's son and the son of their state senator. He just hoped for Kenny's sake no one realized they were the VIP couple Becks mentioned on stage.

A full-on motorcade waited for them at the curb, and the two boys dove into the back seat with Danny. The car was moving before the door closed.

"That was intense." Asher glanced back at the screaming crowd. "You'd think he'd hate all that screaming."

"Becks? Mr. Center of Attention himself?" Kenny quipped. "He loves every second in the spotlight."

"Where to, sir?" the driver asked.

"Riverpass," Asher answered.

"In this car, I am the only one who answers to sir," Danny said. "Take us to the airport, and then escort Mr. Montgomery back to his school in Riverpass."

"Um, no," Asher argued. "I'm not leaving Kenny alone right

now. He's had a bad night. The least we can do is give him a ride back to school."

"It's fine, Ash. I can drive myself."

Asher turned a death glare on Danny. The one that said, "I will lose my shit if you don't treat me like a normal guy right now."

"You know what I'm going to say about unscheduled stops, Ash. Don't give me that look."

Asher turned up the volume on his glare.

"You are not the president, Asher Brooks. I'm sorry, but you don't get unscheduled stops." Danny sighed. "No don't give me the eyes, kid. It's not going to work. Not this time." Danny turned to look out the window but Asher knew he was about to cave.

"Fine. We can send someone ahead to make arrangements." Danny nodded to the driver. "Looks like we're going to Riverpass."

Danny spent the entire drive on the phone making arrangements for an overnight stay at a hotel in Riverpass. Kenny stared out the window, lost in the turmoil of his thoughts, and Asher… fell asleep.

"Hey, Ash?" Kenny's voice was a whisper in his ear.

"What?" Asher opened his eyes, confused for a moment.

"We're almost there."

"Oh." Asher blinked. He'd fallen asleep on Kenny's shoulder and somehow ended up tucked under his arm and snuggled against his side. "Sorry." He sat up, rubbing his eyes to buy him a moment to clear his head. That didn't stop the warmth spreading across his face. He'd made a big show of being there for his friend, and then he fell asleep. *Good job, Ash.*

"You can fall asleep on me anytime," Kenny whispered, squeezing his hand.

That made Asher blush even more, eliciting a chuckle from Kenny.

"Thanks for riding home with me."

"Yeah, sure, anytime."

"Okay, Mr. Montgomery, here we are, safe and secure at Defiance Academy," the driver said. "Where is your dormitory?"

While Kenny gave directions to the driver, Asher and Danny had one of their silent arguments. Danny didn't know it yet, but Asher was staying with Kenny for as long as he needed someone.

"Thanks again, Ash." Kenny moved to exit the car. "Maybe we can—"

"I'm coming with you." Asher slid across the seat.

"Yeah, no, you aren't." Danny slid Asher back to his side.

"Follow me if you must." Asher shrugged out of Danny's grasp.

"Just so you know, Defiance Academy has every bit of security Asher's school has in Washington. Probably even more since so many VIPs send their kids here to live on campus," Kenny offered.

"Sir, couldn't we let the kid have a moment?" one of the other agents said. "Remember what, er, Victory and Voyager said before we left?"

"Yeah, I remember." Danny's shoulders slumped. "It still goes against my better judgment."

"That's our cue to leave." Asher took Kenny's arm and headed toward his dorm.

"I live in that building over there." Kenny pointed at the building behind them.

"Yeah, you should probably lead the way." Asher nodded.

The two boys took off across the lawn, leaving the security team arguing about the best ways to keep Asher safe on an impenetrable campus. Of course, Danny sent two agents to follow them.

"You know, we could ditch Super Danny for the night if we can get inside this building before he realizes it locks behind me." Kenny took out his access card and swiped it at the door.

"Danny will just call security to let him in after he tries to kick in the door."

"Takes his job seriously, that one."

"You have no idea." Asher rolled his eyes. "It's like having a third parent." Asher winced at the mention of parents, not wanting to remind Kenny of his current family situation.

"Take one step inside that building without me and you're really going to find out how much of a prison the White House can be." Danny came charging up the steps to the door.

"After you." Kenny held the door open for him. "Just try to keep it down so you don't get me in trouble for breaking curfew."

"You missed curfew?" Asher asked.

"I always miss curfew." Kenny shrugged, following Asher into the foyer.

"Where's your room?" Danny asked.

"Second floor, last door on the left. And try not to give my roommate a stroke when you go in there."

"You can come up after we sweep the room," Danny said.

"You have a roommate?" Asher hadn't planned on that. Not that he'd really thought this through.

"Yeah, Will's not much of a bother. He'll be in his room by now."

"You have separate bedrooms in your dorm?"

"We have a roommate suite. It's tiny, but our bedrooms are connected by a shared space."

"So, let's go watch a movie or something," Asher suggested. "I'm guessing you won't be sleeping much tonight, so let me keep you company."

"Where's your entourage going to stay?" Kenny's half-smile sent Asher's heart skipping.

Asher shrugged. "I guess we'll figure that out later." Asher took the steps two at a time, trying to ignore the secret service following them to Kenny's dorm room. This was starting to feel way more like a date, but with so many eyes watching them, it was impossible to enjoy it. That, and Kenny's current family situation. Neither parent had bothered to call their son to check on him. That had to hurt nearly as much as his mother's affair with his advisor. If Asher could continue to distract him, it was the least he could do.

"All right, this is how this is going to work." Danny met them at the door to Kenny's room. "The roommate is in for the night. We did a quick background check, and he's squeaky clean."

"Dan." Asher groaned. "That's so rude."

"I don't care. You two can stay out here and watch one movie. I'll be in Kenny's shoebox of a room to give you some privacy. We have agents stationed at the door to this room, all over the grounds and at the front door of the building. After your movie, we're going to the hotel we've arranged for you, and then we leave for Washington in the morning."

"Thank you, sir." Kenny nodded. "That's more than fair."

"But wouldn't it be easier to just—"

Kenny kicked him before Asher could finish protesting.

"Thank you," Asher muttered.

"If you need me, I'll be in Kenny's room moving heaven and earth to make arrangements for our flight in the morning." Danny's voice was gruff, but when he shut the door to Kenny's room, he shot Asher a wink.

"You have to learn to pick your battles, my friend." Kenny flopped onto the small couch in front of the wide-screen television. The room was small, but the furnishings were high end. "What should we watch?"

"Anything. You pick."

"You realize if you don't choose I'm turning on a hockey game?"

"What game?" Asher sat down beside Kenny and propped his feet up on the coffee table.

"The Jackets are in Tampa, and we may actually have a shot at beating them."

"You're a big Columbus fan, aren't you?"

Kenny looked at him like he was stupid. "I'm from Ohio."

"Yeah, but that could also mean you're a penguins fan or a wings fan."

A dark look crossed Kenny's face. "You take that back."

Asher shrugged. "It's true. Only people in Columbus are really Jackets loyalists."

"How do you know? I doubt you even follow hockey."

"You'd be surprised."

"Name the teams. All thirty-one of them."

Asher's eyes widened. "Are you serious right now? We're really arguing about if I like hockey?" He sighed. "Fine." He named every team.

Kenny didn't look impressed, but Asher figured fighting about hockey was a good distraction from the craziness that was his family.

Kenny crossed his arms. "How?"

"What?"

"How do you know anything about the NHL? Back when we were friends, you couldn't care less."

That stung Asher. He'd gone to all of Kenny's games, hadn't he? So, he didn't give one lick about the hometown Washington Capitals. He was more of a casual fan than anything else. He wouldn't admit he'd read up on it more after the last time he'd seen Kenny. And he definitely wouldn't admit to watching games on TV after Kenny abandoned him as some kind of masochistic act full of self-pity. He'd missed his best friend even after said friend refused to accept him. He hadn't been able to help it.

Instead of letting all those confessions vomit out, he shrugged. "We going to watch this? I'm always up for a game."

"You may live to regret those words." Kenny grinned as he turned the game on and sat back against the couch, looking somewhat relaxed after the terrible night he'd had.

Kenny's phone buzzed in his pocket.

"Do you need to get that?" Asher asked.

"It's Kyle. I don't want to talk to him." Kenny didn't even look at his phone. "Of all the people she could have cheated with, why did it have to be Kyle?"

"It has nothing to do with you, Ken. This thing with your parents, it's between them. Kyle is a good advisor, and he cares about your future in the NHL."

"If he cared, he'd have kept his hands off my mom." He ran a hand through his hair in frustration. "Ugh, I can't even talk about it without feeling nauseous."

"Sorry." Asher wasn't sure if he was helping or hurting the situation. He just knew if it was him, he wouldn't want to be alone.

"It's not your fault. And for the record, I'm glad you're here." Kenny squeezed his shoulder. "Want anything to drink? I think we've got some cookies too if you're hungry."

"I can help myself." Asher stood. "You just sit and watch the game and try not to think about it." Asher moved to the little kitchenette behind the tiny living room. After checking the cabinets and the fridge, he poured them each a drink and stacked a plate of cookies.

"Did you just make me milk and cookies?" Kenny stepped up behind him.

"Um, yeah. I don't care how cool you are, no one is too cool for milk and cookies. Especially Oreos." Asher grabbed the plate and tried to turn around, but Kenny didn't move out of his way. Instead, he took the plate from Asher and set it back on the counter.

"You're so adorable I can't even handle it." He took a step closer, pressing Asher back against the counter.

Asher lost the ability to think when Kenny stood so close. "Is that good or bad?"

"I'm not sure I know how to answer that." Kenny's laughter reminded him of much simpler times when they were just kids and nothing more complicated than the question of what game to play stood between them. "I screwed up your first kiss." It wasn't a question. "I'm sorry about that." His fingertips trailed down Asher's face. "I'd like a chance to fix that."

Kenny leaned in, pressing his lips against Asher's, the pad of his thumb grazing Asher's jaw. Nearly as surprised as he was the night of the pool party, Asher froze, but only for a moment. Kenny's kiss was gentle this time. The sense of urgency was there, but the pressure wasn't. This was how it was supposed to be. Asher tilted his head back and went with it, sliding his arms around Kenny's waist. A moan escaped him as Kenny pulled him closer, wrapping his arms around Asher, deepening their kiss with a touch of his tongue.

Kenny broke the kiss far sooner than Asher would have liked, but he pressed his forehead against Asher's taking a deep breath—as if the kiss had affected him as much as it had Asher. "Whenever you remember your first kiss, remember that one. The first one didn't count."

"That's what I said." Asher tried to hide his trembling hands, grabbing a cookie from the plate beside him. He could play this cool. *For once in your life, Ash, try to pull this off.*

"Oh, you've been talking about me?" Kenny grabbed the plate of cookies, and Asher brought the two glasses of milk, following him back to the couch.

"I needed help translating the naked man pic." Asher shrugged, taking his place on the couch. He tried not to show his disappointment when Kenny sat on the opposite corner, quickly becoming absorbed in the game again.

Asher studied his profile. Kenny seemed at ease after their kiss—their earth-shattering kiss—but he immediately grew distant, leaving Asher to wonder if this kiss meant more to him than to Kenny.

Chapter 17

Kenny

Shouting jerked Kenny from the best sleep he'd had in ages.

"You're my son, and this is how you treat me?"

Ohh, crap. His dad.

Kenny tried to sit upright, but a weight held him down on the couch. Asher. They'd fallen asleep watching the game and lay curled around each other. Asher's hand found its way up Kenny's shirt sometime in the night.

Yep, this was the scene his dad just had to walk in on.

"Dad, it's not what it looks like."

"The hell it's not." He lowered his voice. "It's not enough to embarrass me with your antics with Nicky St. Germaine over the summer. Now, you're using Asher Brooks to get back at me."

"It's not like that, Dad." Kenny averted his eyes from his father and found Danny shutting the door into the hall. Sunlight streamed in through the windows overlooking the grassy hill rolling down toward the quad.

"Tell me, son. What is it like?"

Asher groaned as he started to wake. "Ken?" His eyes opened, and he took in his position with alarmed eyes. Was it really that bad to be here with him?

Kenny didn't have time to consider that. There were more pressing issues. Like his fuming father or the secret service agent who for some reason allowed Asher to stay all night.

Pushing Asher off him, Kenny stood to face his father. He scanned him from head to toe, noticing not a thing out of place. The man's wife was caught in an affair the night before, and he strode in looking like it was business as usual.

"You're not perfect." Kenny's voice was so quiet he wasn't sure his dad heard him, but the words weren't for his benefit. For so long, his parents held themselves up as the ideal. They were what everyone should strive to be, a united couple chasing success at any cost.

And it was all a lie.

Kenny spoke louder this time. "You're not perfect, Dad."

His dad bristled at that. "Ken—"

"Let me finish. You've had eighteen years of telling me exactly what to think and do. Now it's my turn."

To his credit, his dad nodded for him to go on.

"It's okay not to be perfect. That's an impossible standard. For so long, I tried to live up to your expectations. You had no flaws other than your obvious disregard for your son. But even that I thought was my fault. I'm not a politician, Dad. I don't want to wake up one day and realize I've only ever tried to project this image of myself that isn't real."

He took a deep breath. It was now or never. Time for courage. Time for truth. "I'm bisexual."

His dad stared dumbfounded, but he didn't respond.

Kenny rubbed the back of his neck. "And I think you know that. You've known for a long time. All that media crap over the summer? Nicky didn't attack me. I dated him for two years before the infamous kiss. It sucked to be outed that way, but it would have been okay if my family supported me rather than trying to cover it up and shove me right back into the dark." He breathed heavily.

Danny stepped toward Asher. "We should go. The rest of your security is waiting."

Asher shook his head, not taking his eyes from Kenny. What did he see? A coward who'd waited this long to stand up to his dad?

Kenny didn't think he'd been a coward, but he knew what the world saw of the closeted. He just hadn't been ready. Even now, he wasn't sure he was, but he knew the time had come.

"I needed you, Dad. And Mom. But you were both too absorbed in your image of the good conservative family. You abandoned me." He glanced back at Ash. "Just like I abandoned someone." He was no better than his dad.

"Kenneth." His father sighed. "Your lifestyle does not fit into our world."

"That's just it, though. It's not a lifestyle. It's just a life. I don't want to be someone I'm not anymore. Trying to be who you want me to be has cost too much." Anger burned in him when his father looked away. "You're cold, Dad. Maybe that's why Mom had to find love somewhere else."

The back of his father's hand struck him before he even saw it coming. Kenny stumbled back, rubbing his face and staring at his dad.

His father ran a hand through his hair. "I'm sorry, Ken. I shouldn't have done that." Far be it for the man to lose control. "Your mother..."

"She left you, didn't she?"

He nodded.

"For Kyle?"

Another nod.

Even after all their problems, Kenny wanted to reach out to his dad, to still be his family. He just didn't know if that was possible anymore.

"I'm going to fire him."

"You don't have to do that." His father blew out a shaky breath. "Kyle has been instrumental in getting NHL scouts to come watch you. Don't let your mother and I mess up your dreams."

It wasn't what he'd expected his dad to say. For so long, he'd wanted Kenny to become a politician, saying the odds of making it in hockey were too low.

But he didn't get a chance to ask. Throwing a stern look at Asher, his father turned. "I just came here to make sure you were okay after the news released. I'll see myself out."

When he shut the door, it was as if all the air suddenly poured back into the room, and Kenny could breathe again.

He collapsed back onto the couch beside Asher.

Asher looked to Danny. "Gotta say, I'm surprised to still be here. Why didn't you wake me up to go to the hotel?"

Danny shifted his eyes away. "I...uh...fell asleep."

Kenny barely heard their exchange because his mind was still on his father. He'd come to check on him? It surprised him his mom hadn't called, but during what must have been a terrible time for him, his dad showed up.

It was hard to reconcile that image with the man who refused to accept him.

I'm bisexual.

Those words actually left his mouth in his father's presence.

Asher bumped their shoulders together. "You told him."

"Yeah." Kenny buried his face in his hands. Coming out to his dad should have been freeing, but all Kenny could think was "what now?" Was he expected to openly date a guy? He'd never even crossed that line with Nicky.

Would he open himself up to the entire world of judgment? It wasn't like hockey was a particularly accepting sport.

Could he have both his dream and be himself openly and proudly?

"You know it's going to be okay, right?" Asher whispered.

Was it? Kenny replayed their kiss from the night before. In the moment, he'd been desperate to forget the night's events, and yes, he'd wanted to kiss Asher. But it couldn't be more than that. Not with Asher Brooks.

That would be like stepping from his closet into a circus.

Yet, sitting there next to him gave him a comfort few things ever did. "Ash." He sighed. "I think I need some space to think."

"Oh." Asher's face fell, and Kenny hated himself for the disappointment he saw there.

Danny jumped in. "We have a plane to catch back to Washington, anyway. Asher, your mother is not happy you're here."

Asher stood and flattened out his wrinkled shirt. "She'll understand. There was a time Kenny was like a son to her. She wouldn't have wanted him to go through this alone."

He started to walk away, but Kenny reached out and grabbed his hand. "Ash…thank you."

Asher turned a sad smile on him. "I'm glad you've finally let me see who you are, Ken. For the record, your parents are missing out."

"So are all the guys who missed out on your first kiss."

Asher's smile widened into a grin. "I assumed we weren't mentioning that."

Kenny shrugged. "Everything is shit right now. I've got to remember the good stuff."

"Good is boring. Try epic."

Leave it to Asher to be able to make Kenny laugh at a time like this. "Okay. Epic. Whoever gets your next kiss, they'll never top that."

Asher's smile dropped slightly, and he turned quickly, following Danny out the door.

Kenny laid his head against the back of the couch and closed his eyes, wishing he could be the guy who got Asher Brooks' next kiss.

They had so much history, a lot of it bad, he didn't see how Asher could ever feel anything for him.

Will's door opened, and he stumbled out into the common room, rubbing his face. "Did I hear yelling this morning?"

Kenny eyed his shirtless roommate, almost laughing at how disheveled he looked. "Yeah. My dad showed up and found me asleep with Asher Brooks."

Will froze.

Kenny didn't say the word bi but Will could put it together. They all knew of the pictures of him with Nicky.

He groaned. "I must need coffee because I think you just told me the president's son spent the night in our dorm." He collapsed into a chair.

"I did."

"Oh, well, okay, man. Asher is hot, so go you."

"Uh…"

"Don't get your panties in a bunch. I'm totally straight and not after your man, but can't a heterosexual male call a spade a spade?"

"Please don't call him hot again."

Will threw a pillow at him. "Why not? Afraid of some competition?"

"You don't care that I like a dude?"

A raised eyebrow was Will's only expression. "Why would I?

What I do care about is that we're teammates, and I have never once seen you checking me out in the shower."

"You're disgusting. Gay guys or bi guys or whatever-they-want-to-be guys don't go ogling every man we see."

"Yeah, but I'm a prime cut of beef. A little attention would be nice."

Kenny threw the pillow back, laughing in satisfaction when it struck him in the face. He hadn't realized how worried he was to tell his teammates. They all speculated, but now they'd know.

And Will didn't care. It was a start.

Getting to his feet, Kenny shook his head. "I'm going to shower."

"Pizza with the guys at noon?"

He rarely got together with the team anymore, but it had been tradition in previous years when he took his leadership role seriously. "Yeah, man. That sounds great."

As Kenny waited for Will to get ready, he turned on his phone for the first time since the night before.

Nicky and Becks had both texted, but he knew they'd only be checking to see how he was.

Asher's name popped up next.

Asher: Last night at the concert was actually fun.

Kenny smiled.

Kenny: Don't tell Nicky.

Asher: Absolutely not.

His smile fell when he noticed three missed calls from Kyle. It wasn't a surprise. Kyle had a few NHL players as clients, but in terms of draft prospects, Kenny was the most high profile.

With a sigh, he tapped Kyle's name and brought the phone to his ear.

Kyle answered immediately. "Kenny, thank God. I've been trying to reach you all night."

"I know."

"Look, son—"

"I'm not your son, Kyle. For better or worse, only one man can claim me as his son—my mom's husband."

Kyle was silent for a moment. "Ken, you and I have been together for a while. I've brought scouts that have helped raise your draft profile."

"No, my play has raised my draft profile. But you… I will admit you've always been good to me."

"I have."

Kenny rubbed his face. "That's what makes this all suck so much. Kyle, even when my parents didn't care, you and I were a team. But you've destroyed my family."

"What family, Ken? Your mother was not happy in that farce."

"Then she should have divorced him. I don't care whatever excuses you and Mom give me, nothing makes this okay. I had to look into my dad's eyes today and know everything he'd worked toward was falling down around him. We may not agree on much, but he's my dad."

"And she's your mother."

"Then maybe she should try acting like it instead of sleeping with the one man I thought I had on my side." Kenny breathed deeply as he tried to control his temper. "Look, Kyle, I've come to realize I don't have room for toxic people in my life. I'm trying the honest thing here. You're fired."

"You can't fire me."

"Actually, I can. I'm sorry it came to this." He hung up without a goodbye just as Will came out of his room.

"You hear that?" Kenny stood.

"Yeah, sorry, man. Families suck."

He thought of Asher's parents and the sometimes embarrassing amount of support they gave him. "Sometimes, they do." There'd been a time the Brooks supported him too. He wanted that back.

He wanted it all. Asher. His family. Suddenly, the spotlight didn't matter so much.

"I think I might be in love with Asher Brooks." He hadn't meant to say it out loud, but the revelation hit him stronger than anything. Maybe he always had been, and that was why he'd pushed him away when Asher came out as gay.

Because it became possible.

And that was terrifying.

No matter what Kenny said, he didn't want Asher's next kiss to be with someone else. Yet, he also couldn't tell him, and he knew exactly why.

There was no way Asher felt the same way. Not after everything they'd been through.

Will clapped him on the back. "I've gotta say, man, you aim high. I like it."

Kenny shrugged him off and walked into the hall. Will followed. "You going to ask him to winter formal? That would be quite the scene."

"No." Kenny laughed. "There is no way I can bring the president's son to a high school dance. Besides, he wouldn't say yes."

"Where is the Kenny confidence? Weren't you the one who went naked into the dunk tank? We all know you've got man bits of steel."

"Don't say man bits. That's gross."

"Fine, I'll quit. But I know you'll miss me next year when you're off in Boston, and I'm stuck here another year."

He would. Kenny had never imagined he'd miss Will Dalton.

Since they weren't allowed to leave campus without permission, pizza with the team meant eating in the dining hall.

Students packed the tables, and Will led Kenny to where the team sat huddled over plates piled high with pizza. After saying hi, they went into the line for food and returned. Kenny slid in next to Killian.

Killian leaned in. "Heard you weren't on campus last night."

Kenny shrugged. He trusted Killer, but could get in a lot of trouble. Though, he doubted his secret was really a secret since Asher's bodyguards had accompanied them to campus.

Will pounded on the table for the team to quiet down. Voices faded. "Our own Kenny Montgomery has something he needs to talk about."

Kenny froze. He hadn't planned on telling the team like this, but news traveled fast, and they'd find out some way.

Will met his gaze. "These guys here are your brothers whether you've acted like one of us this year or not. We want our Kenny back, and that starts with honesty and ends with us being here for you."

Kenny sucked in a breath. Will was right. Before this year, the team had been his family. He didn't want to hide anything from them.

"I'm…" He cleared his throat. "I'm bisexual."

They looked at him dumbfounded.

Kenny sighed. "I like girls, but I like guys too, maybe more."

Will gave him a strange look. "Uh, Ken, I meant we were here to talk about your parents if you wanted us to. Totally wasn't outing you, bro."

"Oh." Well, Kenny felt like an idiot now.

Travis, a sophomore winger, laughed. "And, what, you think we didn't know?"

A few others nodded their heads. Some just shrugged like the news didn't matter to them.

Will grinned. "See, Ken. We're brothers. Can't believe you'd think that would matter to us."

What surprised him the most were Killian's words beside him. "I'm gay." He shrugged as if that term was as normal as any other, like he'd just said, "I like pizza" or "I'm a goalie."

Maybe, they were normal.

Or, maybe, they could be.

This was the support he'd been hoping to find in his parents. They hadn't been capable of it. How was it a team of teenage athletes who enjoyed pounding people into the boards had more compassion, more acceptance than two grown adults who were supposed to love their son?

Killian, the ever stoic—and gay—goalie nudged his shoulder. "How does it feel?"

"Really freaking weird. I spent a lot of time hiding it."

"Dude, if you wanted to hide your sexuality, maybe, you shouldn't have kissed Beckett Anderson's boyfriend and ended up in the media for it? Just a thought."

"Yeah." Will laughed. "You'd make a terrible spy."

Kenny picked a piece of pepperoni off his pizza and flung it across the table. It hit Will's cheek. "I'd be an awesome spy."

"No." A new voice joined them as Wylder plopped herself down on the opposite side of Kenny. "You'd be awful." She paid no mind to the rest of the team as she studied him. "I heard the cat is out of the bag with a certain burnt ember."

"Burnt ember?"

"Oh, don't pretend not to know who I'm talking about. He

talked to Nicky, and Nicky talked to Becks, and Becks talked to me."

"All in like two hours?"

"You underestimate our meddling power."

So much for not telling Nicky they'd had a good time together. He couldn't hold in a laugh. "You're all ridiculous."

"Thank you." She smiled as if it was a great compliment. Wylder was so much like her brother, just maybe a broody version of the country star.

"I don't want to talk about it."

"Fine. Then let's talk about Winter Formal."

"I wasn't planning to go."

She huffed. "And why wouldn't you ask our ember friend?"

He leaned in and lowered his voice. "You can say Ash. No one will connect the dots."

"That's not as much fun."

He shook his head. "He wouldn't say yes. This whole... being honest thing is kinda a big deal for me. I need to take it all slowly. And taking a guy to the dance is not slow."

She pursed her lips. "Fine. Then you're taking me."

He lifted a brow. "You don't have a date already?" His eyes scanned the table of his teammates, and more than a few of them were watching Wylder. If she stopped her anti-academy-friend movement, she could have her pick of guys.

"The guys at this school are boring." She grabbed his arm. "Save me. Please. We can spend our time mocking our classmates' penchant for spending too much money on an outfit for a dance they won't even care about a few weeks later."

He liked the sound of that. Hanging with Wylder was fun, and that wasn't something he'd ever thought before.

"Okay, it's a date."

She clapped her hands together. "Perfect." Leaning around

him, she lifted her voice. "Killian, you're coming with us. You are not sitting in your room during this dance."

The look on his face told them that was exactly what he'd planned.

"What about me?" Will pouted.

Wylder barely looked at him as she stood. "No."

She walked away, leaving the table rolling in laughter.

Kenny couldn't remember the last time he just sat with his team and joked and had a good time. He'd been so stuck in his own problems he'd forgotten how much he needed them. After a while, once his stomach hurt from all the food, Kenny wandered back to his dorm alone.

Practice wasn't for a few hours so he planned to sleep off the food baby and try to forget about his dad and his feelings for Asher.

That didn't work so well when the boy in question messaged him.

Asher: Heard you're going to the formal with Wylder.

Kenny:... news travels fast?

He could imagine what Asher was thinking. There goes Kenny, trying to be straight again, only choosing one side of his sexuality. The truth was, yes, Kenny liked girls. They were nice smelling and soft. But he wasn't nearly as drawn to them as he was to boys like Nicky or Asher.

Sure, he could pass as straight. He'd been doing it long enough. But he didn't want to.

Asher: She's Nicky's best friend. You know they talk more than any two sane people ever do, right?

Kenny: Doesn't explain how you know.

Asher: I hope you have a good time with her.

Kenny: I'm not into Wylder.

Asher: Didn't think you were.

Kenny: Okay…

Asher: I just wanted to tell you to have fun.

The dance wasn't for another week. Kenny unlocked his dorm and walked into his room, throwing his keys on the desk but keeping his eyes on the phone. Was he hoping for another message? One that explained whatever Asher was trying to say. Have fun? What did that even mean?

Kenny: Ash…

Before he could send the last message, a new one from Asher popped up.

Asher: Don't overthink everything.

He still knew him too well. He knew Kenny would sit staring at his phone long after the conversation was over.

But he didn't know how much Kenny wanted to prolong it, how talking to Asher felt right. Listening to Ash, he stopped thinking altogether and pressed his thumb down on Asher's name. Immediately, it started ringing, and he wanted to hang up.

His nerve slipped, but before he could end the call, Asher answered.

"Kenny." There was laughter in his voice, but Kenny didn't know why.

"Hey." His brain short-circuited. "What do you need?"

Asher laughed. "You called me."

"Right. Yeah."

"Is Kenny Montgomery flustered? That's normally my job."

A call beeped in, but as soon as Kenny saw Kyle's name, he ignored it. "My mom still hasn't called. Kyle won't stop. You saw my dad come by. But nothing from her. No apologies or explanations. She blew everything up, and it's like she doesn't care."

"I'm sorry." He was quiet for a moment. "Are you...okay?"

"Yeah." He realized he was. "My parents' problems have never been mine. I came out to my team today."

"Ken, that's amazing. I'm so proud of you."

Kenny's face glowed with the praise.

"How did it go?"

"Better than I ever expected. None of them seemed to even really care. They didn't make it a big deal."

Asher hummed his approval. "No one should care. Being gay or bi or trans or anything you are isn't brave, Ken. It's who we are. Saying it's brave is like claiming we have a choice to be anything else. Coming out shouldn't be any bigger of a moment than a straight dude saying he has a girlfriend. I'm sorry it was for you."

"You should be an inspirational speaker."

"Ha." He could practically hear Asher's grin through the phone. "I'm way too awkward for people to listen to me."

"You're not awkward, you're adorable." His cheeks flamed. Had he really just said that? "I mean—"

"No take backs. You said it, and now it's forever stuck in my brain."

"Okay, I'm going to hang up now before I make an even bigger fool of myself." He ended the call and sank onto the corner of his bed.

You're adorable?

How much more of a weirdo could he be?

Chapter 18

Asher

Leaving Kenny with his father was harder than Asher expected. The part of him that had always been Kenny's friend wanted to stay to make sure he was okay. The part of him that was crushing on the senator's son just wanted to know what that kiss meant.

"You've been quiet the whole trip home." Danny's voice trailed off as they walked across the south lawn to the Residence. "Are we doing the presidential walk of shame here?"

"Ew, no." Asher shoved him, laughing when his efforts yielded him nothing. It was like shoving a boulder. "We just fell asleep watching a hockey game. What's your excuse, Mr. Diligent? Why didn't you wake me up?"

"That kid's dorm room bed was the most comfortable thing that has ever touched my backside. I was just going to stretch out for a minute, and then I was a goner." He shook his head in disbelief. "I've never fallen asleep on the job like that, but you two were on the most boring date ever."

"I don't think it was a date." Asher looked up at the entrance to the White House. "The whole setup you guys planned was a waste of time."

"What setup?" Danny frowned. "I don't know anything about a setup."

"You're a terrible liar."

"Listen, kid. You two were having a good time until the shit hit the fan with his family life. Give him time to deal with that mess, and he'll come around. It was just bad timing last night. But you did a nice thing for your friend, not leaving him alone at that stuffy boarding school."

"A nice thing, huh? Maybe next time you won't give me such a hard time when I'm trying to be there for my friends?"

"Not likely. But I respect the gesture of kindness."

"You're such a pain in my ass."

"That just means I'm doing my job."

Danny's face went blank like it did when one of his minions spoke to him through his ever-present headset. "Come on, your mom wants to see you." He steered Asher toward the West Wing.

"Of course, she does." Asher rolled his eyes. "What, was she in on the setup?"

"I know nothing."

Asher followed him into the building, brushing a careful hand over last night's clothes, trying to smooth the wrinkles from his shirt.

It was the weekend, but his mother was always working. It came with the job, but she still managed to make time for her kids. Something he was beginning to realize he'd taken for granted.

"Asher, did you have a good time at the concert?" the Chief of Staff asked as she stepped out of the Oval Office.

He was used to everyone knowing his business, but he loved his mother's Chief of Staff. She'd served as his father's Chief of Staff as well, so he'd known Lillian since he first came to the White House.

"Yeah, it was a blast."

She glanced at her watch. "Nora's in a meeting, but she'll be back in about ten minutes. Your dad will meet you both here, and then IT will set up the video conference."

Lillian was already halfway down the hall before Asher could ask her what videoconference she was talking about.

"You know anything about that?" Asher turned to Danny.

"No idea." He held the door open to his mom's office, taking his usual stance at the door to await the President's arrival.

"You don't have to wait with me, you've gotta be tired."

"I'm good," Danny insisted. "I'll take a break after you're settled back in the residence. Just promise me no overnight trips again anytime soon."

"Can't guarantee it." Asher gave him a smirk. Danny was rarely away from Asher's side when he wasn't in his own rooms, and Asher suspected the guy never slept.

"Hey, Ash." His dad walked in with his nose buried in some protocol binder. "Have fun on your date?"

"It wasn't a date." Asher sighed, feeling like more of a loser knowing his parents played a part in last night's set up. That had to be a new level of pathetic, even for him. "But we all had a good time."

"Good, good."

"What's this I hear about a video conference?"

"Let's wait for your mother. She'll kill me if I tell you before she gets here."

"That sounds ominous."

"It's not ominous, Asher." His mother stepped into the room from her private study. "You always suspect the worst."

"Hey, Mom." Asher yawned. He still didn't know how he felt about spending the night on the sofa with Kenny, but he was exhausted from his trip. "What's up?" All he wanted was a shower and a nap.

"First, how was your date?"

"It wasn't a date," Asher and his father announced together.

"Well, did you at least have fun?"

"Yes, Mother, I had a great time." He was a hundred percent certain she'd received a full report on his activity, including the night spent on the couch, but she had the decency to pretend she knew nothing. "Now, what's this about a video conference?"

"A prestigious, cutting-edge art school has been trying to get in touch with us since your art show, but the recruiter obviously had a hard time reaching out."

"I talked to the woman briefly yesterday," Asher's father said. "It sounds like an amazing opportunity, so we made arrangements to speak with her today."

Asher ran a hand over his tired eyes, stifling another yawn. "Not the best timing." He wasn't remotely interested in hearing some college recruiter kiss their asses for the next hour.

"She only wanted a moment of your time, son." Asher's dad stepped aside to let the IT guys set up the call. "I really think you'll like her."

"What's the school?"

"Manhattan College of New Arts."

Asher frowned. "I've never even heard of it."

"It's new and really kind of exciting," his mom said. "But we'll let Roxie tell you all about it."

"Roxie?" Asher's eyebrows shot up. "The recruiter's name is Roxie?"

"You'll love her. She's from Australia and she's so cool."

"Great. I can't wait." Asher would be more excited to talk about foreign policy at this point than any talk of his future.

Ten minutes into the conference call, and Asher could see why Roxie was their best recruiter. She got extra points for not falling to pieces when greeting his parents.

"So what makes Manhattan College of New Arts a better choice than NYU or The Rhode Island School of Design?" Asher leaned toward the screen.

"The short answer to that question is we aren't living in the past with our heads stuck in the sand, oblivious to how the world has changed in the last century."

"So this is not a classic program of fine art?"

"Far from it, Asher."

He liked the way she said his name with her Aussie accent. He could listen to her talk all day.

"How many times have you heard someone say an education in the arts is a waste of time and money because you can't make a living as an artist?"

"Everyone says that, and it's a scary thought."

"Right? To put yourself through so many years of school, losing sleep, living on ramen noodles and caffeine just to graduate and never find a job in the creative arts. It's heartbreaking. But at MCNA we have a perfect record, placing all of our students in jobs they've been trained to do. We have that high level of success because we will never just teach our fine art students how to paint a beautiful piece of art without also teaching them how to sell it and market their brand as an artist. But, you're into the digital arts. Photography, film, graphic arts. Those are all skills that are in high demand. Think about a world where art doesn't exist. There would be no entertainment. No music, no film, no beautifully designed buildings and interiors. No art of any kind."

"That's a bleak image," Asher said.

"Exactly. We can't even fathom it because the best things about our world revolve around art. So why do we have so many starving artists, vying for the same few jobs? Because the art education system is flawed and no one is doing anything about it."

"That still doesn't really answer my original question." Asher fidgeted on the edge of his seat. He liked everything she'd said so far, but it still felt like a sales pitch.

"Our classrooms are different, and our curriculum is always changing. We listen to our students and their intuition because it's that raw creativity that leads to the next new thing. Take photography, for instance. In a traditional program, you would take intro to photography as a freshman, and you'd learn all the fundamentals. All the does and don'ts that have been taught for decades. At MCNA, your intro photography class will include the fundamentals, but you'll also learn to develop your own brand and your social media presence through Instagram and other online outlets. You'll learn how to implement a variety of mediums into your photography class based on the interests of the student. And your work shown at the Long View Gallery is a prime example of the kind of multi-medium work that can come from a photography class or even a printmaking class. We will always push our students to explore their boundaries, their limitations and listen to their instincts."

"How did you find me? I mean, other than the obvious I'm the president's son."

"Listen, I don't give a rat's arse who your parents are—no offense, ma'am, sir. Our acceptance rate is *seven* percent. We don't have the time, resources, or the inclination to kiss booties or make room for a flashy celebrity student. We care about the art and the talent. And you, my friend, have the talent. I stumbled onto your work through Caitlin Moore on Instagram. She's a talented student I've had my eye on for a while. But my eye went right to your silkscreen work. It has so much heart and you have a lot to say through your work. I didn't care who you were, I just knew from the one piece I saw that I wanted to meet you."

"What would be our next steps, Roxie?" Asher's mom asked.

"We'd love to invite you all to come for a visit to tour the campus and meet with some of our teachers. Asher can come alone or with a family friend if that's easier, ma'am. I know you're busy."

"We will make the time to come for a visit."

"I think I'd like that, but I'd need to think about it and talk to my parents about it before committing to anything."

"Of course. In the meantime, I'll send you some information on the school along with our current curriculum and job placement programs."

"Sounds wonderful, thank you, Roxie." Asher's father smiled and ended the call.

"Well." His mom beamed with excitement. "What do you think?"

"It sounds like a great place. If I decide to do the art thing, it would probably be my first choice. I'm just not sure yet."

"Take some time, son. Think about it over the holidays, and after the first of the year, we can take a trip to New York and check it out. It would be so nice to have you just a train ride away. Unless, of course, you decide to go to school here in Washington, and then you can just stay at home with your mom."

"You know that part is never going to happen, Mom."

The president sighed. "I know, but a momma can wish."

"On that note, I'm going to take a shower and a nap. See you at dinner." Asher made his way across the gardens to the residence with a lot on his mind.

Talk of college was a good distraction. He was more interested in MCNA than he'd let on, but he just wasn't ready to make that decision.

No, Asher's thoughts were still with Kenny, wondering how he was doing. Scrolling through the news articles he'd found on the scandal, Asher read all about how Kenny's mother and his advisor had carried on an affair for over a year, using her son's hockey events and potential career in the NHL as an excuse to meet in private. It seemed she'd spent a great deal of time in Twin Rivers on the pretense of seeing her son to meet with her lover instead.

Asher's heart broke for Kenny. He remembered Kenny's mother from when they were kids. She'd never been the kind of warm, motherly type his own mother was. Victoria Montgomery treated motherhood as a chore, pawning her duties off on nannies and her husband.

Asher stared at his phone, trying to find the words to say to help his friend through such a tough time. No matter what the kiss meant or didn't mean, he felt like they were finding their friendship again, and he refused to leave Kenny to suffer through this alone.

> **Asher:** Thanks for a wonderful night at the concert. I had a blast and it was great reconnecting after all this time. I just hate that our night ended so badly for you. I'm here for you if you need to talk … or if you just want to talk about hockey or the weather, or whatever. I'm here.

He stared at the screen, hoping to see the three dots dancing, but he didn't really expect Kenny to answer. He had more on his mind than a former best friend he might be crushing on now.

Asher tossed his phone down on the bed to go take a shower and get his mind off Kenny and that kiss.

Just as he grabbed a fresh towel from the linen closet, his

phone chirruped. Asher dived headfirst onto his bed to grab the phone.

"Get it together, Ash." He pulled up his texts, hoping to see something from Kenny, but it was Nicky.

Nicky: You make it home okay?

Asher: Yeah, I finally got back to my room just now.

Nicky: How did it go with Kenny last night? I mean up until the date crashed and burned with the news of his crappy mother.

Asher: It wasn't a date, Mr. Meddling Meddler.

Nicky: It was so a date.

Asher: I think you think he's way more in to me than he really is. I think we're just friends.

Nicky: Was there a kiss?

Asher: Sort of, but it was more like he thought he owed it to me.

Nicky: Owed it? Was there tongue? If there was tongue, it wasn't a favor kind of kiss. Was he a closed off dick-bag after?

Asher: Yes and yes.

Nicky: See he likes you. If he didn't, he wouldn't freak out and he definitely wouldn't kiss you. Give him time. He's got family drama that makes it unnecessarily hard for him. With this new mess his mother's created, he'll need all his friends to be there because his instinct will be to pull away from everyone.

Asher: That I can do.

Nicky: You need to think about making a grand gesture.

Asher: What? Why?

Nicky: Kenny is not going to realize you like him, like him unless you hit him over the head with it. Grand gesture style. You know, once the drama settles and he's had time to come to terms with his cheating ass mother.

Asher: Who says I like him, like him?

Nicky: Oh please, it's all over your face. He's perfect for you, and you'd be so good for him. Think about it. Grand Gesture.

Asher finally stepped into the shower, letting the hot water cascade over his shoulders, washing the grime of the night away. His mind filled with thoughts of Kenny and grand gestures. What exactly did a guy do to show another guy he was in it for the long haul? Because Asher was pretty sure he wanted to be all in with Kenny. He didn't have much to compare it to, but he didn't think kisses like that happened every day.

Chapter 19

Kenny

Kenny hated formal wear. Political life basically sucked the joy out of a lot of things other people enjoyed. But a winter dance wasn't a stuffy fundraiser or a stupid ball. This was supposed to be fun.

With a sigh, Kenny tightened his tie and examined his slicked-back hair. He looked like his father. Why was he even going to this thing?

Oh, right. He had friends now, and friends were pushy pains in the butt.

Sitting on the edge of his bed, he pulled on his black shoes, shined to perfection just as his father taught him. There'd been a lot of fatherly lessons, just none of the normal stuff. Geo-politics, yes. How to throw a football, no. Dressing to impress had been a constant lecture, but there'd been no advice on navigating the dating world. Basically, his father had been more of an etiquette teacher while his mother was nothing more than a bystander.

And now, what were they?

His mom still hadn't called. Two weeks and nothing. To his surprise, his dad texted him occasionally. They'd never had a texting relationship. It was never anything important, and he wondered if his dad just wanted to make sure he was still there, that his family wasn't gone.

Wylder and Killian were late, but Kenny wasn't in a hurry to get to the academy banquet hall. He pulled his computer onto his lap and opened a folder with old photos in it. He'd only heard from Asher once since he talked to him last. Asher wanted to see how he was, but Kenny didn't let himself speak the true answer.

Hockey was good, never better. The team played as more of a cohesive unit than they ever had with Kenny and Killian leading the way. They'd been unstoppable.

School was easy.

The parentals were absent.

Basically, everything was as it should be, but something was still missing. Scrolling through the pictures, Kenny stopped on one of two boys sitting with their feet hanging into the pool behind the West Wing. Asher wasn't the only one who grew up in the White House. Kenny spent more time there than at his own home.

And he'd been happy.

It was only when he ran from it everything changed.

In the picture, Asher had his arm draped around Kenny's shoulders and his head thrown back in laughter. He'd always been too good for Washington. Even then.

And now?

Kenny fingered the end of his tie as he continued scrolling through pictures. He wanted Asher here. He wanted to be able to walk side by side into that dance with the boy who'd been his best friend, and to kiss the guy he'd become.

Even if Kenny had asked him, he wasn't delusional enough to think the president's son could come to a high school dance. Kenny's life of classes and hockey was so beneath such a high figure. Kenny belonged in locker rooms and gyms. Asher was destined for art galleries and champagne toasts.

A knock sounded on his door, and Kenny stood. He knew who it was without opening the door because Wylder wouldn't have knocked.

Killian stood with his hands in his pockets, looking so out of place in the gray suit stretched across his broad frame.

"Don't laugh," he grumbled. "The suit isn't mine, and it's a bit small."

"Wouldn't dream of it." Kenny bit back a grin as he let Killian in.

Will appeared from his room, waving to them as he raced out, probably to go pick up his date.

Killian sat on the couch. His slacks rose, revealing a lack of socks. This dude was hopeless.

Pressing a hand down one of the many expensive suits his father thrust on him, Kenny made sure not a wrinkle could be seen. He pretended he didn't see Killian's scowl.

"Okay, Ken. Ground rules. Just because we're going together does not mean I'm your date."

Kenny nodded, trying not to laugh.

Killian continued. "I like my men smart."

"I feel like I should be insulted."

"That's because I just insulted you."

The door burst open, revealing Wylder in a short rainbow dress that barely reached mid-thigh. It wasn't what anyone would consider formal. She looked like cotton candy.

Taking them in with raised eyebrows, she shook her head. "You two are hopeless."

"Me?" Kenny's suit was designer.

She smirked. "Yes, you." Reaching for his collar, she undid his tie and pulled it off. "If you're going to be on my arm, you will not look like a stuffy politician." She unbuttoned his collar, leaving it open, and ruffled his perfectly done hair to give it a wild look. Surveying him, she nodded. "Passable."

Her gaze turned to Killian. "Take the jacket off. If the suit doesn't fit, you're not wearing it." He obeyed without question, leaving him in his white button-down shirt.

She smiled. "Now, I won't be embarrassed. How about me?" She twirled, and the tulle skirt formed a circle around her.

"You're wearing a rainbow…" Kenny gripped her shoulder to stop her from spinning.

She grinned. "Solidarity, boys. I'm going to have a G on one arm and a B on the other. Now I just need to find L, T, and Q, and I'll cover everything. Except P. Why isn't there a P? It should be LGBTQP. Or as my brother says PLGBTQ because he wants to go first with all his pan business."

Kenny snorted. "Sounds like Becks."

Killian eyed Wylder skeptically. He hadn't been exposed to Becks or Nicky or even Wylder much. They had their own brand of ridiculousness. But Kenny had come to realize they were crazy in all the best ways.

She pursed her lips as if her question sent her deep into thought. Finally, she snapped out of it and held out a hand to Killian. "Come on. I want to get there before someone else has a chance to spike the punch." She tapped her purse.

"Is she serious?" Killian asked when he followed Kenny out the door.

"As a heart attack," she sing-songed, sliding an arm around each of their waists.

They navigated the halls among others trying to get to the dance before stepping outside and walking down the hill to the quad. The banquet hall, used only for school fundraisers and dances, had trees lining the walkway lit with white lights that reflected off the snow.

Powder crunched under their shoes.

Once inside, they handed off their coats in the front room before following the crowd to the hall that had been transformed into a fairy tale. An ice sculpture of a castle sat at one end. Blue and silver silk draped from chandeliers over white cloth-covered tables and chairs.

At the far side of the room, a band played recent hits in front of a crowded dance floor. Buffet tables lined one wall with every kind of dish they could imagine. Waiters in black tuxedos filled water glasses and served hors d'oeuvres. After the meal, they'd push dessert carts down the aisles.

Defiance Academy spared no expense for their student events. Their philosophy was that giving kids activities on such a grand scale kept them from trying to leave the safety of the academy walls.

Two years ago, Kenny used to host parties at his house in Twin Rivers, but then the crackdown on security came.

Wylder released a breath. "Wow."

Kenny grinned down at her. "I forgot this is your first year at Defiance Academy. Twin Rivers High didn't have dances like this?"

She laughed. "Um, no. They threw us in a smelly gym with a bowl of punch and a bad DJ." She let out a distressed sigh.

"What?"

"How am I going to spike the punch when there's no punch bowl?"

Killian barked out a laugh. "Yeah, that's always my first thought when walking into an event like this too. Don't we all get upset it's not more pedestrian?"

"Pedestrian?" Wylder bristled at that. "My friends and I always had a great time at our *pedestrian* dances. Okay, my friend and I. Nicky. It was Nicky. He was my only friend. Ugh, you two are like the broody twins torturing information out of me."

Kenny draped an arm around her shoulders. "I seem to remember an epic party you threw in an empty school building at the end of last year."

"Yeah," she sighed. "It was my swan song to Twin Rivers High."

"We're not so bad, are we?"

"I never thought I'd be around Kenny Montgomery and not want to punch him in the face."

Killian laughed.

Kenny shrugged. "I'll take it."

"My food baby makes this dress even tighter." Wylder leaned back in her chair.

"Maybe you shouldn't have eaten so much." Kenny smirked.

"Maybe you rich kids should learn to have less delicious food. Who needs spiked punch when they have all that glorious cheesecake." Her eyes swept the table of mostly hockey players and their dates, most of whom had only had a quarter of the food she'd consumed. "Ugh, I should not hang around athletes. You guys are no fun when you won't shove food down your throats."

Killian's lips tipped up. "That's some imagery."

"We have practice tomorrow." Will shrugged. "None of us want to puke."

At the front of the room, Headmistress Jones stepped onto the stage and up to the podium. A screen descended from the ceiling behind her. "Welcome to the Winter Formal." She smiled. "I hope you're all having a wonderful time."

Several people cheered. Their principal was more popular than any of the teachers.

Mrs. Jones waited for them to quiet again. "Defiance Academy has always been a place where students are protected from whatever life their high-profile parents live. We take pride in letting teenagers be teenagers. Well, our school is entering a new phase, one which will see us expand and grow. Our fundraising campaigns have exceeded our expectations and I'm happy to report we will be able to take in many more students next year."

She paused. "Finding the right students is key. We want young men and women who uphold our ideals."

Kenny leaned toward Wylder. "Basically, students who can pay."

She laughed. Wylder was one of the few academy students without wealthy parents. Kenny was pretty sure Becks had gotten her in when he agreed to do the commercial and probably paid a boatload of cash.

Mrs. Jones looked to the screen behind her. "We have finally finished our first commercial. It won't be used publicly as this school must maintain our anonymity. But this video will be our best recruitment tool. What better time to reveal it than when our wonderful students are already gathered?"

She lifted a clicker in her hand and pressed her thumb down.

A student Kenny recognized as a lower classman appeared on the screen talking about what Defiance Academy meant to him. The image transitioned to views of the state-of-the-art facilities before Becks' grin appeared.

"I'm Beckett Anderson." He sat on the steps outside one of the buildings on the quad. "My sister goes to Defiance Academy, and I couldn't imagine a better place for her. She's happy here." His face faded away and the new image that appeared was Becks standing at center ice with his guitar. He strummed a few chords before starting to sing. As his song took over the video, images of him shooting on the NHL draft prospect goalie flashed across the screen, followed by picture after picture of student activities.

Toward the end of the song, Becks appeared again. He flashed the camera a grin moments before his skates flew out from under him, and he landed on the Knights' logo. He winced as his gaze found the camera once more. "Whether you're planning for a future in hockey, politics, business, or even music, Defiance Academy will get you there."

The screen faded to black, and applause sounded.

Wylder sat in her seat, shaking with laughter. "Everyone just saw my brother fall on his butt. Priceless."

Killian stared at the table, his cheeks flaming in embarrassment for having such a prominent role.

Kenny clapped him on the back. "Good job, man."

Killian opened his mouth to respond, but he was cut off when the doors to the hall burst open and a line of men in black suits marched in.

Mrs. Jones ran from the stage to find out what was happening.

Two of the men walked the perimeter while the others searched the room. The entire student body sat stunned. Some shrank into themselves in fear at this intrusion on their dance, but others were only curious.

It wasn't until three of the men stopped behind Kenny he realized what was going on. Men in black suits. Their completely obtrusive entrance. Not caring how this looked. Yep, secret service. Also known as a giant pain in the butt.

All eyes fell on Kenny as they realized the burly men were there for him.

He knew the questions they'd ask. What did Kenny do? Was he being arrested?

"You need to come with us," a gruff voice commanded.

Kenny threw his napkin on his plate. "I'm going to kill him."

Why would Ash send secret service here? Kenny glanced back at the door, hoping to see a certain adorable guy. But he wasn't there.

"Mr. Montgomery, we're serious." He crossed his arms.

"Why?"

"You're under arrest."

Will spit water all over the table. All around the room, jaws hung open.

"For what?" Anger burned through Kenny. Had he been wrong? Were these not secret service? Maybe FBI? Maybe it wasn't him. Maybe his dad or his mom did something horrible.

The man scowled. "You'll find out soon enough."

Kenny looked to Wylder helplessly, but she showed no expression. She didn't try to help him or backtalk like she normally did. Was the sassy Wylder Anderson intimidated?

Mrs. Jones appeared. "I can't let you take one of my students without proof of who you are."

He showed her something that made her take a step back. Great, there went his last bit of help.

Rising from his chair slowly, Kenny faced them. One of the men grabbed him by the shoulder and turned him so they could cuff his wrists together. The metal scraped his skin as they pushed him toward the door.

Kenny glanced back at the room full of his peers one more time, wondering how the night had gotten so messed up.

The agents forced him across the quad, and Kenny had no idea where they were going until they stood in the shadows of the arena. The winter air chilled him, but they hadn't allowed him to grab his coat.

"Why are we here?"

"No questions." One of the men shoved him through the doors and down the long hall to the ice entrance.

As the icy air hit his face, a familiar voice had his head snapping up. "Boys, you didn't have to cuff him."

Kenny met Asher's eyes and didn't know if he wanted to kiss him or punch him.

Danny sat near the swinging door. "Ash, you did tell them to arrest him."

Asher skated toward the tunnel where a secret service agent unlocked the cuffs on Kenny.

"I hate you." Kenny scowled.

"No, you don't." Asher grinned.

"That was ridiculous. Arrest me?"

He put a hand on the half wall. "Do you remember when we were kids and always wanted Danny to arrest anyone we didn't like."

"Yeah." He remembered everything.

"Well, this wasn't like that."

"Okay…"

"This time, I had my agents arrest someone because I do like him. More than like. Kenny—"

Kenny cut off his words by leaning forward and pressing a kiss to his lips. Asher skated backward, and Kenny walked out onto the ice so it wouldn't break their kiss.

Needing some air, Kenny pulled back and gripped Asher's chin between two fingers. "You, Ash, are mean. Everyone back in that banquet hall now thinks I'm on my way to a jail cell."

"Everyone except Wylder." He grinned. "This was her idea."

Kenny laughed and released Asher. "That doesn't surprise me."

"Ken?"

"Yeah?"

"I came here because I needed to ask you a question."

Chapter 20

Asher

"You were saying you had a question for me?" Kenny turned with a knowing smirk as Asher skated in a close circle around him on the ice.

The asshole knows what he does to me. But Asher couldn't wipe the smile off his face. He felt it in Kenny's kiss this time. The aloof, I-don't-care attitude was gone. Coming out to his father seemed to have lifted an enormous weight off Kenny's shoulders.

Now, if only Asher could do the same.

"Right." Asher came to a stop in front of Kenny, closing the already narrow distance between them. "This is stupid." Asher's shoulders sagged. He followed Nicky's advice with the grand gesture, and now, it just felt silly.

"Hey." Kenny tilted his chin with the tip of a finger. "Nothing you do is ever stupid."

"All right." Asher took a deep breath and grabbed Kenny's hands in his trembling ones. "I'm crashing your Winter Formal because I want to be your date tonight, but I'm still not a hundred percent certain this is what you want. I just...know it's what I want. So...here I am with the big gesture, probably making a giant fool of myself, but for once, I don't think I really care about that."

"I've made a mess of everything. Haven't I?" Kenny ran a hand through his hair. "I'm sorry, Ash. I ruined your first kiss, and I was an ass about the second one too. My life is a mess right now with my crazy mother and Kyle's betrayal. I don't know who I can trust. My dad is being weird, and I have all these new meddling friends trying to set us up, and I almost ruined the best thing that's happened to me, *again*."

Asher chose to focus on that last part. He grabbed the lapels of his immaculate tux and pressed his lips to Kenny's, partly just to shut him up. But the moment Asher's lips met his, a weight lifted from his shoulders. This was so right. For so many weeks, they were headed for this moment—finally on the same page like it was always supposed to happen this way. Kenny's arms wrapped around him, and all the tension melted from both of them. After all the drama, mixed signals, and misunderstandings—they finally made sense.

Asher reluctantly pulled away. "So…was that a yes?"

"No." Kenny stepped back. "I have something to say."

Asher's stomach sank to the ice beneath his feet. This was not how he'd envisioned this night going.

"I owe you an apology. A long overdue one." Kenny took Asher's hands in his. "You were my best friend, and when you came out, you were so confident about it. It scared me. I was only thirteen, and it confused me about my own struggles. I didn't understand how I could be attracted to you and the girls in my class at the same time. They were pretty and sweet, and I literally liked *all* of them. But they weren't nearly as scary or confusing as all the other boys thought they were. *You* were what scared me, Asher. So, in true Kenny fashion, I was a dick and abandoned you when you needed a friend most. Sure, my parents didn't want me to have anything to do with the gay kid, but we know they're bigots. I hid behind their beliefs because I was too scared to confront my own feelings—and too terrified to face the rejection of my own family. I've been scared ever since. I dated Nicky for two years. He's probably the best person we know, and I treated him like a dirty secret. He didn't deserve that, and I didn't deserve him. Just like I don't deserve you now. But I want to, Ash." He reached to cup his face, his brow furrowed with fear and confusion. "I want to be good enough for you. I want a chance to make it up to you—to start fresh."

Kenny's eyes were so earnest and full of hope, like he thought Asher might turn him down.

"So…what you're saying is, you've had the hots for me since we were thirteen?" Asher couldn't hold back his smile.

"That's what you got out of my soul-baring speech?" Kenny rolled his eyes and pulled Asher into his arms, his laughter bouncing off the ice.

"Seriously, if we can be friends again and have this too"—Asher reached to meet Kenny's lips again—"then I'm the happiest guy in the world right now. I missed you."

"I missed you too, Ash. Every day."

"So is that a yes to my original question?"

"What was that? I forget." Kenny's face-splitting grin did things to Asher's insides.

"Can I be your date tonight? Are you ready for that?"

"Yes! Let's go." Kenny grabbed his hand. "I want you to meet my friends."

"You have friends?" Asher couldn't help the teasing tone in his voice as he changed from his skates, back to his dress shoes.

"Yes, I have friends. They refuse to go away, so I guess I'm stuck with them."

Asher walked with Kenny across the snow-covered campus with the sparkling night sky shining down on them. The secret service followed at a discreet distance. Asher was used to it, but it was a lot to ask of a date—or potential new boyfriend.

"Listen, before we go in," Asher said, pulling Kenny to a stop outside the ballroom. "I come with a lot of baggage." He gestured at Danny and his team. "They're going to go in there and cause another scene. I've lived with it almost all my life, but I know it's a lot to ask of anyone. So if you're not ready for that kind of attention, I completely understand."

"You're too adorable for words, you know that?" Kenny leaned down to kiss him again. "I'm proud to walk in there with you. You and all your *baggage*. Just as long as Super Danny knows I'm going to need some serious alone time with you very soon."

Asher grinned and took Kenny's hand as they walked into the ballroom together. Everyone was still eating dessert, and they stopped and stared the moment the secret service returned. Asher felt all eyes on him—not a new sensation for him, but one that always felt creepy no matter how many times it happened.

"Sorry, my date was late and decided to pull an epic prank on me. Carry on." Kenny waved at the crowd and, with a nod from Danny, steered Asher across the room to his table. "Save us any dessert?"

"Will was about to eat yours, so we had to sit on him," Wylder said.

"Hey, I'm still hungry." Will stood to greet Asher with a curt bow. "It's nice to actually meet you this time, young sir."

"Ignore him." Kenny said, pulling out a chair for Asher. "You get used to him after a while."

"Ash isn't the queen of England." Wylder gave Will a shove. "Sit down and try to be cool, man. We know you can do it."

"Sorry about the theatrics earlier," Asher said, taking his seat. He really wanted Kenny's friends to like him. Wylder he could count on, but the rest of his teammates were a big deal. "A good friend told me to go for a grand gesture, so a fake arrest seemed like a good plan."

"You should have seen his face," one of Kenny's teammates said. "I thought he was going to piss himself." His stony face cracked to reveal a semi-smile. "I'm Killian, by the way. Nice to meet you, Asher." The way he said it sounded so normal, like he didn't give a crap who Asher was. He liked him already. The others went around the table introducing themselves, but Asher was afraid he'd never remember all of their names.

Asher and Kenny split a huge piece of black forest cake as everyone settled down and the stares and whispers died down.

"I hope you don't mind I stole one of your dates." Asher elbowed Wylder sitting next to him.

"Nah, it's fine. I have a spare." She gestured at Killian.

"She forced me here." Killian rolled his eyes. "She just hasn't realized I'm terrible dancing with girls."

"What? You need me to lead?" Wylder shot him a glare. "I know I have all the scary girly parts, but I also have two feet and a pair of arms. How hard is it to dance with a girl? I mean, that's why you're here."

"You're too damn small." Killian frowned. "I might break you."

"I'll dance with you, Wylds," Asher laughed, relieved there were other gay kids at this school.

"He'll dance with you later." Kenny leaned over him. "He's mine first." Kenny took his hand and led him to the dance floor where others were starting to gather as the first slow song of the evening began to play.

It was a little awkward at first, but they found their rhythm together, and to Kenny's credit, he didn't seem the least bit worried about what anyone thought of them together.

"I'm proud of you," Asher said.

"Of me? Why?" Kenny smiled down at him.

"You've been on a long road to here, Ken. I've never seen you so comfortable with who you are. It's kind of amazing to witness."

"I feel good." Kenny nodded. "Better than I have in a really long time. A lot has changed for me recently. Some of it good. Some of it I'm still not sure about, but one thing I am sure about is you. I should have been this guy for Nicky, but I wasn't. We weren't right for each other. Not like he is with Becks and I am with you."

"We do have a pretty big problem though." Asher didn't want to ruin their night, but it had to be said.

"What's that?"

"Distance. You're here and I'm in Washington."

Kenny shrugged. "I have a feeling I'll be spending a lot more time in Washington soon anyway so I'll be a frequent White House visitor. We'll be fine, Asher." Kenny pulled him closer, whispering into his ear. "I don't want you worrying about that. Just think of all the events where I get to be your plus one. Think about all the private late night pool parties we'll have sneaking off together at those dull parties. How much fun we're going to have driving Danny crazy like we did when we were kids."

"You're pretty good at this boyfriend thing." Asher winced. He didn't mean to us the B word. It was too soon.

"I plan on getting much better at being your boyfriend." Kenny guided them in a slow dance to the beat of the music. They were in their own little bubble, oblivious of the couples dancing around them. Kenny's lips pressed against his, hard and warm, and a little more demanding. He could get lost in those lips, but now was not the time or the place.

"I'm cutting in." Wylder announced, breaking the spell between them. "You've had the good dancer to yourself for like three dances. And Killian is *awful*." She eyed Kenny with her death glare.

"He's my boyfriend, you know that, right?" Kenny laughed.

"And you don't do fast dances."

The music had changed, and they hadn't even noticed.

"I will leave you in the capable, yet terrifying, hands of Wylder before she starts kicking my shins. But I'll be back." He kissed Asher's cheek. "You get one, Wylds." He left them with a wink and Asher couldn't help watching him go. He liked watching him leave just as much as he liked watching him approach.

"Hey, eyes on me, Ash. You know, your friend, Wylder?"

"Oh, sorry." He smiled, taking her hand as the beat of the music grew and the lights dimmed.

"You two are hella cute together," she admitted. "Just don't tell Ken doll I said that."

"You know he hates that name, right?" Kenny loathed the nickname when they were kids. He'd even wanted to change his name once when he was eleven. Asher had talked him out of it.

"He likes it when I say it because it's said with love." Wylder shouted over the music. "And just so you know, if you hurt my friend, I'll have to hurt you."

"Hey, I was your friend first." Asher whirled her around, a silly grin on his face.

"I'll have the talk with him too before the night is over. Just like I did with Nicky and with Becks when they first got together."

"You have a *lot* of not-so-straight friends, Wylds." Asher frowned down at his friend, wondering if she maneuvered herself into these friendships to avoid any real relationships of her own. "We need to find you a nice boy you can boss around. No…more like one that can actually give as good as he gets. Or a girl. That would be cool too."

"I'm not into relationships right now. If I was, it would be a guy, but it's way too much drama for me. I just live vicariously through my boys. And I'm perfectly happy on my own." Her brilliant smile lit her face, and he knew she meant what she said.

Wylder was the kind of girl who didn't need to find her happiness in a boy. She had it in spades on her own. Asher just wondered what kind of guy it would take to break through all of that sass to find the sweet but broody girl underneath it all. He hoped she'd find him soon. She deserved someone great.

"All right, Anderson, you've had two dances." Kenny towered over them. "Can I have my boyfriend back now?"

"I suppose so." Wylder grinned. "You boys have fun." She turned to go. "Just not too much fun," she called over her shoulder, her laughter like a chorus to the music.

Kenny's hands slid to Asher's waist as they fell into another slow dance.

"Wait, is this your first school dance?" Kenny asked.

"Yeah, actually." Asher's cheeks flushed. "I never bothered going to our formal events since I never had a date. Besides, my school is Quaker, so no dancing. Our events are more like the stuffy Washington banquets. It's like they want to prep us for a lifetime of that scene, and I've already had my fill of it."

"Well, I have a secret." Kenny leaned in closer. "It's the first school dance I've ever enjoyed."

Chapter 21

Kenny

A Political Dynasty Has Fallen.

Kenny couldn't believe the title they'd tacked on to the article about his family. Nobody had fallen. His father still held his influential position. His mother got what she wanted and just disappeared from their lives.

And Kenny?

He stared at the two images in the article. In one, his mom leaned in close to Kyle in a restaurant. In the other, Kenny and Asher danced at the Defiance Academy Winter Formal. How did they even get the picture when the media couldn't get onto campus?

Both pictures were meant to harm his father. First, his wife left him, and then his now-out bisexual son fell for his political rival's kid.

The dance was just days ago, yet it felt like another lifetime. Asher was back in DC, and Kenny was stuck sitting through civics class. He didn't hear a word the teacher said as he scrolled through the article on his phone. Less than two weeks until the holiday break, but it wasn't like Kenny had anywhere to go.

Maybe to Washington? He'd have to train for most of his time off, but maybe Asher could score him an invite for Christmas at the White House?

The thought of spending the holiday with Asher put a smile on his face. They were boyfriends now, but the only guy Kenny had ever dated was Nicky and their entire relationship was spent in a closet.

Part of him worried he'd mess it up like he always did.

Those worries flew out of him when a text popped up on his phone.

Asher: Guess the cat's out of the bag.

He must have meant the article talking about their relationship.

Kenny: And it's a really fat cat.

Asher: You'd tell me if you were second guessing stuff, right?

Kenny's thumbs paused over the screen. It surprised him that in this new media nightmare, the one thing he hadn't second-guessed was how he felt about Asher.

Asher: If you don't answer me, I'll assume you're freaking out.

Asher: Kenny…

Kenny grinned as the texts came in rapid succession.

Asher: You aren't allowed to break up with me.

Asher: Not after that epic dance.

Asher: So help me, Kenneth Montgomery, don't make me come to Ohio and strangle you.

Kenny: I didn't know you were that Kinky, Ash.

Around him, the room cleared out as class ended. He slipped his books under one arm and pressed his thumb over Asher's name before bringing the phone to his ear.

Asher answered after a single ring. "Tell me the truth. Are you freaking out right now?"

Kenny chuckled, but didn't answer.

"I like that sound."

"What sound?" Kenny asked.

"Your laugh. It completely betrays your broody asshole persona."

"Careful, Ash. If I didn't know better, I'd think you had a crush on me."

"In your dreams, buddy."

Kenny sighed. "I wish you were here."

"Me too. This kinda sucks. Are we worth it, Ken?"

It was a question he'd asked himself so many times. Was Asher worth blowing up his life?

"Yeah. We're worth it."

"That's what I was hoping you'd say."

Kenny walked down the Cambridge Hall steps and onto the quad where red brick paths crisscrossed snowy grass. He was so focused on Asher he didn't watch where he stepped and hit a patch of ice. A scream left his lips, and he slammed into the ground, the jarring force vibrating up his spine.

His phone clattered to the bricks.

"Ken," Asher yelled. "Kenny!"

With a wince, Kenny reached for his phone. "It's okay. I stuck the landing."

"You're flat on your back right now, aren't you?"

"Of course not. I'm a hockey superstar. I don't let a little ice trip me up."

"Superstar, huh?"

"Yep." He suppressed a groan as he picked himself up. His entire body ached, but at least it didn't seem like he'd hurt himself.

His phone beeped, and he looked at who was trying to call. "Ash, I've gotta take this."

"'Kay. Talk later. Don't go slipping on anymore ice."

"Hardy, har, har, funny guy." He switched over to take the call from the McCullen Agency. They were the ones who'd assigned Kyle as his family advisor a few years ago with the expectation he'd become his agent when he went pro.

"Kenneth Montgomery?" a deep voice asked.

"Uh..." Kenny bent down to pick up his fallen books as he wedged the phone between his shoulder and his ear. "Yes. That's me."

"It's Albert McCullen."

He straightened. The head of the agency? "Hello, sir. How can I help you?"

"Young man, forget the sir business. Call me Albert."

Kenny couldn't believe it was Albert McCullen on the other line. He'd had a decade-long NHL career before starting his agency, and now represented some of the biggest names in the game. "Yes, s—Albert."

"Now, the reason I'm calling is that I need to apologize to you on behalf of the agency."

"Why?"

"We have a moral code here at McCullen, a code of conduct all our agents sign when they come on board. Kyle Henderson did not act in your best interests, and with this media storm, he has harmed the integrity of our agency. He has been fired, Kenny, and I wouldn't blame you if you looked for representation at a different agency when it comes time to turn pro."

"Honestly, I haven't really thought about what I need to do next." He was ashamed to admit it. The draft was in six months, and he'd been too distracted to focus on his future hockey career. Distracted by his mom's mess, but more importantly by Asher and just coming to terms with himself.

"Kyle always spoke very highly of you, Kenneth, and we think you have a bright future. We'd like to keep you. I never handle the draft-eligible kids myself, but I want to be your advisor."

Kenny found his way to a snow-covered bench and sat down, not caring how the snow soaked into his pants.

"You don't have to give us an answer right away. I know our agency has probably lost your trust."

"No. I mean yes," Kenny blurted. "I want to stay."

"That's good. Very good. We're happy to have you on board. I'll email the paperwork today. You and a guardian will need to sign it and send it back. I'm looking forward to getting you to the NHL, son."

He hung up and Kenny sat there in a daze. The first time he'd been approached by Kyle his freshman year, he'd been told a pro-hockey career was possible.

Now, it seemed more than possible. He'd get there.

That night, he played hockey as if all the weight had lifted from his shoulders, and he could enjoy the game again. The media still circled his family, but that wasn't anything new, and he'd get through it. He always did.

This time, there were no more secrets, nothing left to hide.

The Defiance Academy Knights won their game in Columbus in an uneven score with Kenny leading the way.

The team cranked the music in the locker room as they showered and changed. Kenny couldn't help but smile at the texts rolling in.

Wylder: Dude... why am I watching this game online? Being friends with you is hard.

She was not a sports person.

Nicky: You played a-wait for it-mazing!

He'd binged too much *How I Met Your Mother*. Kenny laughed.

Killian dropped onto the bench next to him. "Stop the smiling. It's weird, dude."

Kenny shrugged. For the first time since he was a kid, he had true friends. His family may have been messed up, but he wasn't alone anymore.

"Someday, Killer, I'm going to laugh when you meet a guy who wipes that scowl off your face."

"Not happening. I'm a sad sack by nature."

Coach appeared in the doorway of the visitor's locker room and motioned for Kenny to join him. They stepped into the hall.

"Yeah, Coach?"

"You played your best game tonight, Montgomery." He met his gaze. "But that had nothing to do with the points you scored. You were a leader out on that ice like I always knew you could be."

"Thanks, Coach."

"I wanted to check in after the news article this week. How are you doing?"

Kenny shrugged. "I'm okay." He wasn't about to spill his guts to the coach. He wouldn't tell him he couldn't stop thinking of his dad or that the new advisor contracts burned a hole in his hockey bag, lacking a parent's signature.

"You're a strong kid, Montgomery. Remember that. Not everyone is as strong as you." He eyed him one final time before entering the locker room.

Kenny stayed in the quiet hall, alone save for the occasional trainer walking by. *Not everyone is as strong as you.*

After a few moments, he went back in, ignoring the jibing of his teammates as he dug through his bag and pulled out the folder holding Albert McCullen's contract.

"Killer." He looked up. "You drove Will's car, right?" Killian and Will drove up separately to haul some extra equipment.

"Yeah, I think they're packing the trunk right now."

"I need the keys."

Killer stared at him for a moment, not asking the questions anyone else would ask. After a bit, he reached into his bag and pulled out the keys, tossing them to Kenny. "I'm telling Will you stole these from me."

"Thank you." He lifted his eyes to Killian's. "Really."

Killian only shrugged as Kenny slung his bag over his shoulder and raced from the room. He barely noticed anything as he left the rink behind and found Will's blue BMW in the parking lot.

Sliding in, he started the car and peeled out of the parking lot. He had over six hours to figure out what he was going to say when he got there.

The familiar townhouse sat on his right with its brick facing and intimidating oak door. Glancing at the clock, he cursed himself for the millionth time for coming to DC on a whim. It was four in the morning, but Kenny wasn't tired. If anything, the adrenaline pumping through his veins made him more awake than ever.

His dad wouldn't be awake for another two hours, so Kenny left and spent time driving around the town that had seemed like home once upon a time. He passed the White House, picturing Asher curled up on his bed and wishing he was with him. But this trip wasn't about Asher.

At a quarter of six, he stepped inside his favorite bakery and picked up a sack of bagels and two coffees. They were going to need them.

He found himself back at his family's townhome a little after six. It was early, but his father was a creature of habit, and Kenny doubted even his life falling apart would break that. At this moment, he'd be walking down the stairs to make his coffee before heading into the office early.

Some people aren't as strong as you.

Kenny gathered all his strength to knock on the door. It swung open only a moment later, revealing a disheveled looking senator. His suit looked like he'd slept in it, and his hair stood on end.

"Kenneth." He stepped back to allow Kenny in out of the cold. "I didn't know you were in town."

You're using Asher Brooks to get back at me.

Your lifestyle does not fit into our world.

His father's words rumbled through his mind as he looked at the man, and he suddenly didn't know why he'd come.

"I brought coffee and bagels," he said dumbly.

His father nodded and took the coffee from his hands. "I was just doing some work in the office."

"But it's six in the morning. You never get up before then."

"There are things to be done, Kenny." He led him into the

kitchen where dirty dishes littered the normally immaculate counters.

Looking from his dad to the mess, he scrunched his brow. "Are you sleeping, Dad?"

He refused to look at Kenny as he took a long pull of coffee. "Like I said, there are things to do. The job is all I have left, so I must give it everything."

Sympathy he hadn't expected to feel for his dad curled inside him. "It's not all you have, Dad."

For a moment, he wasn't even sure his dad heard him. "She's gone, Ken. And I don't think she's ever coming back."

"I wasn't talking about Mom. I'm right here, Dad. I've always been right here in front of you." And never seen. He'd tried to be a good son, but nothing ever made his parents proud.

His father turned away from the counter to look at his son, but didn't respond.

Kenny had to get the rest out before he broke down. He set the bagels on the counter. "Nothing I ever did was enough to make you proud. I'm good at something, really good, and you only said hockey wasn't enough. I abandoned my best friend when he needed me because you didn't approve of him. I hid a relationship for two years! All because I didn't want to disappoint you. But I can't live my life that way. I can't live it for you."

His father walked on unsteady legs to lower himself into a chair at the table. Resting his elbows on the solid wood, he hid his face in his hands. "I struck you last time we spoke. My own son. Maybe I deserve to lose you too."

Kenny sighed. "Yeah, you probably do. But I don't deserve to lose my dad."

"When I was a young man, Ken, I had all these ideals. I wanted to serve in public office because I could make a difference. I lost my first election. I'd run on a platform of inclusiveness and fighting for all peoples. It wasn't until I married your mother that I started to play the game."

"The game?" Kenny sat across from him.

"That's what politics is, son. Say the right thing, move forward two spaces. Make a mistake, return to the beginning. Calculate every move, every word. Your mother won me this seat in Congress that I've held ever since. Do you want to know how?"

Kenny nodded.

"She told me if I wanted to win a conservative seat, I had to run a conservative campaign. And once you go down that road, you can't come back. In the age of the internet, our words are never forgotten, our positions aren't allowed to change."

"Are you trying to tell me you've had to be against your own son because of politics?"

He lifted his face. "I've never been against my son."

"That's what you don't understand, Dad. You can't pick and choose which parts of me you accept. Either you love me or you don't. There is no in between, no gray area. My sexuality isn't just a shirt I put on or a phase I'm going through. It's me, Kenny Montgomery."

"I do love you, Kenny."

Kenny sighed. "I think that's the first time in years I've heard those words."

"I'm…trying. You're right, as much as I deserve it, I haven't lost everything." He rubbed his face. "When you were born, it was the happiest day of my life. I wanted to be a good father, but I never have been."

"I'm only eighteen, Dad. You still have a lifetime to be a good dad. But I won't keep trying to make someone accept me if they aren't capable. I deserve more than that."

His dad stood and walked into the kitchen. He opened the bag of bagels and pulled two plates out of the cupboard. After slathering both bagels with cream cheese, he set a plate in front of Kenny. "You deserve so much more, son. And I can promise you I'll try to get there."

"Try?" Kenny wanted more than that; he needed more.

"Kenny, I need you to understand something. I don't disapprove of you or who you choose to love. It has never been about that. I used to think I'd win this game at all costs, but now I think some costs are too high. Having a bisexual son may be like putting a bomb in the middle of a conservative position, but not having my son is like putting a bomb in the middle of my life. I don't want to be alone, son. Whatever happens with your mom, I need my family. You."

Kenny slid his chair back and stood. "I don't want to be alone either."

Shocking both of them, his dad pulled him into a hug. Kenny couldn't remember ever hugging his dad, but he closed his eyes, letting a tear slide down his cheek. It would take some time, but it was a start.

"Son, can I ask you a question?"

"Yeah."

"Did it *have* to be Asher Brooks?"

Kenny laughed and pulled away. "It couldn't be anyone else."

He rubbed the back of his neck with a wry grin. "I'll never hear the end of this from Nora." His face sobered. "Kenny, I'm… I'm…"

"I know, Dad." His dad didn't need to actually say the word sorry. It might take some time, but he believed they'd be okay.

His dad blew out a breath. "Will you stay for a couple days? I have to head into work. We have an important vote today, but you and I have some more talking to do."

He thought of everything waiting back at school. Classes. Practice. Not to mention the fact he had Will's car. But nothing could have stopped him from agreeing. "Oh, wait, before you go, I need you to sign something."

He ran out to the car and returned with the folder. His father read over the documents before glancing up. "Albert McCullen. Even I know that name. I thought I said you didn't need to fire Kyle."

"I didn't. The agency did."

His dad reached for a pen but stopped with his hand hovering over the signature line and looked up. "Hockey is truly what you want, son?"

Kenny nodded. "It's all I've ever wanted."

"And you're good enough?"

"Would it matter if I wasn't?"

"No, I guess not if it's what you love."

Kenny didn't recognize the man before him. "But, yeah, I'm kind of awesome."

His dad shook his head with a wry smile. "It won't be easy for you, will it?"

"Dad, nothing in this world is easy for people like me, but we still have to live our lives." He lifted one shoulder in a shrug. "And who knows? Maybe I can make it easier for the next person."

His father signed the form. "I'm…proud of you." He handed him the papers. "I'm just sorry this is the first time I've said those words out loud."

Kenny tried his hardest to keep his eyes from welling up. He'd been so scared to face his dad, so scared of being turned away again. He hadn't been prepared for this.

"Thanks, Dad." He coughed to cover the emotion in his voice.

With a single nod of his head, his dad stood. "I need to shower and get to the office. But dinner tonight?"

Kenny nodded.

As his dad showered, Kenny picked up the house, hoping it would help his dad feel less like everything was falling apart.

His mom's silence even after the constant articles spoke louder than words, but for the first time in years, he was at an understanding with his dad and that made everything okay again. He just hoped his mom found whatever she was looking for.

After his dad left for work, Kenny sat on the couch and turned on the news where they spoke of today's vote his dad mentioned.

The senate was set to decide on a bill that would allow states to continue passing their freedom bills, discriminating against people based on religion and sexuality.

With a sigh, he pulled his phone out of his pocket and texted Asher.

Kenny: You awake?

A few moments passed.

Asher: I am now. Thanks for that.

Kenny: If you didn't want my awesomeness to wake you, then set your phone on silent.

Asher: I wish you were here so I could kiss the smirk off your face.

Kenny: How do you know I'm smirking?

Asher: ... Ken

Kenny: What if I told you I could make all your dreams come true?

Asher: You can bring me Chris Hemsworth?

Kenny: Better.

Asher: Sorry, man. There is no better.

Kenny: I'm in DC.

Asher: I stand corrected. Tell me where to send my secret service to arrest you.

Kenny laughed, remembering the dance. Asher was the most ridiculous person he knew and also the best. Standing from the couch, he crossed the room to the front door and practically ran out to his car.

With everything going on, he just needed Asher's calming presence. He needed him to say everything was going to work out as Kenny hoped it would.

Chapter 22

Asher

"You should come spend Christmas here with us." Asher linked his fingers through Kenny's. It was another lazy Saturday afternoon spent on the couch in the White House solarium. Kenny's second weekend visit in a row. This room was quickly becoming their spot. It was one of few places where they could truly be alone. Asher gazed out the huge windows and across the promenade, watching the snow fall outside. Christmas at the White House was magical, and it was Asher's favorite time of the year. He was already on holiday break and Kenny would be too in a few more days.

"I was going to try to find a way to invite myself." Kenny chuckled, his breath warm in Asher's ear. "I have to train over the holidays, though." Kenny laid his free hand on Asher's chest. His other arm was Asher's pillow. Who knew he loved snuggling so much?

"So, you'll come here on the weekends, and I'll come visit you during the week. But I'd like to spend the holiday with you if we can work it out."

"I'll be at my dad's for Christmas. He's pretty down these days, so I don't want to leave him alone. But I will definitely come here as much as humanly possible." Kenny turned them so he was the big spoon, pulling Asher back against his chest.

Asher worried about the long distance thing, but they were both going to college soon. They'd make it work. Somehow.

"Asher? Did you forget about our meeting with Roxie? She'll be here soon," his mother called from the entrance.

"What meeting?" He sat up in a panic, not prepared to think about his academic future right now. "Is she here now? Today?"

"Whoa, babe, calm down." Kenny's soothing voice brought him out of his initial panic. "It'll be okay. Who's Roxie?"

"Babe? I could get used to that." Asher smirked. "She's just the college recruiter I was telling you about earlier."

"Did I forget to tell you she asked for a meeting?" His mom crossed the room, a frown wrinkled her brow. "I swear I told you."

"Mom, really?" Asher ran a hand over his hair. He was a mess.

"Sorry, it was last minute. I don't think it's an official interview or anything serious you'd need to prepare for. Just take a deep breath, son. We have a few more minutes until she arrives."

Asher smoothed his hands over his shirt, tucking it in. Glancing at his hair in the mirror behind his mother, his eyes widened in horror. He was so not ready for this.

"You look handsome as ever. Don't worry." Kenny chuckled. "You've got this."

Over the last few weeks since his initial chat with Roxie, Asher had grown more and more excited about the prospect of going to Manhattan College of New Arts. He'd spent every waking moment not obsessing over his relationship with Kenny, obsessing over his portfolio. He'd submitted his official application and portfolio for review just two weeks ago.

Asher's shoulders slumped. He wanted to spend the rest of the day in a snuggle bubble with his boyfriend. Not stressing over a college interview.

"Kenny," his mom said with a kind tone she seemed to reserve just for him. "It's good to see you again. I didn't think you'd make it back until this afternoon."

"Sorry, Madam President, I got in late last night and headed over first thing this morning." Kenny gave her his best smile, but she was already putty in his hands.

"Enough with the madams, Kenny. I've known you since you were in diapers, call me Nora." She pulled him into a hug. "I'm so sorry about your mother, honey. How's your father doing?"

"He's doing okay. He does think you'll never let him forget this, though." He grabbed Asher's hand with a smirk.

"Pfft. Your father and I might spar on a regular basis when it comes to politics. Lord knows, this town is nothing more than a big boxing ring full of angry opinionated toddlers. But when our kids are involved, the gloves come off. He needn't worry. It's no secret I get a kick out of needling the Ohio senator, but you kids are off-limits. Besides, I quite like the goofy smile you put on my son's face."

"Mom," Asher groaned, but said smile was still plastered on his face. He couldn't seem to stop it when Kenny was around.

"Well, it's true." His mother wrapped an arm around each of them. "And, Kenny, you're welcome here anytime. Come for Christmas if you can."

"Thank you, Ma'am. Er, Nora." Kenny was adorable when he was flustered.

"Madam President, Asher's visitor is here," Danny announced.

"I'll let you meet with your advisor." Kenny turned to leave.

"Stay," Asher said. "I'd like your opinion on this weird non-traditional school."

"We'll just meet in here, then. Danny please have secret service escort her up here, and if you can find my husband, that'd be great. Seems I forgot to tell him too."

"Will do, ma'am."

"Do you know what she wants?" Asher turned pleading eyes on his mother.

She winced, throwing her hands up. "I can't remember. Sorry."

"Oh my God, Mom. After this, Dad is in charge of all college related parent phone calls. He's busy but not as much as you are."

"You know me, I want to be involved."

"You are, Mom." Asher gave his mom an indulgent smile. "Don't ever think you're not. Honestly, you could probably take a smidge of a step back and still be involved plenty."

"You're impossible."

"And you two are too cute together," Roxie said at the entrance. "Oh, sorry." She glanced up at an annoyed Danny. "Was I supposed to wait for you to announce me? I don't really do formal, so I hope you'll forgive me, Nora." She held her hand out for the president, totally not intimidated.

"Lovely to see you again, Roxie. Please have a seat. You'll have to forgive us. It seems I forgot to tell Asher you were coming."

"Nearly gave me a stroke too." Asher stepped forward to shake her hand. "It's wonderful to meet you in person. I'm so sorry, I'm not prepared for your visit."

"Relax, kid, this is my favorite kind of visit. You got all the hard stuff behind you with the essays, forms, and portfolio review. Now, for the fun stuff. But first, I have a really important question to ask."

Asher took his seat next to Kenny, not at all in the frame of mind to answer any important questions.

But Roxie turned to Kenny instead. "Kenny Montgomery, centerman for the Defiance Academy Knights, right? I have to ask what team you're hoping to play for after the draft?"

"Me?" Kenny sat up straight.

"Hockey's kind of my jam, and the draft this year is going to be amazing. You know we have some great teams in New York."

"Well, I don't really know," Kenny said, his ears turning pink. "I'll pretty much play for anyone who wants me. It's the draft, we don't get a choice. Really, I just want to make it to the NHL."

"But you're going to play in college, right?"

"Yes, ma'am. Boston College."

"Ooh, that's a great team." Roxie's eyes widened with excitement. "And just a quick train ride from New York. I will definitely come down to see you play sometime."

"Thanks." Kenny fumbled with his hands in lap. "I'm looking forward to playing in Boston."

"We'll all be there for your first game, Kenny," Asher's mom promised. "And wherever Asher decides to go to school, hopefully, it won't be too far." She smiled.

"I see what you did there, Nora." Roxie sat back with a knowing smile. "That's why I'm here, Asher. You'll be getting an acceptance letter from Manhattan College of New Arts after the holidays, and I really hope you will accept the offer."

"Wow, really?" Asher's eyebrows shot up. "That was a fast decision." He hung his head, studying the carpet beneath his feet for a moment. It always came back to this. Did he get in on his own merit or was it simply a no brainer that they would accept the president's son to the program? The program that only accepted a mere seven percent of their applicants. Did he really even deserve the spot?

"And that look on your face is exactly the reason I'm here." Roxie leaned forward to get his attention. "We had hundreds of applicants this year. Yours was one of the last portfolios to come in before the deadlines. We take our portfolio review seriously. But this year, we had several high-profile applicants. Very attractive applicants with wealthy parents—quite the temptation for a brand new college. We had to decide if we wanted to be like every other prestigious art school out there and take tuition payments from anyone who could afford it, regardless of their talent? Or if we wanted to stick with our mission statement to set the bar higher and choose our students based on their raw talent and design skills they can bring to our school? It was an easy decision. We needed to remove the temptation. So this year, and likely every year from now on, we opted for a blind portfolio review.

"The selection was quick and dirty. From over three hundred candidates, we whittled it down to twenty-two students for the entire incoming freshman class—and your anonymous portfolio was one of our top choices. Asher Brooks, I can tell you with one thousand percent honesty, you got in all on your own. I'm not sure any other school can make that promise."

"Wow." Kenny breathed. "That's impressive, Ash."

Asher gripped his boyfriend's hand, grateful for his presence.

"Your work speaks for you, Asher. And you've got something important to say with your art. We want to help you say it."

"Thank you, Roxie. It means so much that you came here to deliver such good news in person. I-I don't even know what to say."

"Well, don't say anything yet. We want you to take all the time you need to make this decision with your family and your boyfriend." Roxie shot a wink at Kenny. "We know you're going to be hearing from a bunch of schools who will want you just as badly as we do. We hope you choose us, but we know it's a big decision for any high school senior. But I also have a financial offer to go over with you."

"Did I arrive just in time for the money talk?" Asher's dad said as he rushed to join them. "Sorry I'm late. I didn't get the memo. Kenny?" He stopped and shook Kenny's hand. "Good to see you hanging around this place like you used to." He clapped Kenny on the back and turned to Roxie. "Did I hear something about a scholarship?"

"Yes, Mr. er, Former President, sir. I was, um, just getting to that." She fumbled with the stack of papers in her lap, clearly flustered, like most women were around his charming father.

"Please, call me Ben." He sat on the couch beside Asher.

"I'm sorry, sir." Roxie hid behind her stack of papers. "I didn't vote for you." She winced. "But I did vote for Nora."

"Eh, story of my life." He waved her concerns off with a laugh. "She's always been more popular than me anyway."

"Sorry, I just had to get that off my chest."

"Scholarship?" Asher tried to steer them back on course.

"Right. Every year we award a few merit scholarships to our most promising freshmen. This year, during our blind portfolio review, every professor scored each candidate based on certain criteria. Those scores are added to the score your written application received. The scores are averaged and the top five are awarded a financial package. Asher received one of these awards. It will cover your first year at MCNA. If your performance continues to impress your teachers, you can expect to receive additional financial awards next year too."

"Asher, I'm so proud of you." His mother beamed. "But I'm afraid we cannot accept the financial award. We would be happy to pay Asher's tuition, but the award should go to a student in dire need of it."

"Yes, please," Asher added. "I'd rather use my own college fund my grandparents set up for me."

"I thought you might say that." Roxie pulled another stack of papers from her briefcase. "The award is Asher's. If refused, it will not go to another student. But perhaps you'd like to sponsor a few students through our financial assistance program instead? Your donation dollars will go much further, and you'll be able to assist many students who really need the help."

"That sounds like a fine idea," his mother said.

"I'd like to pay for that with my college fund," Asher added. "If I'm getting a scholarship, then I'd like to use at least some of my college money as a donation."

"You're such a good kid, Asher." Roxie beamed at him.

A warm hand slipped around Asher's waist, giving him a gentle squeeze.

"And these two together are too cute for words."

Asher placed his hand over Kenny's. It was tempting to accept the offer simply to be close to Kenny at Boston College, but Asher didn't want to make such a huge decision based on that alone. "Well." Asher gave him a look. "What do you think, Mr. Cutie-cute?"

"I think we need to talk about terms of endearment, babe." Kenny's laughter eased some of the tension in Asher's shoulders. "But this is your decision, Ash. I'll be in Boston either way. I'd love to have you that close, but I also want you to choose the best school for you and what you want to get out of your education."

"How far is a train ride from New York to Boston? I need to look that up."

"I already did." Kenny smiled. "It's only four hours. Long enough to do homework on the train but short enough to see each other all the time."

Asher nodded, secretly thrilled that Kenny was thinking the same thoughts Asher was. "Considering I was pretty sure I wanted to go to MCNA back when I still thought you were an asshole, I think it's a win-win for all of us."

Asher caught his mother looking at her phone. "Need to get back to work, Mom?" His tone was teasing; he knew what she was doing.

"What, I wanted to know how long the train ride was to New York from here. Sue me."

"And how long is it?" Asher's dad asked.

"Three and a half hours." She smiled. "The boys can come home as often as they want. I quite like this arrangement, although I'm terrified of my son living in New York all by himself."

"I'll be fine, Mom. It's not like Super Danny isn't coming with me."

"I meant the takeout bills. You're a foodie, Ash, and New York is expensive. We're going to have to put you on a budget."

"So, is that a yes?" Roxie clapped her hands together.

"Looks like I'm moving to New York." Asher's smile made his cheeks hurt, he was so excited.

"Excellent." Roxie shot out of her seat to shake his hand. "I'm thrilled to hear it. You're going to love our campus. You'll be receiving all the necessary information in the mail. You can apply for your dorm assignment as early as March, and you can opt for a roommate or a private room."

"Private room," both Asher and Kenny said together.

"Oh that sounds like the cue for momma to leave." Asher's mom stood. "I do need to get back to the West Wing, but thank you so much for everything, Roxie."

"My pleasure, Nora.

"Ben, I take it you'll handle that conversation." She pointed to Asher and Kenny. "Private rooms." She shook her head. "Give him four roommates. Loud ones."

"Why do I get all the hard conversations?" His dad looked like a deer caught in headlights.

"Because I'm the president." She grinned as she left the room. "Congrats, Asher." She blew him a kiss from the hall. "And, Kenny, make sure you stay for dinner. We're going to celebrate."

"I want to be her when I grow up." Roxie beamed. "Okay, where were we? Dorm rooms, right. And security. Our campus security will work with secret service for whatever Asher needs while he's a school. The fall course schedule will be available in March. That's when you'll need to come up to the campus for a few days and meet with your advisors to select your coursework for the semester."

"Sounds wonderful." Asher stood to see her off.

"I will get out of your hair now and let you get to that important Dad talk."

"Or you could just stay for dinner."

"Sorry, kiddo, you're on your own. Kenny, nice meeting you. Good luck at the draft."

"Here, let me walk you out." Asher's dad was quick to follow Roxie out of the room.

"Well, that just happened." Asher fell back on the couch next to Kenny. He couldn't stop smiling. Just a few months ago, Asher lived in a bubble all on his own, feeling like the White House was a prison he'd never escape. And now, he had this amazing future to look forward to with a great guy.

"I'm so glad you said yes." Kenny tackled him, and they fell off the couch in a tumble of arms and legs on the floor. His lips crashed against Asher's in a rough kiss that chased all thoughts of college and the future out of his mind. This moment was all that mattered.

Asher's hands slid through Kenny's silky brown hair as Kenny's hands inched slowly up the back of Asher's shirt. Their kiss slowed, deepening as Asher's heart tried to pound out of his chest. He finally broke away, taking a deep breath. "I don't have anything to compare that to, but that has to the most amazing kiss ever."

"No contest." Kenny kissed him again. "Every kiss with you is the best ever."

"That's a good line, keep that one in your repertoire. It'll work on me every time."

"It's not a line." Kenny's teeth grazed along Asher's neck before he finally pulled away. "I'm serious, Ash. It's never been like this with anyone else for me. Not even close."

"Me either." Asher grinned, feeling like he got it right the first time.

"We have college plans." Kenny draped his arms around Asher, and they quickly returned to the snuggle bubble.

"We do. That happened so fast I can't even think. But that's probably more from all the kissing." Asher turned to face him. "I'm proud of us. We're each pursuing our passions and doing our own thing, but we get to keep this too." He raised his hand for a fist bump. "Go us."

Kenny's laughter vibrated in his chest, but he met Asher's fist bump. "You're too adorable, babe. Don't ever change."

"All right, guys. I had to ask Google first, but I think it's time for that talk." Asher's dad stared down at them with an amused smile on his face.

Chapter 23

Kenny

The biggest day of Kenny's life came, and he couldn't seem to move his feet. His eyes scanned the arena he'd been in many times before. Fans filled Nationwide Arena to the brim for the NHL draft.

They crowded into the outer concourse and stood in lines to get their picture with the Stanley Cup.

Kenny stood near the announcer's desk right outside his section and focused on the men huddled around tables on the arena floor. Excitement buzzed through the building. On this day, many dreams would come true.

Day one of the draft would only see first round choices made. If they didn't pick Kenny, he'd come back for rounds two through seven tomorrow.

But he didn't want to come back.

The scouts below knew who he was. He'd been through the scouting combine and the many many interviews. They knew his story, a story that would take on another life as soon as his name was called.

A hand slipped into his clammy palm, and he turned to see Asher smiling at him.

"You ready for this?"

Was he? Kenny took a deep breath. "I think I am."

Asher squeezed his hand. "No. No thinking. This is the day your dreams come true, Kenny. Be ready for it."

"How do you have so much faith in me?"

Asher's brow arched. "Not faith, Kenny. I love you and as the man who loves you, I get to peer into your future."

Kenny laughed. "Oh, really? And what does this future look like?"

"One day, an entire arena will be chanting your name. And do you know what you'll be doing?"

"What?"

"Thinking about me."

Kenny threw his head back and laughed. "Naturally."

Asher glanced at his phone. "Wylder, Nicky, and Becks are watching the draft on TV and they're all texting me incessantly to see how you're holding up."

"Why don't they text me?"

"Nicky won't let them distract you. Not today."

Kenny grinned. His friends were more supportive than he could have imagined. He thought back to when he'd become friends with Nicky again and had to teach him the hockey basics. Wylder didn't care to learn the rules, but she still watched him.

And who knew what Becks thought about all of this?

Releasing Asher's hand, he wrapped an arm around his shoulders. "Thanks for coming."

Asher looked up at him. "You think I'd ever miss this?"

Kenny couldn't help himself. He kissed his boyfriend right there in front of everyone. If any of the scouts or GMs looked to the balcony, they'd see him. But Kenny realized a long time ago if a team didn't want him because of who he was, they weren't the ones for him.

And if that meant he fell to the second round, so be it. Hockey was important to him, but it wasn't all of him.

He led Asher to their section. Danny and a few other secret service followed closely. They'd gotten much better at giving them a little space in recent months.

Albert McCullen waved from his seat, beckoning them to him. He grinned. "I forgot how exciting the draft is. I haven't had an amateur client in years."

Kenny sat next to him. He'd gotten to know the older man quite a bit and liked him. They definitely had a future together. Hopefully. If Kenny was even drafted.

He rubbed his face as his thoughts ran wild with every scenario. He'd pored over draft rankings, seeing himself anywhere from thirteen to forty-five. Yet, part of him waited for it all to fall apart.

Maybe that was residual fallout from everything with his mom. He'd talked to her once since she left six months ago, and it hadn't gone well.

His dad was a different story. They were trying.

The commissioner gave his speech and then started calling teams up to make their choices. They went through the song and dance of giving jerseys and getting pictures. Number thirteen passed by, and before Kenny knew it, they'd reached twenty.

"Who has twenty-one?" Kenny asked.

Albert glanced at his list. "Washington."

"How ridiculous would it be if you ended up in Washington after I left it?" Asher laughed.

Kenny only shook his head. Whoever drafted him probably wouldn't want him to compete for a spot for at least a year or two. He was going to Boston College no matter what.

Albert stared at his phone. "There's a rumor Columbus is

trying to trade to get another first round pick so they can take the Ohio boy."

Kenny tried to suppress any excitement. Playing for the Jackets would be a dream.

Albert's phone rang as Washington drafted a goalie.

He grinned as he hung up. "Welcome to the NHL, kid."

"What?" Kenny only stared at him.

"That was the GM of the New York Islanders. They're going to go up there as soon as Washington is done and take you with the twenty-second pick."

"The Islanders?" New York? Where Asher would undoubtedly want to be after college.

Commotion came from the end of the row as people stood to let someone through.

"Sorry. Excuse me."

Kenny recognized the voice, but his mind continued to work furiously. An NHL team was going to call his name.

"Asher," the voice said.

"Senator." Asher stood and moved a seat away. Kenny wanted to call him back, but then his dad dropped into the seat.

"I'm not too late, am I?"

"You came." Kenny's voice was no more than a whisper.

He smiled, a new look over the last few months. After torpedoing his standing among his conservative base, it was like a darkness had been lifted from his dad. "Of course, I came, son. This day—"

His words were cut off as Kenny's name boomed across Nationwide Arena. "From the Defiance Academy Knights, the New York Islanders take Kenneth Montgomery with the twenty-second pick."

A cheer rose up for the hometown Ohio boy, and Kenny's

shoulders shook as Albert took hold and jerked him up from his seat.

"Kenny," Asher called. "That's you."

Right now, every TV tuned to the draft no doubt broadcasted his stunned face. Was this what it felt like to have all your dreams come true?

Kenny stood on shaky legs and hugged Albert and then his dad. Asher tried to hug him as he passed, but Kenny pulled him into a bruising kiss. The cheers grew louder.

Danny and the other secret serviceman pounded him on his back as he passed. Ushers guided him across the arena floor to the stage where a jersey waited with Montgomery ironed across the back.

Officials from the team shook his hand and congratulated him, but as they lined up for pictures, Kenny's gaze drifted to where Asher still jumped up and down in the stands.

Who was he kidding? His dreams came true six months ago. This was just icing on the cake.

And it was a damn good cake.

Epilogue

Asher: Three Years Later

"How are you still so nervous about these things?" Kenny massaged Asher's shoulders. They'd crept back up around his ears again with the anxiety he always went through before a big reveal. And this was the biggest one yet.

"You're one to talk." Asher relaxed a bit as he smirked at his boyfriend. "I seem to remember someone dry heaving over a toilet before last month's NHL awards ceremony."

"You know that's only because I was terrified I'd actually win and have to go up and give a speech."

"You play in front of almost twenty thousand people regularly. How does a room full of other hockey players scare you?"

Kenny wrapped his arms around Asher from behind. "I just figured no one would want to hear what I had to say."

Asher turned in his arms to meet his gaze. "Uh, Ken, in case you forgot, there were like a million articles written about you after you were nominated for the King Clancy award. It didn't even matter that you didn't win. They recognize your work with *Hockey Is For Everyone,* making sure kids of all races, sexual orientations, and incomes can fall in love with the sport. It was incredible."

Kenny shook his head. "I could never make as big an impact as you. This show is what's incredible."

In his time at MCNA, Asher had participated in some of the most amazing projects, but this one was his baby. And the stakes were high. He felt like he was about to strip naked on the world stage, but Kenny's words made it feel more worth it than any reporter's or art critic's.

"I'm so proud of you." Kenny wrapped his arms around Asher's waist, pulling him close. It was Asher's favorite place to be and it immediately relaxed him. "I know this is a huge deal for you, but your mural makes everyone speechless. It's beautiful."

"No one has seen the finished piece yet. Not even you. I just want people to interpret it for themselves. This isn't about my thoughts and views. It's supposed to help the American people express theirs."

"And they will."

"It's Times Square." Asher took a deep breath. He'd spent his summer break painting the mural on a massive brick wall on campus. But the mural was just the study piece. It was practice. Once he'd completed it, Asher photographed it and spent most of the fall semester creating a digital masterpiece that was about to go live on the largest billboard in Times Square. It was his first step toward becoming a political artist. It wasn't controversial. That wasn't what Asher was about. His work was meant to get the American people talking about the issues of the day. Because talking lead to action, and though he had no desire to enter the political ring himself, it would always be in his blood.

"POTUS has arrived. Everyone is waiting for you, Asher," Roxie said. "It's time."

Kenny took his hand and led him out to the waiting crowd. His mother and father stood near the podium with secret service keeping the crowd at bay. She was nearing the end of her second term as president. In little more than a year, the White House wouldn't be home anymore. It was kind of scary and exciting all at once.

"Ready?" Roxie asked.

Asher nodded. It was almost sunset and the reveal would happen in just a few moments. It was time to make his statement.

"Good luck, babe. I love you." Kenny squeezed his hand one last time before Asher stepped up to the podium. The crowd was huge and most had no idea what they were about to see.

"Good evening ladies and gentlemen." Asher cleared his throat. "I apologize. I did not get the public speaking gene from my parents. So, I will let my art and the poet, Emma Lazarus speak for me. She said it best in her poem *The New Colossus*."

> "Give me your tired, your poor,
> Your huddled masses yearning to breathe free,
> The wretched refuse of your teeming shore.
> Send these, the homeless, tempest-tost to me,
> I lift my lamp beside the golden door!"

Asher's hands shook as he folded his notes. "I'm no politician. My sister got that gene too." He paused for the laughter from the audience. "Caroline is definitely the rising political star in this family. So I'm not here today to talk politics. I don't care if you're Republican or Democrat. Right wing or left or somewhere in the middle. We are all people who yearn to be free."

Asher took a step back and looked up at the enormous screen. No one had seen the finished piece yet. Not even his best friend, Harper. She'd only seen bits and pieces of the mural in progress.

Asher stuck his hands in his pockets and waited beside Kenny and his parents.

"I'm so excited," his mother murmured just as the LED screen flickered to life.

The first frame showed a line of ships sailing across the ocean in a single line. The Spanish Conquistadors, Pilgrims seeking religious freedoms, slave ships, ships carrying Irish peasants and European prisoners bound for the New World. The ships evolved as time progressed in an endless march across the sea, bringing immigrants from all over the world. Ellis Island and Lady Liberty came into view, the immigration lines teeming with huddled masses. From there came a march of refugees from every war the modern world has ever known. From the first World Wars, Korea and Vietnam to The Cold War, The Persian Gulf War, the war in Afghanistan, and the war on terrorism. Through the end of slavery to the liberation of Holocaust survivors, the crumbling of the Berlin wall, and the dissolution of Japanese internment camps. Syrian refugees with nowhere to go. Latin American's searching for a better life. No matter what stood in their way, they all made it here. Every fiber of the American heartbeat was represented in Asher's work. The ancestors of every American alive today. The melting pot of languages and cultures that made America one of the greatest nations in the world.

Silence fell across Times Square. Even the traffic came to a stop.

"Marry me?" Kenny whispered, looking to Asher with tears in his eyes.

"Yes—what? No wait—what?"

Kenny looked back up at the mural. "The man who can say a thousand words without uttering one. The guy who can stop traffic in Times Square because his heart is so big. That's *my* guy. The only one I will ever love. Marry me?" He met Asher's gaze, his eyes burning bright under the dazzling lights of Times Square.

The crowd began to stir, but Asher was only dimly aware they were softly singing the National Anthem. His mother was bawling, but Asher smiled as his anxiety vanished. "Yes. You've always been the only guy for me."

Asher and Kenny now have their happily-for-now, but are you more of the happily-ever-after type? **Sign up for your bonus chapters at www.subscribepage.com/DatingWashingtonBonus**

Next up, Killian gets his story told! Get Dating Texas on Amazon now. Turn the page for a preview.

DATING TEXAS

CHAPTER ONE: KILLIAN

There was only one thing Killian "Killer" James wanted in his life, only one plan. Hockey. More specifically, stopping the next puck. That was as far as he let himself look into the future. Each puck coming for the enigmatic goaltender represented a new chance to be great, a new path toward his dreams.

He slid back closer to the crossbar, squaring his body up with the opposing shooter streaking through the neutral zone. His winger raced to catch up with him, but Killian saw how it would all play out. With the defense stuck chasing the play, it was only him and the centerman.

It happened in slow motion. The shooter drew his stick back, telegraphing his play, and Killian slowed his breathing. The sounds of the crowd no longer reached him as he tracked the puck. It flew toward the upper corner of the net, a perfect shot.

Killian barely moved as he stuck his glove out, plucking the puck out of the air. The impact reverberated up his arm, and the silence in his mind shattered, allowing in the excited chants from the stands.

"Killer, Killer" wound around the arena, but he didn't acknowledge them.

Kenny Montgomery, a teammate, slapped him on the back. "Nice save."

Killian only grunted. Defiance Academy had the best high school hockey team in the Midwest, but something felt off that night. The forwards bungled passes. The defensemen missed hits. It was the last game before winter break, and their minds were already on the three weeks off.

Kenny lined up to take the face-off, but the puck only glanced off his stick before careening toward the far corner.

Guys from both teams scraped along the boards, trying to push the puck free. It popped out of the melee, coming right to the stick of a defenseman standing near the open corner of the net.

Killian dropped his leg out, sliding into the splits as he shifted from post to post, taking away the shooter's easy angle. The puck hit Killian's leg before the opposing shooter tried to stuff in the rebound. Killian whirled around as three opposing players jammed the net.

He didn't know how many saves he made in a matter of seconds, but by the time he managed to cover the puck, his name once again drifted toward the domed ceiling.

Lifting his eyes, he took note of the time. Four minutes left. A tie game. If his teammates couldn't score, Killian could at least give them the tie.

After winning the face-off, Kenny took off down the ice, only to have his shot blocked by the opposing goaltender who steered his rebound to his own man. All ten skaters bore down on Killian. He made stop after stop and didn't see it coming.

The hit.

As he lifted his blocker, a big body slammed into him, and the two collided with the goalpost, knocking the wind from Killian. A sharp pain speared through his shoulder, and he dropped to the ice as a whistle rang in his ears.

"Killer?" Kenny bent over him. "You okay, man?"

Killian looked back at the dislodged net. He didn't know who'd hit him, but the douchebag just skated away.

"Yeah." He grunted, trying to push away the pain. "I'm fine." As he tried to push himself up, he gritted his teeth and fell back, agony spreading down his arm.

The trainer walked out onto the ice as every eye fell to Killian. Along with Kenny, he helped him to his feet. The crowd roared their approval.

"I can finish the game." Killian met the trainer's eye.

Coach Ryan joined them. "Where are you hurt?"

"Nowhere, I'm fine."

"Don't lie to me, James. We all saw the hit you just took."

Killian clenched his jaw, refusing to tell his coach about the pain snaking along his shoulder. He was a hockey player; he'd played with worse. The team needed him. He glanced at the scoreboard. Two minutes. He could play through any kind of pain for two minutes.

"Let me play."

Kenny gave him a nod of respect, but Coach didn't look nearly as impressed. "No. If you're hurt, you could make it worse. Go to the locker room. We'll put Matthews in net."

Matthews sucked, but Killian wasn't about to say that out loud. The truth was, no one who made the Defiance Academy team sucked, but it had been Killian leading them in net for the last two years. He couldn't stand the thought of someone else coming in now.

Coach Ryan pointed to the tunnel. "Go."

Anger burned through Killian, fueling each step as he left the ice. He didn't bother grabbing his skate guards before storming down the tunnel and into the locker room. Ripping his mask off, he hurled it at the concrete wall, wincing at the pain the movement caused.

He could have stayed in the game. His breath rasped in his throat, and his chest heaved. No one would ever claim Killian James was a calm guy. Not when it came to hockey. To him, the game was life. He'd make it pro no matter what kind of pain he had to play through.

There was no way he'd return home to Texas after high school when there was so little for him there. Hockey was his only way to a different kind of life.

Sitting in his stall, he started unlacing his skates and pulled them off just as noise reached him from the hall. Moments later, the team burst into the locker room. They didn't speak, but their sullen body language said it all.

Defiance Academy had lost. Killian tried not to blame the backup goalie, but he couldn't help thinking if he was in net they'd at least have stayed tied.

Yeah, he was cocky but deservedly so.

The truth was, Killian shouldn't have even been there right then. He should have been playing for Team USA in World Juniors, but he'd been passed over for that just like everything else in his life.

Never quite good enough.

Coach entered the room, his eyes scanning the faces surrounding him. "You boys played well."

"We lost." Kenny hung his head. "And if it hadn't been for Killer, we'd have lost by a lot more than we did."

Coach Ryan sighed. "Hit the showers, boys. You all leave for winter break soon, and we don't have any games until after the holidays. Rest and come back with fresh memories. This loss is now in the past."

Killian closed his eyes and leaned his head back against the wall. Coach Ryan's favorite speeches revolved around having short memories, but you couldn't erase a loss.

When he opened his eyes again, Coach stood in front of him. "How are you feeling?"

"I told you I was fine." Killian tried to stand, but Coach put a hand up to stop him. "Take a shower, and then one of the trainers will drive you to the hospital."

"Coach…"

"Nonnegotiable, James. I saw how your shoulder hit the post, and I see how you're holding your arm now. I want you to get an X-ray and an MRI. If it's just me being an overprotective coach and nothing is wrong, at least we'll know that. But I've seen guys struggle to come back from injuries, and I will not have the best goalie I have ever coached lose his bright hockey future because he was too stubborn."

"Fine." Killian bit back the words he wanted to say. Coach didn't deserve to bear the brunt of Killian's anger. "I'll go."

By the time Killian returned to campus, the halls were eerily silent. Defiance Academy had strict rules about things like curfew. All students had to be in their rooms by ten at night. They said it was for safety reasons. The academy was the kind of rich-kid school Killian never thought he'd set foot in. Children of politicians, CEOs, and celebrities attended because their parents were assured certain protections from the media.

And there was Killian James, poor nobody from San Antonio, Texas. The day they'd sent him a scholarship offer to play hockey changed his life. He went from ranch hand and casual hockey goalie to NHL hopeful within a few years' time.

It was a rise that had been written about in the *Hockey News*, but Killian never saw why they felt the need to talk about his humble upbringing. He might not have had much, but he had the best mom in the world.

A mom who'd called three times since seeing the game streamed online. She never missed one.

Killian stared down at his vibrating phone as he leaned against the wall next to his door. Bringing the phone to his ear, he sighed. "Hey, Ma."

"Killian James! What is the matter with you, boy? I have to see my son get the sense knocked out of him and then wait hours for him to call his dear old ma to say he's alive."

A smile curved his lips. Even in his exhausted state, hearing his mom's thick Southern voice made him wish she was there. "It's nothing. I promise. They checked me out for a shoulder tear, but it's just a sprain."

The breath *whooshed* out of her. "You're going to drive me to my grave, you know that?"

"I love you too, Ma."

"Your sisters want to say hi to you. It's late, and I tried to make them sleep, but they worry just as much as I do."

He smiled at that. Being away from home was hard, and Defiance Academy wasn't exactly the most welcoming place for scholarship kids.

"You're a jerk." That was Zoey, Killian's thirteen-year-old—and every bit the age—sister.

"Hey, Zoe. Miss you too."

"If you missed me, you wouldn't make us think... He—" Her yell was cut off when another voice came on.

"Sorry, Zoe. Killy just wants to talk to me."

He laughed at six-year-old Rory's words. Even on such a crap night, his sisters could always make him feel better.

"Are you coming home for Christmas, Killian?"

He hated the words he had to say and hated even more that his mom hadn't told Rory yet. "Rory… You're going to have a great Christmas, but I won't be there."

She started crying. "Why not?"

How did he tell a six-year-old their mom couldn't afford to fly him home for both winter and summer breaks so he had to choose? "I'm going to be home in the summertime."

"But, Killian, Baby Girl needs you." He smiled at that. Baby Girl was what she'd named the horse he'd taught her to ride. They didn't own her, and her real name was Jasmine, but she belonged to the ranch their mom worked at. Their mom was a cook and housekeeper. During the summer, Killian mucked stalls and exercised horses.

"You'll just have to explain it to her, Ror. Tell Baby Girl I love her and I wish I could be there with her, but sometimes, we don't get what we want."

Rory's soft sobs came through the phone for a moment before another voice rang in his ears. "I'm so sorry, Killian." His mom had always felt guilty for not being able to provide more for her kids after their dad left them. Killian didn't blame her though. She did the best she could. The ache in his shoulder intensified, and all he wanted was go to sleep and forget this day ever happened.

"It's okay. I've got to get some rest."

"Okay, I love you, honey."

He hesitated for a moment longer before hanging up. It was the second year in a row he'd miss being with his family for the holidays, and it didn't get easier. No matter how busy he was, or how focused, he couldn't stop missing them. On his tough days, he sometimes wished he could just go home and live a simple life.

But then he'd put on his hockey pads and remember he was never meant for simple.

Pushing into his room, he stopped when he caught sight of his roommate, Diego, hunched over his keyboard. Diego didn't look up from his massive computer screen as Killian dumped his hockey bag near the foot of his bed.

Taking an ice pack out of their shared freezer, he placed it under his shirt over the compression bandage and sighed as the cold seeped into his skin.

Still, Diego didn't notice him. His eyes darted back and forth across the screen. Code appeared as he typed it, but it wasn't like Killian understood any of it.

After living with Diego all semester, the only thing Killian really knew about him was that he loved his computer more than people and was the son of some wealthy tech genius.

Pushing his glasses up into his dark hair, Diego rubbed his eyes and looked up, noticing Killian for the first time. His gaze darted from the ice pack to Killian's face, but he didn't ask if he was okay. That would have required him to speak.

The truth was, Killian was pretty sure he scared Diego. He was a big Texan hockey player at a school that worshiped hockey. When they'd first met, it amused him. But then Diego never snapped out of his wide-eyed fascination, and it started annoying Killian to the point he avoided his room.

After staring at each other for a moment longer, Killian lay down on his bed and turned away from Diego. "Don't type on your computer all night. I need some sleep."

Diego didn't answer, but the typing never resumed.

Sharp pain woke Killian the next morning. He groaned as he

turned over, realizing he'd shifted onto his sprained shoulder in his sleep.

As he opened his eyes, he jerked back. Diego stood over him, bent down so he looked straight into his face.

"What are you doing?" Killian breathed through the pain.

Diego straightened. "You…l-looked like you were in pain."

"I was, but that doesn't explain why you were standing over me." This dude was weird.

Diego removed his glasses and cleaned them on his shirt. "I… You were in pain." He cocked his head to the side as if that was reason enough to act creepy.

Sure, Killian might have woken up groaning, but he must have missed the part where he became friends with Diego. It wasn't that he disliked the guy, but Diego had never made any effort, and Killian saw Defiance Academy as only a means to an end. He had little desire to get to know the privileged kids like Diego who had a career set up for them at their family companies before they were even born.

"It's fine. I'm fine."

Diego went to the freezer and retrieved an ice pack. Holding it out to Killian, he didn't say a word.

Killian struggled out of his T-shirt and unwound the compression bandage before placing the ice pack directly on his skin.

All the doctor told him to do was rest and ice. He said if he did enough of both, Killian would probably be ready to go by their next game in three weeks.

His phone rang from where he'd left it on the desk. Diego snatched it before he could. "Someone named Zoey is calling you. Is that your girlfriend?"

"No." He took the phone and shut it off without answering. Zoey would only be checking up on him for his mom. "What time is it?"

"Almost noon."

No wonder his stomach growled. Reaching into the bin under his bed, he retrieved a protein bar. "Shouldn't you be packed to go home?"

"Home?"

"Yeah, the place where people live when they're not stuck in a shoebox room with another dude."

"I'm not going home." He sat in front of his computer, turning his attention away from Killian.

"What do you mean you're not going home?" Killian got out of bed, realizing how sore his entire body was after that game.

Diego shrugged. "My father isn't big on holidays, and I have things to accomplish here."

He spoke more like a businessman than a teenager. The anger Killian was known for crept up, and he had to hold it back. His winter break wasn't supposed to be spent sitting in a crowded room. The only thing he'd looked forward to was having space for the first time in months.

"You have things to accomplish?" Killian loomed over Diego's shoulder.

Diego didn't answer him. He'd already disappeared into the lines of code streaking across the screen.

For a moment, Killian had forgotten about his shoulder, and all he wanted to do was convince Kenny to take practice shots on him so he too could lose himself.

But then the throbbing intensified. Gingerly pulling a shirt over his head, Killian walked to the door. "I'm going to the dining hall."

Diego didn't respond. Sometimes, Killian wondered if his roommate even lived in the real world.

DATING TEXAS

CHAPTER TWO: DIEGO

"This is next-level disgusting." Diego carefully placed the last pin correctly labeling the pig's respiratory system. He needed AP biology on his college résumé, but he questioned whether it was worth it. Honestly, he needed high marks on every possible science he could fit into his schedule, but dissecting a baby pig was the very last thing Diego Jackson ever wanted to do. It was inhumane, and he couldn't help but wonder why someone hadn't come up with a synthetic alternative. Anything would be better and much less gross than this pitiful creature.

"At least it's not a cat." His lab partner, Van, poked their pig with a sharp utensil, trying to locate each lobe of the lungs. "Last term, the junior class got cats. Can you imagine?"

"I saw them in the lab fridge. They really didn't look like cute cuddly kittens." Not that the pig was remotely cute either. "They were kind of terrifying. I didn't open that fridge for the rest of the semester."

"I get the importance of studying from the real thing," Van said, squealing as a stream of formaldehyde splattered across her safety goggles. "But this is never going to be my idea of a good time."

"Remember the frogs in ninth grade?" Diego scribbled his observations in their lab journal, labeling each of the respiratory parts without looking at his book or the pig. When it came to the sciences, Diego didn't struggle like some students. It was in his blood.

"You tried to lead a protest against using real animals for high school dissection exercises." Van shook her head with a smirk. "You didn't get very far."

"Hey, I've never been the leader type, but I got three students on my side. Four if we count you."

"And two of those girls just didn't want to touch the frogs."

"I'm used to people not getting me now. I'll keep my 'save the world, save the animals' ideas for my apps."

"How's the new one coming?" Van sorted their tools and started cleaning their lab station.

"It's slow." Diego sighed. "I'm tackling an enormous project all on my own, but it'll be worth it if I can ever get it into beta testing."

"I still don't get why you don't just ask your dad for help."

"Dad's more focused on saving the financial industry than the planet. He's not going to be impressed with my little project."

"You should talk to him about it while you're home for the holidays. Tell him it's a project for your STEM club and you just want to pick his brain."

"I'm not going home."

"What? Why? You can come home with me if your dad's not going to be around."

"It's not that. I want to stay."

"Why?" Van wrinkled her nose. "Why would anyone want to stay on campus for Christmas? It's not like this is Hogwarts."

"It's three whole weeks of uninterrupted work. I wouldn't give that opportunity up for anything. If I go home, Dad's going to feel like we have to spend time together or go on some lame vacation. Here, I can just work without anyone bothering me."

"You have strange priorities, my friend."

"Vanessa, you can pack up for the day. You guys are done," Mrs. Cone said. "Good job, both of you. I know this isn't your thing. Diego, the headmistress would like to see you before your next class. You can head out early."

"Thank you, Mrs. Cone." Diego grabbed his things and headed to Headmistress Jones's office. He was hoping she had good news for him.

"Diego," Mr. Wilson, the school secretary, greeted him as he entered the administrative office. "The headmistress is waiting for you."

"Thank you." Diego shouldered his way into Georgina Jones's office, dropping his bag at the entry.

"Diego, have a seat." She stood on top of her desk on her bare tiptoes, changing the light bulbs in the overhead fixture.

"You know you could just call maintenance for that." Diego ignored her offer and crossed the room to help her, knowing she'd refuse.

"I'm picky about my bulbs. I need soft light, or it gives me a headache. There." She finished screwing in the last bulb. "Well, if you aren't going to sit, come, make yourself useful." She gestured for him to stand next to her desk. She grabbed his shoulder and stepped down onto her chair and back on the floor where she slid her feet into her high heels. She still barely came up to Diego's shoulder.

"How's the app coming?"

Diego flopped into the chair opposite her desk. "It's coming. It's just slow."

"You can write code in your sleep. What's slowing you down?"

"The visual stuff." He scratched the back of his head. "I don't have the patience for it. I'm more into organizing and structuring the app than making it look nice. I'll have to do it eventually, but right now, I'm avoiding it."

"Well, I might have a solution for that." She sat behind her desk, shuffling through her files. "Ah, here it is. Since you're staying on campus for the holidays, I had a genius thought to pair you with a mentor or sorts."

"A mentor? Here in Riverpass?" Diego just managed to hold back his snort, covering it with a cough.

"Don't be such a snob, Diego. Just because our school happens to be in a sleepy little town doesn't mean greatness can't come from outside these walls. There's a graduate from Twin Rivers High who's now a student at MIT."

Diego leaned closer. "MIT? Who is this guy?"

"*She* is the local girl who created the hugely successful app, No BS. Peyton Callahan is a brilliant coder with a talent for the visual components you struggle with. She's in Twin Rivers for the holidays and has agreed to mentor you for the rest of the year. You can get acquainted while she's home, and if it's a good fit, you can continue to work with her for as long as it's mutually beneficial."

"And she's willing?" Diego sat on the edge of his seat. Having an MIT student as a mentor was the best Christmas present he could ask for.

"I've given her a pass to access the campus over the break. She'll meet you this afternoon at the coffee shop in the quad. I know you're not exactly a people person, but Peyton might be the nicest person I've ever talked to."

"I'll make it work, Mrs. Jones. Thank you for setting this up."

"Just do me one favor, Diego." She leaned over her desk.

"Sure, anything, Mrs. Jones."

"Try to have some fun over break. I know you find great joy in your work, but don't forget to live a little too."

"Soy milk vanilla latte with an extra shot." Diego ordered his regular coffee. "And please use my cup." He handed over his stainless-steel travel mug—complete with an annoyed look from the barista—and mentally calculated the points that would earn him once the app was in beta.

Diego turned to scan the crowd at the coffee shop. He spotted Peyton sporting an MIT sweatshirt, looking out of place among the more fashionable Defiance Academy girls. He liked her already.

Grabbing his coffee, he went to join her. He wasn't exactly nervous with new people. He just wasn't good at small talk, and most people either thought he was weird or rude.

"Peyton?" He moved to sit opposite her.

"Diego, it's so nice to meet you," she gushed.

Ah, crap, she's a talker.

"Your headmistress has told me so much about you and your app. I designed my first app when I was in high school, and it was one of the hardest things I've ever tried to do. It didn't really start to come together until I realized there was only so far I could take it on my own. Once I knew I didn't have the skill set to see it through to the end, it became more about what No Bs needed and less about whether or not I did all the things or someone else did some of the things."

Peyton beamed a beautiful, happy, energetic smile at him, and Diego wondered what it was like to be friends with someone like her. She looked at him like it was his turn to talk.

"Oh, right." Diego fidgeted in his chair and glanced at his

phone. He was better through email and text messages. "I guess that's where I am now with my app. I'm still making progress, but it's slow."

"What's it called?" Peyton leaned across the table, sipping her latte.

"No idea. I can't seem to land on a name I like."

"Tell me about it. Mrs. Jones told me a little, but I want to hear more about your vision and what needs to happen to get it there."

"It's a habit trainer disguised as an adventure game. Players do small things to help the environment, and they earn diamonds to purchase key components to the game, which they'll need to level up. There are even real-world prizes they can win based on the player's overall points. The more beneficial an act is to the environment, the more diamonds they'll earn."

"I love it." Peyton grinned. "I would totally play that game. So, what kinds of tasks do players need to do?"

"Little things like opting to have your morning latte in a reusable cup rather than a disposable one. Switching from plastic straws to stainless steel. Those kinds of tasks are worth ten to twenty-five diamonds and can add up over time when done daily. Bigger tasks like participating in a community cleanup or a recycling drive are worth tons of diamonds. Making real donations to climate change studies can earn a player huge in game rewards."

"How do gamers prove they've actually done these tasks?"

"I'm working on a system that involves checking in on Facebook and uploading a selfie of gamers performing a task."

"Wow, that's impressive. Is it working?"

"Sort of." Diego smiled. "I still have some bugs to work out before it will be ready to beta test."

"What are the most challenging parts for you?" Peyton sat back, crossing her arms over her chest.

"The pretty stuff." Diego shrugged. "I have the game set up with a rudimentary layout while I finish mapping out the levels of gameplay, but it's not cute."

"I can help you with that. I can meet with you several times over the holidays to work out a basic visual plan, and then we can keep working on it after I head back to school. We can have this thing in beta before spring break."

"That would be amazing, Peyton. But are you sure? MIT is no joke. I don't want to take up too much of your time."

Peyton waved his concerns away. "I'm happy to mentor you and help with the visual stuff. That's the easy part for me, and it's the part I enjoy the most. Really, it'll be like a break."

"Sounds incredible. Thank you so much." Diego didn't really know how to respond to such kindness. Peyton wouldn't really get anything out of this arrangement.

"Now, the important question." Peyton eyed him with a serious look. "MIT or CalTech?"

Diego laughed. "MIT all the way, and not just because it's not California."

"Good answer. I'm looking forward to working with you, Diego."

"When do you have time to meet again?"

"Thursday, and I have homework for you." She slid a sheet of paper across the table.

"Homework?" He tried not to smile. Diego had a small tribe of nerds and geeks who spoke his language, and they typically got him. Peyton was not like any of them, but he sensed she would still fit into his tribe. He skimmed the list of questions and to-do items she wanted from him. It was quite a list, and she wanted it in less than two days. But after reading her notes, one thing was clear. Peyton spoke his language.

"All right, let's do this."

Get your copy on Amazon now!

ABOUT ANN MAREE

Ann Maree Craven is an Amazon bestselling author of Young Adult Contemporary Fiction and YA Fantasy (her Fantasy fans will know her as Melissa A. Craven). Her books focus on strong female protagonists who aren't always perfect, but they find their inner strength along the way. Ann Maree's novels will appeal to audiences of all ages and fans of almost any genre. She believes in stories that make you think and she loves playing with foreshadowing, leaving clues and hints for the careful reader.

Ann Maree draws inspiration from her background in architecture and interior design to help her with the small details in world building and scene settings. (Her degree in fine art also comes in handy.) She is a diehard introvert with a wicked sense of humor and a tendency for hermit-like behavior. (Seriously, she gets cranky if she has to put on anything other than yoga pants and t-shirts!)

Ann Maree enjoys editing almost as much as she enjoys writing, which makes her an absolute weirdo among her peers. Her favorite pastime is sitting on her porch when the weather is nice with her two dogs, Fynlee and Nahla, reading from her massive TBR pile and dreaming up new stories.

Visit me at Melissaacraven.com for more information about the series and discover exclusive content.

ALSO BY ANN MAREE CRAVEN

Redefining Me:

Dating My Best Friend

Dating the Boy Next Door

Dating My Nemesis

Discovering Me:

Dating Nashville

Dating Washington

Dating Texas

Emerge Series (Written as Melissa A. Craven):

Emerge: The Awakening (Book 1)

Emerge: The Edge (Book 1.5)

Emerge: The Scholar (Illustrated Character Journal)

Emerge: The Volunteer (An Emerge Short Story)

Emerge: The Judgment (Book 2)

Emerge: The Catalyst (An Emerge Short Story)

Emerge: The Captive (Book 3)

Emerge: The Assignment (An Emerge Novella)

Emerge: The Heir (Book 4)

Emerge: The Betrayal

ABOUT MICHELLE

Michelle MacQueen is a USA Today bestselling author of love. Yes, love. Whether it be YA romance, NA romance, or fantasy romance (Under M. Lynn), she loves to make readers swoon.

The great loves of her life to this point are two tiny blond creatures who call her "aunt" and proclaim her books to be "boring books" for their lack of pictures. Yet, somehow, she still manages to love them more than chocolate.

When she's not sharing her inexhaustible wisdom with her niece and nephew, Michelle is usually lounging in her ridiculously large bean bag chair creating worlds and characters that remind her to smile every day - even when a feisty five-year-old is telling her just how much she doesn't know.

See more from Michelle MacQueen
and sign up to receive updates and deals!
www.michellelynnauthor.com

ALSO BY MICHELLE MACQUEEN

Redefining Me:

Dating My Best Friend

Dating the Boy Next Door

Dating My Nemesis

The Invincible series:

We Thought We Were Invincible

We Thought We Knew It All

Discovering Me:

Dating Nashville

Dating Washington

Dating Texas

The New Beginnings series

Choices

Promises

Dreams

Confessions

Fantasy and Fairytales (Written as M. Lynn)

Golden Curse

Golden Chains

Golden Crown

Glass Kingdom

Glass Princess

Noble Thief

Cursed Beauty

Legacy of Light (Written as M. Lynn)

A War For Magic

A War For Truth

A War For Love

www.ingramcontent.com/pod-product-compliance
Lightning Source LLC
Chambersburg PA
CBHW020554310726
48979CB00008B/1207/J

* 9 7 8 1 9 7 0 0 5 2 0 4 6 *